The Golden Rock

The Golden Rock

by
Théo Varlet

translated, annotated and introduced by
Brian Stableford

A Black Coat Press Book

Visit our website at www.blackcoatpress.com

ISBN 978-1-61227-134-7. First Printing. December 2012. Published by Black Coat Press, an imprint of Hollywood Comics.com, LLC, P.O. Box 17270, Encino, CA 91416. All rights reserved. Except for review purposes, no part of this book may be reproduced or transmitted in any form or by any means, electronic or mechanical, including photocopying, recording, or by any information storage and retrieval system, without permission in writing from the publisher. The stories and characters depicted in this novel are entirely fictional. Printed in the United States of America.

TABLE OF CONTENTS

Introduction

Le Roc d'or by Théo Varlet, here translated as *The Golden Rock*, was originally published in Paris by Plon in 1927. Two of the other three stories included here first appeared in the short-lived periodical *Le Beffroi*, and are among the author's earliest prose works, written while he was still affiliated to the Symbolist Movement; "Le Tonnerre de Zeus," here translated as "The Thunder of Zeus," appeared there in 1904; "Le Dernier satyre," here translated as "The Last Satyr," in 1905. Both stories were reprinted in the author's first short story collection, *La Bella Venere*, in 1920, and then again in the expanded "édition définitive" of that collection issued in Amiens 1923 by Edgar Malfère as *Le Dernier satyre*. "Messaline," here translated as "Messalina," was one of three further items added to the later collection, and was probably original to it, although some bibliographies give an original date of 1922.[1]

Le Roc d'or was Varlet's first solo *roman scientifique*, although he had previously written two based on original versions by Octave Joncquel, collectively known as *L'Épopée martienne* (1921-22)[2], and

---

[1] It is possible that the 1922 date arises from a confusion, because Edgar Malfère published a novel entitled *Messaline* in 1922 by an author using the unlikely pseudonym of Nonce Casanova, whose true identity remains undetermined. Varlet probably read it, and he was doubtless also familiar with Alfred Jarry's similarly-titled novella, published in 1900.

[2] tr. as *The Martian Epic*, ISBN 978-1-934543-41-2.

one on an original version by André Blandin, *La Belle Valence* (1923)[3]. He published one other during his lifetime, *La Grande panne* (1930)[4], but the sequel to the last-named, *Aurore Lescure, pilote d'astronef* [Aurora Lescure, Spaceship Pilot], was only issued posthumously. Varlet was also an important pioneer and practitioner of "cosmic poetry" reflecting scientific notions and astronomical discoveries.[5]

In a preface added to a 1936 reprint of *La Grande panne*, Varlet complained bitterly that it had been reported to him that the fundamental premise of that novel—microbes developed from extraterrestrial spores causing havoc on Earth—had been subsequently used in a story in an American pulp science fiction magazine, which circumstance he interpreted as plagiarism. He was, perhaps, being slightly inconsistent in so doing, given that *La Belle Valence* explicitly borrowed H. G. Wells's time machine as its initial premise, and *Le Roc d'or* is, in effect, a variation on the theme of Jules Verne's posthumously issued novel—revised for publication by Michel Verne—*La Chasse au météore* (1908)[6].

It is possible that, if he had been charged with this inconsistency, Varlet might have used the same defense as Oscar Wilde, to whom it was pointed out when he complained bitterly about one of his ideas being stolen,

---

[3] tr. as *Timeslip Troopers*, ISBN 978-1-61227-078-4.

[4] tr. as *The Xenobiotic Invasion*, ISBN 978-1-61227-054-8.

[5] A more detailed account of Varlet's life and career can be found in the introduction to *The Martian Epic*, and there are some additional observations in the introduction to *The Xenobiotic Invasion*.

[6] tr. as *The Chase of the Golden Meteor* and *The Hunt for the Meteor*.

that he was a frequent borrower of ideas himself. Wilde replied that when he saw a beautiful flower with four petals, it was only natural that he should be inspired to produce one with five, but that he could not see for the life of him why anyone would want to produce one with only three. Whether or not Varlet would have made that reply, however, it is actually the case that the history of speculative fiction is replete with instances of authors taking up the innovative ideas of others and developing them further, or in different directions, and that that capacity is one of the strengths and glories of the genre. Although *Le Roc d'or* does use the same premise as Verne's novel, it extrapolates it in a very different fashion; it is far from being a mere copy, and its supplementation enhances the interest of the two works, viewed as a pair.

Verne's novel is an amiable comedy whose principal plot-line concerns the dispute between two amateur astronomers in a small American town over which of them deserves priority for the discovery of what would nowadays be called a "near-Earth object," which they have both spotted at the same time. Their quarrel causes a rift between their two families, which threatens to disrupt a projected marriage between two of the younger members. In Verne's story, the stray mass is captured by the Earth's gravitational field and assumes a stable orbit around it, effectively becoming a tiny second moon. When the discovery is made, spectroscopically, that it is made of gold, the bonanza seems to be permanently out of reach, but in a secondary plot-line an eccentric genius builds a kind of ray-gun capable of causing its orbit to decay, so that the object will fall to Earth—a feat that he eventually contrives, bringing the mass down on the shore of an island off Greenland.

The probability that the advent of a meteorite made of gold would inflame the kind of "gold fever" that had provoked "gold rushes" in Australia and California during the early 19th century and the Klondike gold rush of 1897-99 within living memory—the last-named extensively and memorably featured in fiction by Jack London and poems by Robert W. Service—is treated flippantly in Verne's novel, and the potential economic upheaval consequent on a sudden massive increase in the world's gold supply is barely mentioned, although the scientist's banker is able to use his inside knowledge to make a fortune. In the climax of Verne's novel, it is the romantic settlements that take pride of place, while wider implications are complacently swept under the carpet.

In Varlet's novel, on the other hand, the humor is conscientiously underplayed and much blacker in tone, the element of satire is correspondingly more scathing, and the economic and political aspects of the consequences of the meteorite's fall, discovery and exploitation are the principal dramatic focus of the story. Although the narrative does appear, briefly, to be shaping up as a conventional spy story with a formulaic "love interest," that dimension is swiftly marginalized in favor of its cynical analysis of the of the economic and political impact of the meteoric gold on a world whose currencies' long dependence on the gold standard is on the brink of falling apart by virtue of the hectic inflation that followed the fallout of the Great War of 1914-18.

Although we now live in a world in which the gold standard is ancient history—although the price of gold still remains an economic obsession—it is arguable that our current economic troubles, as the world's banks and the euro teeter on the edge of an abyss of irredeemable debt, are sufficiently closely akin to the inflationary upheavals of the 1920s to allow contemporary readers to take a more sympathetic interest in the plot of *Le Roc d'or* than might have been possible in the later decades of the 20th century. Varlet could not foresee the Wall Street Crash of 1929 and the subsequent Great Depression, nor could he anticipate the precise circumstances in which World War II—which he could and did foresee— would actually break out, but he certainly has a clearer consciousness of such apocalyptic possibilities than many other writers of the period.

Perhaps there is an element of whimsical fantasy in *Le Roc d'or*'s depiction of the French people's psychological reaction to the revaluation of the talismanic franc, but it is an element of fantasy with which modern readers can identify quite strongly, as we suffer similar anxieties and preoccupations with regard to the value of our own currencies. In addition, Varlet's cynicism concerning the functioning and achievements of the League of Nations can hardly help but strike a resonant chord with contemporary views of the United Nations, which was set up as the earlier organization's more competent successor. We now know that *Le Roc d'or* was not a prophetic novel, but we also know that it was a novel with its finger firmly on the pulse of real issues and real concerns, which addresses them with an admirable verve and perspicacity.

Although the reputation that economics has of being the "dismal science" has not recommended it strongly for frequent treatment in popular speculative fiction, Varlet demonstrates that its melodramatic potential is by no means inconsiderable. The fact that *Le Roc d'or* carries forward and varies the fundamental premise of Jules Verne's novel makes both works more interesting rather than less, and invites fruitful comparison. Although it might seem the least weighty of Varlet's endeavors in the field of the *romans scientifiques*, he was a consistently ambitious and artful writer in that genre, and his works of that sort all made a valuable contribution to the unfortunately-fugitive development of the genre in the difficult decades following the end of the Great War.

Le Roc d'or explicitly, if somewhat ironically, looks back to the period before the Great War as a kind of Golden Age. It did not seem so at the time, of course, when nostalgia tended to look to a much more remote imaginary past for inspiration, especially in a nation where a "good education" was still held to consist of fluency in Greek and Latin and ability to appreciate the Classics. The three short stories appended to the novel are quite different in their generic affiliations, but exhibit nevertheless the same blithely cynical skepticism, as well as the same preoccupation with the corrosive effects of time and the ambivalence of progress. An essential element of Varlet's career as a writer of prose fiction was the imaginative impetus provided by his realization that the world had changed completely within his lifetime, thanks to the advent of new means of travel and media of communication. The development of this consciousness throughout his career is mapped out by the two pairs of stories included herein, thus permitting another exercise in comparison, more visible now to our historically-educated eyes than it was at the time when the works were produced.

This translation of *Le Roc d'or* was made from a copy of the 1927 Plon edition. The translations of the three short stories were all made from a copy of the 1923 Malfère edition of *Le Dernier satyre*.

Brian Stableford

THE GOLDEN ROCK

I. By Wireless

Jovial and agitated, under pressure as usual—even when on holiday—my friend René Jolliot, the famous film-director, greeted me with open arms at the entrance to the veranda. Then he drew me into the loggia, open to the sea breeze, where his wife the film star was chatting with two people I didn't know, near a table set for aperitifs.

He scarcely gave me time to bow to the nonchalant Lucienne Jolliot, sprawled on the divan with a carnation in her hand and made up as in the Superbo films that had rendered all her quasi-Oriental charm familiar. He introduced me to the two strangers.

"My old friend Antoine Marquin, member of the Barcot expedition, who is getting ready to leave on the *Erebus II* for the conquest of the South Pole."

I bowed to: "Doctor Hans Kohbuler, honorary professor at the University of Basle, and his charming daughter, Mademoiselle Frédérique-Elsa Kohbuler, doctor of mathematical sciences...who wanted to meet you, Antoine, and who also, when she learned that you would be here today at noon, did us the honor of staying to lunch. You'll be taking pot luck, I warn you!"

By way of corrective commentary on this dire augury, which his wife greeted with an indignant "Oh!"

Jolliot launched himself toward the next room with a mischievous wink.

In the dining room, adjacent to the veranda, which overlooked the sunlit sea from the top of the cliff, the beach with its multicolored tents and the roofs of Wimereux, two discreetly-circulating valets were completing the setting of a lavish and promising table. I only darted one grateful glance at it, however, my interest returning to the young female doctor. The sight of her produced a bizarre, hitherto unknown emotion in me; it was as if, in that tall, slim young woman with the blonde hair in a Florentine bob, the soft and serious face and the blue eyes enlivened by black lashes and eyebrows, I had rediscovered an old friend. She looked at me with an undisguised sympathetic curiosity.

I was scarcely able to collect myself in order to listen to her father, who was speaking to me. That individual, with a worldly air, scholarly baldness, a prominent Semitic nose and a salt-and-pepper beard, was looking at me from behind his round spectacles with eyes of a troubling malachite-green color.

"My dear colleague," he said, "since our exquisite hostess has been kind enough to contrive this meeting with you, I'll get straight to the point, with a businesslike frankness—for unlike you, I'm not only a scientist. The necessities of everyday life...

"Firstly, permit me to ask a question. The South Pole has already been discovered, some years ago. Commander Barcot is going back there. Is that to take possession of it, officially, in the name of your country?"

A slight German accent and a hint of veiled aggression beneath the courteous tone prejudiced me against the Swiss professor, but the seduction—or rather the magnetism—exerted on me by be the person I was already thinking of as "Frédérique" attenuated the dryness of my reply.

"Not at all, Professor. Our mission has nothing official about it; its goals are entirely scientific. We're going to explore the higher regions of Antarctica."

"You see, Father?" said the young doctor, in impeccable French, in a contralto voice that made me quiver delightfully.

Without paying any heed to his daughter, the professor said: "I congratulate you, my dear colleague. If I were ten years younger, and if the personnel of the *Erebus II* were not doubtless complete, I'd gladly join you..."

"Oh, Doctor!" said the film-director, impetuously, who was pouring the port and had only heard the end of the sentence. "If I wasn't so busy, I too would offer my services to Commander Barcot. Antarctica! What marvelous films one could shoot there...even our dear star, who's as sensitive to the cold as a snake..." He glanced at his wife. "But Barcot's expedition has been complete for a long time, isn't that so, Antoine? And but for your friend Jean-Paul Rivier..."

He left the sentence unfinished, and lifted his glass to his lips with a complicit smile.

"Monsieur Jolliot is mistaken regarding my father's intentions," the young woman said, serenely. "My father is not asking to join the expedition."

"I only desire one thing," declared Kohbuler, curtly. "To make the acquaintance of the Maecenas whose name has just been mentioned. I have a business proposition to make to him, and since you're his friend, my dear colleague..."

"An old school friend," I confessed. "It's thanks to him that I'm part of the personnel of *Erebus II*...and that wasn't without difficulty. Commander Barcot..."

"Say, Antoine," Jolliot interrupted, if you're still leaving for Marseille the day after tomorrow, you'll have difficulty introducing Dr. Kohbuler to Jean-Paul Rivier."

"Oh! You're leaving the day after tomorrow?" said the Swiss, staring at me. "But I assume you'll be in Paris tomorrow."

The hope of seeing Frédérique again at the same time as her father made my heart beat faster. "Yes, I will, for twenty-four hours, from this evening."

"Well, we'll arrive there tomorrow at eleven o'clock. Do you think that Monsieur Rivier would accept an invitation to dinner at Claridge's...if you were to help me meet him, initially as if by chance, at a café?"

"I think so—providing that he's in Paris."

At that moment an electric bell rang in a corner of the veranda.

"Excuse me," said Jolliot, setting off to answer it. "No, it's not the telephone; it's a wireless bell—a new invention, quite ingenious. The signal signifies that a telephonic transmission from the Tower[7]...twenty past noon? That's unusual. What can it be?"

He sat down to an item of furniture laden with a complex apparatus, and began tripping switches. Bulbs

---

[7] When the novel was written, in the early days of radio broadcasting—when only a few people had their own receivers, often combined with transmitters so that they could communicate with one another—the Eiffel Tower was used as the broadcasting station in Paris, temporarily adding a new dimension to its iconic status.

lit up. With a set of headphones over his ears, he looked at us obliquely, with an astonished expression.

"You don't say?" he muttered, in the midst of our attentive silence. Then, in a louder voice, he said to us: "Sensational news! Do you want to hear it?"

He flicked a switch, and a clear voice emerged from a loudspeaker, captured in mid-sentence.

"…ravaging the North Atlantic. Seven distress calls have been received by the coastguard in the course of the last half-hour. Preceded by a gigantic wave, the cyclone is moving at a velocity of more than a hundred kilometers an hour. The Cunard Company's *Lutetia*, in a message abruptly cut short, signaled the distant appearance of a waterspout and vapor, followed by a formidable explosion…apparently that of a submarine volcano…

"*Au revoir*, Mesdames et Messieurs; a further broadcast will be made at two o'clock to provide supplementary details…I shall repeat, for those who have not heard: Hello, hello, Eiffel Tower here. An unprecedented cyclone is ravaging the North Atlantic. Seven distress calls…"

Jolliot let the voice go on to the end for a second time. Gripped by emotion, I looked at Mademoiselle Kohbuler, sitting bolt upright on the divan, whose eyes, attached to mine, were expressing an acute anguish. The star was looking out at the apparently-impassive sea, breathing in the scent of her red carnation. The attentive Swiss professor took regular puffs on his cigarette.

The voice fell silent—but a curt and imperious "Shh!" from Jolliot cut short the exclamations and comments. He fiddled with his apparatus…and the loudspeaker resumed. Now, however, it was the modulated stridencies of Morse code, unintelligible to the profane. Pencil in hand, the film-director scribbled on a notepad.

"An S.O.S. call…from the Norwegian cargo vessel *Oslo*," he announced, finally.

Then, on another wavelength, the sound of a child's trumpet intoned dots and dashes.

"Another one in distress. Cod-fishing steamboat *Saint-Anne*, from Paimpol…"

It required the insistence of his wife to drag the radio ham away from his passion and remind him of his duties as a host. "Come on—we'll soon find out anyway, via the broadcast from the Tower…"

Pirouetting in his chair, he turned toward us.

"A pity that television's still in its infancy, eh? I'm sure that, in ten years' time, apparatus will exist to give us here in Europe, in our homes, the spectacles that are in the process of unfolding out in the Atlantic, three thousand kilometers away. It must be phenomenal…splendid!"

"Atrocious, you mean, Monsieur," said Frédérique. "But while waiting for television, the simple news that these disasters are happening right now is enough to wring our hearts."

"So many orphans! So many widows!" the star felt obliged to declaim, theatrically.

"Yes," I observed, "henceforth, the whole world will vibrate in unison, thanks to the wireless. Fifteen years ago, this catastrophe wouldn't have disturbed us as much, because we'd only have learned about it from the newspapers three or four days later. The rhythm of life on our planet has accelerated, and humankind is increasingly forming a whole, a single organism palpitating all at once with the same reactions."

"You're forgetting the war, my dear colleague," said the Swiss professor, ironically. "Your 'whole' isn't homogeneous. The races are irreconcilable...charged with different potentials of sensitivity."

The mistress of the house did not give me time to reply. She hated arguments, even courteous ones. She brought the subject beck to the subject of the moment. "At any rate, it's over; after these few disasters, the cyclone will exhaust its force, dissipate and fade away..."

"Hmm," said Jolliot. "You're an optimist, Cienne. The cyclone might well sweep away more ships in its course before arriving here...like all Atlantic storms. We'd better get our umbrellas ready. But that's no reason to go hungry—let's sit down at table. That way, we'll be on the coffee when the Tower makes it next broadcast."

The meal provided a diversion. After the *hors-d'oeuvre*, as everyone tucked into the turbot, a tacit truce was established; the subject of shipwrecks was relegated to the domain of the subconscious, and we talked about other things. The professor and Jolliot launched into a digression on the respective merits of European and American hotels, and even the star became a little more animated.

That gave me a welcome opportunity to exchange a few words with my neighbor, the charming doctor, who had as little interest in the subject of hotels as I did. But what point is there is reporting what we said? Banal and uninteresting for any listener, it simply served to support the marvelous intimacy that had revealed itself between us, and my eyes replied in the same language to the limpid confidence that her blue eyes with the black lashes dedicated to me. In feeling close to her, as in a bath of blissful effluvia, I knew that love had just connected our secret magnetic fields forever.

I asked her the name of her perfume.

"Remember," she said, with a smile. "The name's slightly twee, but I like the perfume. Do you?"

"It evokes the scents of a beautiful summer day by the sea," I murmured, reflectively. "The sun on the sand and the briny breeze…it's as poignant and profound as one of those landscapes that one never forgets…"

She darted a glance of infinite softness at me, her lips parted to reply…

But she did not have time. At that precise moment, a subterranean rumble became audible, muted and prolonged, a kind of roll of thunder. Glasses clinked and the house was shaken as if a heavy truck were passing just outside its walls—but the villa was isolated in its grounds on the edge of the cliff, fifty meters from the road.

"An earthquake!" I exclaimed, remembering one that I had once experienced in Italy.

Unfamiliar with such phenomena, the other guests looked at one another, more surprised than anxious.

"Come on, my dear colleague, your deluding yourself!" the professor from Basle objected, disdainfully. "There have never been any seismic shocks in this region!"

"Even so, it might be more prudent to go out into the open," suggested the star—but without getting up.

We remained on the alert for a minute, napkins in hand, ready to make a move—but the shock was not renewed, and we were ashamed of our alarm.

The clear laughter of the young doctor was the first to ring out. I admired her frankness. "You frightened me, Monsieur Marquin!"

"I'm very sorry, Mademoiselle, and I beg you to forgive me, but I really thought that I recognized the precursory symptoms of a quake. I was in Naples in

1912 during a slight earthquake, and it was exactly like the one just now."

Jolliot consulted his wristwatch. "Thirteen fifty-five. In five minutes, perhaps the Tower will tell us what it was. Shall we go on to the veranda? The coffee's ready."

We were disappointed, however. The radiotelephonic broadcast only mentioned the cyclone, which had increased in extent, causing further disasters.

"We do not know the exact number, because communications with North America by cable and wireless have been interrupted. Given the trajectory of the phenomenon and its velocity of travel, the meteorological office anticipates the arrival of a violent tempest on our Atlantic coasts and in the Channel during tonight and tomorrow morning. Ships presently at sea are advised to seek shelter in the nearest port. Departures are suspended on the Paris-London and Paris-Cherbourg airlines."

The commentaries continued, but I was only listening distractedly. The four o'clock express was due to take me to Paris, and I still had to go to my home in Boulogne to pick up my baggage. Even with the automobile that the film-director had put at my disposal, I would only just have time.

I said my goodbyes.

Lucienne Jolliot wished me *bon voyage* as if it were a matter of an eight-hour excursion. It would not have taken much for her to ask me to send her a postcard from the South Pole. Her husband, who was more expansive, gratified me with a warm accolade.

As for the professor, he renewed the invitation I had given him: "It's understood, isn't it, my dear colleague, that we'll lunch tomorrow at Claridge's? Elsa and I will be leaving Boulogne at seven-thirty in the morning, to arrive in Paris at about eleven. Rendezvous at eleven-thirty at the Taverne Royale—and try to bring your friend Monsieur Rivier."

I bowed, dissimulating my joy. I shook the father's horny hand, and then the daughter's soft and frank one. The last vision of her I took away was of an amicable smile of her blue eyes with the black lashes, which I was glad to be able to admire again the following day.

II. The Atlantic Cyclone

I ought to say immediately that the meeting did not take place, and that it was the first link in the chain that broke in the series of events on which I was counting.

Right on time, I disembarked on to the Parisian asphalt at eight-thirty. I had eaten in the restaurant car. The theaters and cinemas did not tempt me. Having deposited my baggage at the Terminus and sent a telegram to Rivier, I took a taxi and went along the boulevards to spend a couple of hours before going to bed.

In the lukewarm early September evening the crowds of pedestrians and automobiles displayed their boring film amid the civilized apotheosis of electric lights. Once again, as in all of my visits to Paris, I was astonished to find the city insouciant and cheerful, in vesperal fête, in spite of the economic distress and the pound at 460.[8] Only the newsvendors—"*Liberté… Intran!...* Special editions!"—were communicating a hint of anxiety to the flood of passers-by, with their papers hot off the press, which people were buying and scanning rapidly.

---

[8] In the 1920s, the pound sterling, rather than the US dollar, was the international currency by which most exchange rates were judged. 460 francs to the pound would have been regarded at the time as disastrous, but the deterioration—further assisted by World War II—eventually reached such a stage that the old franc had to be abandoned and "new francs" introduced, each worth a hundred old francs. The new franc eventually reached a level of eleven to the pound before the introduction of the euro changed the situation.

To read them, I sat down on the terrace of the Café Cardinal at the crossroads of the Boulevard Haussmann.

Stormy debate in the Chambre on the measures to prevent the devaluation of the franc... Ministerial crisis in prospect... Collision of aircraft at Villacoublay...

With regard to the tempest, the evening papers told me nothing more than the two o'clock bulletin from the Tower. As I resumed following the spectacle of the boulevard with an amused eye, however, a luminous announcement attracted my attention. In the background, on the roof of the *Paris-Projecteur* building, a sequence of characters was unfurling from tight to left.

"Tempest ravaging the Azores. Further maritime disasters... The forty-watt Phoebus Lamp is the sun at home... Loss of transatlantic liner *Zuyderzee*... Drink Kichof aperitif..."

A melancholy developed within me, born of that news, which was transposed on to the egotistical plane. I savored the Paris evening bitterly—the last, for how long? A year, perhaps two, spent in the bleak wilderness of the Antarctic...

No matter, though! I was not leaving anyone behind; I was alone in the world, since my wife and my mother had been killed in Paris in April 1918 by a shell from a Big Bertha. The irony of fate. While my hospital was at Malo, exposed to daily fire from the artillery at Dixmunde... No children, scarcely any family. A few good friends, at the most, like Jolliot and Rivier...

Good old Jean-Paul! He had a durable gratitude, that one! True, the hazards of a bathing-spot, fifteen years before, had permitted me to save his life, but how many others would have remembered, in his situation? I could ask him for a hundred thousand francs tomorrow, and he'd give them to me with a smile... In the meantime, it was to him that I owed the chance to flee my unsatisfactory existence; he was the one who had imposed me as ship's physician, at the last minute, on Commander Barcot, whose cruise he was subsidizing...

My existence...!

And I thought once again about my last nine years, as a nomad doctor, migrating from Paris to Trouville, from Trouville to Sanary, from Sanary to Boulogne, without being able to settle down or find anything else in a few brief relationships but disappointing flirtations...

I saw myself, finally resolved to shake off my old self and put on a new skin, for a regenerative exodus to the wilderness and heroic life of the Pole...

And then, as a young blonde, tall and lithe, in the same blue coat as Frédérique, passed by on the sidewalk, the image of the latter came back to me with an almost hallucinatory acuity, and I sensed once again the same disturbance that had possessed me in her presence. Her perfume—Remember!—evoked in the Parisian evening the splendor of the sun on a summer beach. I saw her smile again...

Frédérique! New light! Oh, life with you would perhaps be sweet...

But I shrugged my shoulders, irritated with myself and my crazy imagination, already enchanted by a future in which the blonde doctor would be my lifelong companion, my spiritual ally...

Go on, fool! You're leaving tomorrow for Antarctica...

Just your luck, isn't it, that windfall *in extremis*, of which you can't take advantage! I'm to see her again tomorrow, and then? A fine affair! Shall we know one another, after having had lunch together? And if our sympathy is increased, it will only poison my departure, which I still considered as a liberation this morning! And her father, the enigmatic Swiss—what does he want from me? What does he want from Rivier? If I do him this favor, will he grant me the hand of his daughter in exchange?

Then again, no! It's absurd. One can't get engaged in that fashion, after two hour-long conversations on the eve of departing for the end of the Earth...

I slept badly that night, having gone to bed too soon in my room at the Terminus-Nord. I dreamed about a cruise in the midst of shipwrecks, with Frédérique as captain and her father amusing himself by fishing with a rod and line for floating cadavers.

I had not drawn the curtains or closed the shutters. When I woke up, it was so dark that I ran to the window to check the time on the station clock. It really was eight o'clock! Rain was falling from a sky the color of antimony, rattling against my windows in furious gusts. It was the storm announced the previous day. My first lucid thought was for Frédérique, who had just boarded a train in Boulogne, in that abominable weather, which was doubtless even worse on the coast.

An initial disappointment awaited me in the Avenue de Villiers, at Jean-Paul Rivier's house, where I arrived at ten o'clock in accordance with my telegram. The banker had left the day before for Biarritz, summoned by a telegram from his wife, and would not be back for two days.

What a blow! Adieu to the hope to fulfilling my promise to Hans Kohbuler...but bah! Too bad for him! The essential thing for me was to have lunch in his company, and above all, that of his daughter...

I still had an hour to kill before the arrival of the two travelers. I spent it at the rendezvous—the Taverne Royale—reading the morning newspapers and watching the rain fall.

According to the latest news, after a whole series of disasters in the Atlantic, the cyclone had reached the French shore in Brittany at about one o'clock in the morning. Boats that had remained at sea in spite of the warnings had been sunk. Even in the ports, and here and there inland, a tidal wave had caused serious damage.

At eleven o'clock, the *Paris-Midi* brought further details, albeit summary and provisional, for the cyclone had blown down the telegraph-poles and interrupted communications with the capital. Even the wireless was only receiving messages blurred by the "static" of a magnetic storm raging over the entire northern hemisphere.

The tidal wave, several meters high, had unfurled successively over all the coasts of Western Europe: Ireland, England, France, Spain, Portugal... In the Channel it had reached Cherbourg at three a.m., Le Havre at five; and, increasing its violence in the bottleneck formed by the curve of the coast extending from the Somme to Cap Gris-Nez, it had swept over the dyke at Berck at half past six, razing several villas, and carried away the iron bridge over the Canche at Étaples.

That would have cut the main line from Calais to Paris, two hours before the passage of the express that was due to bring Frédérique and her father that morning!

By virtue of a last residue of hope—the Kohbulers might have changed their plans and taken an overnight train—I waited another hour...but no one appeared.

I had lunch alone, it did not matter where, furious at that failure, cursing the cyclone and striving to dispel the haunting memory of Frédérique.

After coffee and Benedictine, and having smoked two cigars, I observed that I still had five full hours until my departure. A kind of misanthropic perversity deterred me from making the two or three visits that I had originally planned; I sank back into my sulky melancholy, spending my last afternoon in Paris trailing from one café to another.

The capital was living with a simple sulkiness in the dreadful weather, without any apparent concern for the maritime catastrophe. The continuous procession of mechanical vehicles—buses and taxis—assumed a lugubrious and inhuman aspect beneath the cataract of rain. On the sidewalks, the passers-by, their heads invisible beneath umbrellas clenched in both fists, were striding purposefully: mud-spattered trouser-clad legs, and feminine legs of every curvature and caliber, sheathed in silk, with high-heeled shoes, miraculously intact amid the deluge...

At four o'clock, further special editions helped me to be patient.

The disaster was extending. Mute since the day before, America finally sent its contingent of details, via Pernambuco and Dakar.

Sooner and more violently than Western Europe, the Eastern United States and Canada suffered the effects of an unprecedented tornado. A ninety foot wave—more than thirty meters!—a veritable wall of water, hurled itself upon the coasts of the two countries, initially in Newfoundland, devastating ports, lifting up ships and hurling them against skyscrapers in destructive col-

lisions. As we go to press, the victims are already counted in tens of thousands...

An interview followed, obtained from the head of the Meteorological Office and commenting on the unprecedented anomaly of the "double tempest"—so to speak—"progressing radially in opposite directions toward America and Europe, as if from a common center of atmospheric and marine perturbation."

The seven o'clock express bore me away toward Marseilles, beneath a belated dusk falling from an apocalyptic sky, amid a diluvian mixture of rain and hail that peppered the windows like machine-gun fire. A meal in the restaurant-car...splenetic hours in the first-class compartment, facing an English clergyman and his wife, who stubbornly kept the electric light on all the way to Lyon, in order to read...

The sun, caressing my cheek, woke me up. The flat landscape of the Crau extended away from the windows, beneath an immaculate azure, but the cypresses bordering the track were bending over beneath a furious mistral. At the exit from the Nerthe Tunnel, the Mediterranean was displayed, leaden blue in color, bristling with white crests. The tempest was here too, but it was a dry tempest, and the ships had found safe havens behind the various promontories that extended their arms between L'Estaque and Marseilles, for the transatlantic tidal wave had expired on the threshold of the Latin sea, in the straits of Gibraltar.

At eight o'clock, having disembarked at the Gare Saint-Charles, I took a taxi, with my baggage, through the sunlit streets of the ancient Phocean city, along the picturesque and swarming Cannebière, toward the Old Port, where my ship, the *Erebus II*, was moored at the Quai des Belges.

III. *The Departure of the* Erebus II

The activity of a day of departure reigned on the proud three-master, constructed to brave the ice-sheet, but in which my layman's eyes could see nothing as yet but a steamship like any other. Sailors in red jerseys, with white monograms deformed by the play of their robust pectoral muscles, were busy around a gaping hatchway, into which the crane of a loading-mast was lowering barrels picked up on the quay from an automobile truck. The yellow dust filtering from the barrels and powdering the truck and the pavement I recognized, not without surprise, as sulfur.

The officer on duty at the gangplank took possession of me, however; he took me on to the upper deck, to Commander Barcot, a sturdy quinquagenarian with the clean-shaven and ascetic face, who had been popularized by photos in the weeklies and dailies in connection with his first Antarctic expedition.

With my visiting-card between his fingers, he stared at me with his aquamarine eyes for such a long time that I looked away. Finally, he offered me his hand and said, rather dryly: "Welcome aboard, Doctor...since you're Monsieur Rivier's friend. I didn't think of asking, in my letter, whether you have sea-legs? Yes? So much the better, for we're going to dance tomorrow in this mistral."

He interrupted himself to call to an officer who was supervising the maneuvers a few paces away: "Lefébure!" He went on: "Monsieur Lefébure, my first mate, will take you to your cabin, Doctor. I'll introduce you to your colleagues this evening. Until then..."

I followed the first mate.

Lefébure...Robert Lefébure...from where did I remember that name? As we went down the stairway I inspected the suntanned face of my guide, who winked at me mischievously.

"So, Antoine, you no longer recognize your old friends? Bébert, remember—your schoolfellow at the Lycée de Lille, with whom you swapped postage stamps... and who cribbed your Latin translations."

I uttered an exclamation. What an unexpected pleasure, to find myself in familiar territory, in spite of everything, aboard the ship! And I surrendered my fingers to the warm fist of the jovial mariner.

Having arrived by way of the starboard gangway at the port-holed cabin that was to be my home for long months, Lefébure helped me to stow my baggage, and while I put on the new ship's doctor's uniform I had bought in Boulogne—a blue jacket with braid and garnet lining—he sat cross-legged on the edge of my bed, lit a cigarette, and began my initiation without further delay.

"The old man gave you a frosty welcome eh? Not surprising. He'd already chosen his own nephew as shipboard doctor...but as it's your friend Rivier who's covering the expenses of the expedition, the nephew has been bounced in your favor. That's fine; you're lucky to be a doctor hereabouts—which is to say, virtually independent. If you were an officer, for example, you'd be at risk of having a hard time, or even if you were a member of the technical staff...for, you know, we're taking a naturalist, a cinema-photographer, a geologist-cum-paleontologist, a mineralogist...and entire Academy of Sciences. Not to mention, as you're doubtless unaware, engineers...one, two, three, four engineers! Yes, Monsieur, four mining engineers, to go to the South Pole! It's amazing, but that's the way it is, and you aren't at the end of your surprises. If I were to tell you about the cargo: extraction machines, huts, a conveyor-belt, a decauville[9] with kilometers of rail…and finally—would you believe it?—nine hundred barrels of sulfur!

"You presumably believe, in accordance with that the papers have said, that we're going straight to the Pole, with purely scientific objectives? But it's too soon in the season; it's scarcely spring in the southern hemisphere—and then again, is it usual for a businessman such as your friend Rivier to pay for such an expedition? So, first we're going to the Gabon to drop off the nine hundred barrels of sulfur—the commander's nightmare: 'the bold explorer,' as all the magazines call him, raging at seeing himself transformed into a vulgar cargo carrier! After which…but I'll tell you later. You're dressed now. It's ten o'clock; let's go have an aperitif and lunch on the Cannebière. I'm not on duty, and we're not leaving until sixteen hundred hours."

Arm in arm, heading into the teeth of the mistral, we went to sit down on the enclosed terrace of the Café Glacier. And that was the inevitable topic of conversation over our orange curacaos on such a day: the tempest.

I questioned Lefébure. "I haven't read this morning's papers—what are they saying?"

"Nothing genuinely new since yesterday—still material damage and victims. But as I came down from the quarter-deck a little while ago, Madec, the wireless op-

---

[9] The industrial railway system invented by Paul Decauville in the 1870s and marketed by his company thereafter was so successful—especially in its military applications—that his name came to be used as a trivial noun in France.

erator, told me about a long-wave signal he'd just picked up, which gave the explanation of the tidal wave. It's definitely a matter of a submarine volcanic eruption. A cargo vessel, the *Champlain*, going from Montreal to Le Havre, which was lucky enough to catch the ocean wave—fifty meters high, if you please—head on and not sideways, in which case it would have gone down, signaled that it had seen a new island on its northern horizon, at 43° west longitude and 55° north latitude...approximately, for the ship had been sailing through fog by dead reckoning for two days. Obviously an island of volcanic origin, and as the depth thereabouts is some four thousand meters, you can imagine how much water that mass of lava must have displaced, surging from the ocean bed all the way to the surface!"

We had lunch on the Quai de Rive-Neuve, as the Restaurant de la Cascade, where dockers in short-sleeved shirts and elegant couples whose cars were parked outside rubbed shoulders, in the fine egalitarian tradition of Marseilles. While savoring the shellfish—mussels, oysters and sea-urchins—and the inevitable bouillabaisse, we told one another our life stories since school, each of us speaking for his own benefit and putting on a semblance of listening to the other by way of compensation.

Half an hour before raising anchor, at three-thirty in the afternoon, we headed back to the *Erebus II*, whose funnel was emitting thick swirls of smoke.

An expectant crowd had occupied the quay, where obstructed trams were ringing their bells loudly; a brass band was blasting heroic marches into the wind; at the water's edge journalists were setting up a battery of photographic apparatus, including movie-cameras. It took the combined efforts of two policemen to open a passage for us.

On the ship, however, everything seemed chaotic: men fore and officers aft, open-mouthed and idle, everyone talking in low voices. All eyes were fixed on Commander Barcot, who was striding back and forth on the bridge, arms folded, brows furrowed.

"We're not going!" whispered the bosun, Nerfi, as we crossed the deck. "Minister's orders. The old man's in a huff—watch out, Monsieur Lefébure. Ah, doctor! We've just received a wireless message for you. Hang on—Le Moullec has it—he's looking for you. Yes, the big red-headed fellow chatting to the duty officer, behind the servomotor."

I ran to the man, received the blue form and opened it, my heart beating.

It was signed *Hans Kohbuler*. The professor apologized for missing the meeting and begged me to accept his good wishes for the voyage, and those of his daughter.

My head spun. On the deck of the ship, in the blare of the music and the roar of the mistral, which made the paper flutter in my hand, I thought I was breathing Frédérique's perfume again and hearing her voice: "Bon voyage, Doctor!"

I stayed there for some time, leaning on the bulwark, my gaze fascinated by the shiny water of the harbor...

Lefébure came back, though, and tapped me on the shoulder.

"Not bad news, I hope, old chap? No, your lady friend—it's written all over your face. Lucky devil! By the way, do you know what's happening? We've been requisitioned! And we're waiting for an envoy from the ministry, who'll decide our fate. 'Be ready to sail tomorrow at eight hundred hours,' the wireless said. The old man nearly had a heart attack—he wanted to ignore it and leave anyway. Hang on a minute, while I go and get rid of all these idiots who are watching us. They're driving us crazy with their brass band! Since we're not leaving today..."

It was in those troubled circumstances that I made contact with my colleagues of the general staff and the scientific personnel of the *Erebus II*. The effervescence of hypotheses to which everyone was giving free rein, concerning the requisitioning of the ship, created an attractive atmosphere in which I immediately found myself englobed—and those few hours of discussion did more than days of everyday intercourse to incorporate me into the shipboard society.

Two of my new companions, in addition to Lefébure, seemed to me to be particularly likeable: the mineralogist Isidore Gripert, a young man of about thirty with myopic spectacles, who was also interested in astronomy—my own hobby—and the geologist-cum-paleontologist Maxime Vanderdael, a northerner like myself.

Before spending that first night aboard moored to the Quai des Belges instead of being rocked by the waves of the Mediterranean, I took advantage of the delay to draft a long an exceedingly cordial telegram to *Hans Kohbuler, Claridge's Hotel, Paris.*

By virtue of some administrative red tape, the wireless operator to the *Erebus II*, although he had received a wireless message on my behalf, no longer had the right to send private communications since the requisition. I had to run all the way to the main post office.

At half past seven the next morning the engines were already under pressure; we were only waiting for the ministry's envoy and the order to sail. The mistral was still blowing violently, but this time there were few idlers on the quay—not one journalist and no official representatives.

At eight o'clock precisely, a taxi hurtled up at top speed and stopped at the gangplank. A uniformed naval captain came aboard, saluted us coldly and courteously, and disappeared into Commander Barcot's cabin.

Five minutes later, the two men reappeared, chatting amicably, and went up on to the bridge. The commander, transfigured, seemed joyful in spite of the theoretical division of his authority with the naval officer. The latter, with his hands in his pockets, affected to be uninterested in the maneuvering.

The engine-room bell rang. Orders were shouted. The mooring-ropes were cast off. The propeller began to turn in the greasy water of the harbor. The quay gently slipped away—and with an accelerating speed, the panorama of the two shores filed past our eye, while the Cannebière shrank, as seen in our wake.

The transporter-bridge extended its futuristic arch overhead momentarily; we doubled Fort Saint-Jean; and an initial thrust of the swell caused me to stagger. The telegraph bell regulated our progress with the commander's orders. "Hard to starboard! Increase speed! Full steam ahead!"

And the *Erebus II*, heading south-west, assumed her cruising sped of fifteen knots, in spite of the increasingly heavy swell that came at her obliquely.

Clinging to the rampart of the upper deck, sprayed with mist, my eyes roasted by the ferocious mitral, I watched the coast of France draw away, while thinking about Frédérique...

I was beginning to feel the first symptoms of seasickness when a whistle-blast rang out, and then a sailor touched my shoulder and asked me to go down to the ward-room.

I found the ship's officers and the scientific personnel assembled before the naval officer and Commander Barcot.

"Messieurs," declared the latter, scanning us with his bright eyes, glistening with pride, "we're no longer going to the South Pole! The government of the Republic is sending us on a mission, and I have the honor of presenting to you Monsieur de Silfrage, corvette captain, who is the bearer of the ministerial orders. We're instructed to go and explore the new island, provisionally named island N, which a submarine volcanic eruption caused to surge forth three days ago in the middle of the Atlantic."

IV. On Island N

The first four days of that journey only left me with the memory of an abominable feeling of nausea, and of having been shaken in my bunk by one of those crazily-rotating fairground rides known as "whips." I can still see the porthole of my cabin, pointing toward the gray sky one moment and plunging profoundly into the waves the next, throwing me into a glaucous and sepulchral gloom. I can still see the face of the waiter who sometimes came to offer me something to eat, in vain, and that of Lefébure, who arrived streaming in his black waterproof, shouting through the partly-open door at me; "Still as floppy, then, Doc? Not yet ready to come and care for your scientific colleagues?"

The fact is that everyone on board could have died without my giving a damn—but the only serious accident that occurred in those four days was the disappearance of the geologist Vanderdael, carried away by a wave, and I could do nothing about that except sincerely regret it, when I found out about the death of my unfortunate northern compatriot.

I was not alone in suffering from seasickness. It had cut a swathe through the scientific ranks, and three places still remained empty at the ward-room table when I reappeared there for breakfast on the twelfth of September. The sea was still heavy, but I no longer felt ill and had an appetite worthy of a polar bear.

Following the usual custom of ships that spend long months wintering in the heart of the ice-sheet, and aboard which the members of the expedition tend to group, as much to combat the cold more effectively as to tighten the bonds of camaraderie and create an atmosphere of human solidarity against the hostility of nature, the seventeen members of the general staff—except for those on duty—and the scientific personnel ate together at the same table, over which the corvette captain and Commander Barcot took turns to preside.

"I believe you've found your sea-legs, Doctor!" said the latter, ironically, when I went in—but that was the whole of his vengeance. Thereafter, I must say, his rancor at my appointment was concealed beneath the perfect politeness that he manifested outside of his rare fits of anger, when he became surprisingly coarse and swore—always in English, it's true—in a manner worthy of the master of a Yankee vessel.

My mocking friend Lefébure was on watch, and my neighbors, the mineralogist Gripert and the wireless operator Madec limited themselves to inoffensive jokes. The discovery of the island toward which we were sailing was not, apparently, a goal as heroic as our original destination, but its interest was sufficient to maintain a cordial and indulgent humor. Moreover, the scientist saw me as a colleague, and the ship's personnel accorded to the ship's doctor—an individual almost equal in status to the "master after God"—a consideration to which land-dwellers are unaccustomed.

We were arriving in the probable locale of the island, but the coordinates of latitude and longitude furnished by the steamship *Champlain* turned out to be incorrect; for two days we carried out a search in vain in a northward direction, picked at random.

Although the tempest had diminished, and only a broad swell without breaking crests remained, the sea remained utterly deserted beneath the fuliginous sky. Transatlantic services had not been resumed since the cyclone, and in addition, if the radio messages were to be believed, United States shipping had been "virtually annihilated" and Europe's severely depleted.

Since our departure from Marseilles the news from France and America picked up by out antenna had told us very little, apart from the enormous damage caused around the perimeter of the Ocean by the "volcanic eruption." All countries were organizing subscriptions in favor of the victims of the cyclone, and people were still talking much more about them than about island N. Its very existence had been called into question and, it appeared, treated as a hoax by a certain number of newspapers. In spite of that, on a motion from the French delegate, the League of Nations was busy trying to decide to which country the mandate for the new territory ought to be confided. In the same way that we were sending our messages in secret code, however, the radio broadcasting stations were not breathing a word to the public about the mission of the *Erebus II*, and we had sailed toward the island incognito—with several days' start on our potential competitors, in the improbable case that any other nation had similarly had a ship ready to depart, equipped for a long-distance mission of exploration.

It was on the fourteenth of September that we sighted island N, some two hundred miles north-west of the position indicated, under a cloudy sky, in dismal weather. The cold was extraordinarily sharp for the time of year. A north-easterly breeze was blowing, bringing us a breath of the ice-cap. Rain was falling intermittently, stinging our faces beneath the hoods of our waterproofs. In the interval between two squalls, toward mid-afternoon, the cry of "Land on the starboard bow!" rang out. When the laymen were able to make it out, they saw a kind of snow-capped cone surmounting a pedestal of black cliffs, which stood out prominently against the leaden backcloth of the sky.

The island was about six kilometers long and the peak nine hundred meters high—but what astonished us was that no smoke or vapor was rising from it.

"It's funny, all the same, that volcanic island!" muttered Lefébure—we had both taken refuge in the port lifeboat, set against a deckhouse next to the bridge, which gave us some shelter from the wind and rain. "I saw one once in 1909, in the isles of Sonda, not far from the famous Krakatoa. It was a few hundred meters long, at the most, and scarcely rose above sea level. One might have mistaken it for a sleeping whale. But that one was fuming, I can assure you—fuming like ten factories from all its pores, even two months after its appearance."

While altering course in order to head straight for its goal, the *Erebus II* had reduced her speed. Binoculars to their eyes, the two captains were scrutinizing the island, searching for a landing-point. On the bridge beside them, a helmsman, with his ears to the microphones of the ultrasonic sounding apparatus, was announcing the depth in a loud voice.

Commander Barcot expected to arrive at any minute over the submarine plateau that ought, logically, to serve as a foundation for the new island, but nothing became manifest; the depth-readings were between thirty-eight hundred and four thousand meters.

Meanwhile, the island was becoming distinct even to the naked eye. The cone, devoid of snow in its lower reaches, seemed to be dark red in color, dotted with yellow, and of an entirely different nature from the pedestal, formed of black rock cracked by fissures. One of them might perhaps allow access to the plateau surrounding the base of the snowy peak.

Lefébure pointed out the bizarre form of the latter. "Exactly the same silhouette as Mount Corcovado near Rio de Janeiro, as seen from the Boulevard de Botafogo...but only the silhouette, not the color. What the devil can it be made of, this fake Corcovado? One would swear that it was mahogany, encrusted with streaks of gold!"

As there was little more than two hours of daylight remaining, there was no possibility of making a tour of the island in order to find a more favorable point of disembarkation. In his impatience to set foot on the new land, which we all shared, the Commander set a course for the nearest crack in the black cliff.

We were no more than half a mile from it.

"Four thousand five hundred meters!" announced the helmsman.

"That's implausible!" said the Commander. "Unexpected! The island must have risen up as if on a spike of basalt, like the shaft of a column. If this goes on, there won't even be a means of dropping anchor."

And indeed, over all the visible shoreline, there was not a single islet, reef or unfurling of hidden breakers. The sea-swell beat directly upon the foot of the vertical cliffs, which offered the nudity of a fresh fracture.

At a cable's distance from the chosen creek, the sounding was still four thousand meters.

The *Erebus II* stopped. The motor-launch was put to sea, and the Commander designated a mechanic and four men, plus Lefébure, Gripert, the engineer Fresnel and me, to accompany de Silfrage and himself on that first reconnaissance.

"But we're doubtless going to find ourselves walking on lava that's still hot," he cautioned, "so I'm going to distribute winter boots with asbestos soles. That perfect thermal insulation will protect or feet from the heat, just as it would have protected them from the cold."

Thus equipped, we embarked, and the launch set off, to the rhythm of the sputtering engine, multiply echoed by the cliffs, as if in a cavern. The rain was streaming in floods over our hoods. The melancholy aspect of the location even weighed upon the jovial Lefébure.

The only words pronounced during the journey, except for the maneuvering orders, were by Gripert. He called our attention, with bizarre insistence, to the total lack of mollusks and algae at the foot of the cliffs, their absolute nakedness in spite of the fact that it was low tide.

But what was astonishing about that, since the island had only been in existence for ten days, having been newly-born, so to speak, engendered by the pressure of the central fire?

No one deigned to point that out to the mineralogist.

We were exited, in disembarking on to that soil, virginal of all human imprint, and we trod upon it with a sort of fearful respect. It resonated underfoot like a metal slab. There was not a single pebble to be seen, nor a blade of grass, nor any moss or lichen.

The naval captain had leapt ashore first. In his hand he held one end of a long staff sheathed in waxed cloth. It was a tricolor flag, which he unfurled, stating in a portentous voice: "In the name of the government of the French people, I, Albert de Silfrage, officer of the national fleet, take possession of this new island for my country!"

He punctuated the formula with a revolver-shot, which drew echoes from the gorge; then he searched for a fissure in which to plant the shaft of his flag—but the ground was solid, like a single block, and a sailor was unable to succeed, with powerful blow of a pickaxe, in even striking a shard from it. Only a thin superficial pellicle crumbled under his blows. It was necessary to renounce the task, and the flag was returned to its sheath; one of the sailors was charged with carrying it, awaiting a better opportunity.

As soon as they had disembarked, the mineralogist and the engineer had dropped on to all fours in order to examine the terrain.

"Iron!" muttered the former. "Native iron! Superficial oxidation…obviously! That's what it is—there's no doubt about it."

"Personally, I think it's more likely to be a basaltic rock," the engineer demurred. "Porphyroid melaphyre, if I'm not mistaken. It's a pity that poor Vanderdael is no longer with us. He would soon have told us the nature and age of the terrain."

"You think, then, that a mineralogist can't do that as well as a geologist?" Griper retorted, while getting to his feet.

In his turn, Commander Barcot bent down and felt the ground with the back of his hand. He uttered a cry of surprise. "But this terrain is cold!"

"And you expected to find it hot, Commander?" Gripert queried, ironically.

"For sure! Given that a week ago, the Ocean was here, four thousand meters deep! There must have been a volcanic eruption, an outflow of igneous matter, from the terrestrial core to the marine surface…"

"And that island is constituted by a basaltic rock," said the engineer, supportively. "Of porphyroid melaphyre, or some other kind of analogous lava. The melting-point of lava is about four hundred degrees; it must have cooled—whereas iron, injected in a liquid state…fifteen hundred degrees!…would still be red hot, in spite of a week of exposure to the air and the rain."

"Monsieur Fresnel, I believe that you're mistaken, and that Monsieur Gripert is right," the naval officer declared, politely. "Look!"

And, exhibiting a small compass that he carried in an amulet, he moved it closer to the wall of the gorge. The magnetized needle deviated from its axis, clearly attracted. There was no doubt. The black rock really was iron.

The engineer conceded the point. Embracing the surroundings with his gaze, his expression became suddenly radiant, and he exclaimed: "But then, Messieurs, this island is a mine! An inexhaustible mine! There's more iron here than in all the other deposits in the world put together—and in its native state too, not in mineral form. We have enough here to supply terrestrial industry, even if consumption were to triple or increase tenfold, for thousands of years!"

"It's a fortune for France!" exclaimed de Silfrage. "You don't regret having missed the South Pole any longer, Commander?"

The mineralogist continued his investigations. His searching gaze spotted Lefébure and me in the process of examining a kind of minuscule stream that was running along the other wall down the steep slope of the gorge. By some curious phenomenon, the water was red—blood red.

Lefébure tasted it, but spat it out immediately with a frightful grimace.

"Ugh!" he said. "It's vilely metallic. But you'll see, old Antoine, that your colleagues will declare it excellent for rheumatism or something and install thermal baths here…"

Having arrived at the edge of the stream, Gripert dipped his hollowed hand into it and looked curiously at three little yellow pebbles, about the size of grains of maize, in his red-tinted palm.

"Gold!" I exclaimed, at the sight of them, with a start.

"Gold!" repeated Lefébure, in his resounding baritone. "Yes, great gods! Nuggets...like the ones I've seen at the Cape. Gold!"

The magic word attracted all our companions, including the sailors, in a matter of seconds.

"Perhaps it is, indeed, gold," the engineer confirmed, weighing the grains that the mineralogist, without saying a word, had tipped into his palm.

They were passed from hand to hand. At their cold and dense contact, an enthusiastic emotion gripped us...and an enormous hope."

"Gold!" repeated Commander Barcot. "Where did you get it, Monsieur Gripert?"

"There, brought down by that stream, which obviously comes from the snow-capped peak. That water is loaded with gold chloride...a soluble salt, which is even deliquescent. So, according to all appearance, the peak is constituted, wholly or partly, by a pudding-stone—a magma, if you prefer—of gold chloride and nuggets. Do you remember the appearance it presented, seen from the sea: a red rock speckled with yellow? The rain is dis-aggregating the magma, dissolving the chloride and carrying away the nuggets...at least, that seems probable to me; but in order to be sure, we need to go and verify my hypothesis on the spot, up there."

"Forward march! Forward march!" thundered de Silfrage.

First, however, the commander had to call the four sailors to order—they had started rummaging in the auriferous stream and we filling their pockets with nuggets—and threaten to put the mechanic in irons if he left the launch.

The ascent began. After a hundred meters, the gorge narrowed between the high iron walls, to the point at which it was nothing more than a zigzagging corridor, a narrow grove only one or two meters wide. It was necessary for us to walk in Indian file and paddle through the red water, beneath the rain and snow that were swirling in a lugubrious semi-darkness. Our asbestos soles, designed for walking on snow or ice, were ripped to shreds by the asperities of the metallic ground.

Devoured by curiosity, we went forward nevertheless, without paying any heed to the dusk that was falling.

After half an hour of that troublesome march, however, the man who was preceding us as a scout uttered a cry of angry disappointment. The corridor ended in a vertical wall, down which the red water fell in a cascade, mingled with rebounding nuggets. The walls were as smooth as skin and a hundred meters high. There was no means of getting through the cul-de-sac.

We had to give up. Having collected a few grains of gold, we went back down the gorge, already plunged into almost complete darkness. Soaked and exhausted, with our feet bruised—for the asbestos soles were in tatters—we resumed our places in the motor-launch.

Five minutes later, in the gathering night, we were on the *Erebus II* again, where everyone hastened to his cabin in order to change clothes.

V. An Astronomy Lesson

We met up again in the ward-room, with exclamations of well-being. The electric lights were shining; the radiators full of warm water were maintaining a comfortable atmosphere, in contrast to the cold and damp outside. A strong hot toddy was distributed, and completed the restoration of our spirits. When the smoke of pipes and cigarettes rose up, the talk, scattered and fragmentary until then, finally became coherent. We were able to recount our discovery to our comrades who had stayed aboard. Everyone expressed his impatience for tomorrow to come, in order to attempt a further climb to the upper plateau of the iron cliff, in order to reach the snowy peak and make sure that the gold carried by the red stream really did come from there.

No one, however, really dared believe entirely in that prodigious wealth. In spite of the specimens that everyone rattled in his palm, we retained a few doubts. An island of iron and gold, surged from the waves by eruption and cooled down in the space of a week to the ambient temperature! No, that was absurd, impossible!

The Commander appointed himself the interpreter of everyone's desire. "Monsieur Gripert, you must have an opinion about that. I'd be obliged if you'd communicate it to us."

With his second glass of grog in his left hand, the mineralogist was busy warming the right, stained by acid, on a radiator. He turned toward us.

"Gladly, Commander. My conviction is settled, and I can summarize it briefly. That island is not the result of a volcanic eruption. It is not even of terrestrial origin.

Only the oxygen that has coated its surface with a thin layer of ferrous oxide has been borrowed from the gas that we respire, during the few seconds when that surface—and only the surface—was raised to incandescence by virtue of atmospheric friction.

"In other words, Messieurs, if no innate heat is any longer manifest on the ground of the island, itself constituted by a mass of iron and gold visibly extracted from geological layers hundreds of thousands or millions of years old, it's because we have in that island a block of matter that has come from the depths of space: the debris of some unknown planet...a minuscule star fallen from the heavens...a giant aerolith...a bolide!"

There was a general outcry.

"What are you saying?"

"It's absurd!"

"Nothing like that has ever been seen!"

"A bolide that size! It would have smashed the Earth's crust!"

"Someone would have seen it fall; it would have been perceived as a heavenly body in the preceding days..."

Monsieur Gripert stood up to the storm. "And why not? What if the bolide had struck the sea obliquely, and ricocheted as if skimmed, perhaps pirouetting several times on its axis, exhausting its momentum before settling on the ocean bed, on the terrestrial crust...which is a good fifty kilometers thick?"

"Monsieur Gripert," the Commander went on, "would you care to be a little more explicit?"

"Do you want a lecture?"

"Yes, yes!"

"Speech! Speech!"

"Go on, Gripert!"

"In that case, Messieurs, a little hush!" said the mineralogist, folding his arms, placing his index-finger at the corner of his mouth.

He collected himself. Silence fell. And, as if he were lecturing in front of his students, he placed his hands flat on a table and began:

"First, allow me a little digression into the domain of astronomy—a science that is fortunately not alien to me, by virtue of a exception of which I am justly proud, in these times of excessive specialism, which make scientific synthesis so difficult...

"Messieurs, intersidereal space is not the absolute void that the ignorant imagine. Without paying any heed to the multiple energies that are incessantly interwoven in the ether—electromagnetic waves, lines of force, gravitational fields—space is populated by unevenly-distributed material particles, of which shooting stars are witnesses familiar to everyone. The latter generally follow fixed orbits around the sun at cometary velocity. They're currents of particles strung out like chaplets, through which the Earth passes at determined times of the year. There are, in consequence, the Perseids in August, the Leonids in November, and the Geminids in December. But shooting stars are trivial in dimension—a few grams at the most—and their inflammation by friction the upper layers of the atmosphere suffices to reduce them to gas, volatilizing them without residue.

"There are other celestial materials of larger size: fragments of dead stars, including an ancient tiny satellite of the Earth that was disaggregated, according to Stanislas Meunier;[10] blocks hurled out by volcanoes or

---

[10] Stanislas Meunier published his *Recherches sur la composition et la structure des météorites* in 1869.

the moon or the smaller planets, according to Émile Belot;[11] and material subsisting from the primitive chaos of the original nebula—the science is not very definite. These materials circulate in space unknown to us. Space is populated by them, but we only perceive them when they happen to penetrate the terrestrial atmosphere and are heated up by it superficially to the point of incandescence, like shooting stars.

"Some only shine momentarily, and then escape terrestrial attraction, flying away at a tangent and continuing their vagabond course. They are never seen again. Others—a few hundred every twenty-four hours, for the entire Earth—are captured by attraction, either reach the ground intact and are embedded there, or explode in mid-air and fall in fragments. Since its origin, therefore, it has been calculated that the Earth has received several cubic kilometers a century—and the other planets too, of course—and since the discovery of radioactivity, it is believed that the sun itself extracts from that external supply the material necessary to maintain its radiation. 'Suns,' Arrhenius[12] has written, 'nourish themselves on aeroliths as herbivores do on meadow-grass.'

"It is only in the last hundred years that official science, too prudent in this respect, has recognized the ex-

---

[11] Émile Belot published eight books on cosmogony between 1911 and 1932, although he became more famous as an engineer and technologist, promoting the progress of automation in State factories.

[12] Svante Arrhenius, presumably in *Das Werden der Welten* (1908; tr. as *Worlds in the Making*). The speculation regarding the "refueling" of the sun is false, but it was not until the possibility of nuclear fusion was calculated in 1929 that the true source of the sun's radiation could become evident, and not until 1939 that the theory was consolidated by Hans Bethe.

traterrestrial origin of bolides—since the remarkable fall at Laigle in the Orne in the early years of the nineteenth century. Since then, thousands of instances have been observed, and all public and private museums included blocks of meteoric iron of various sizes—for it is iron, Messieurs, of which these tiny celestial bodies are most frequently formed. The Greek name Sideros, which designated the metal iron as well as a heavenly body, proves to us elegantly that the intuition of primitive peoples did not have to wait for the decree of the Académie des Sciences to identify bolides with the blocks of meteoric iron from which they preferred to forge their tools and weapons, because of the ease with which they could work it, and its particular qualities due to the traces of nickel and manganese generally enclosed therein.

"The size of meteoric rocks collected or identified thus far varies from a few grams to hundreds or thousands of kilos. You can see in the Museum of Paris a mass of iron of 625 kilos, found at Caille in the Alpes-Maritimes. Nordenskjold discovered fifteen on the island of Sosko, south of Greenland, which weighed between 8000 and 20,000 kilos. In Diablo Canyon in Arizona there is a crater 7000 meters in diameter, which is two kilometers in circumference, hollowed out by a meteorite 150 meters in diameter—but that one burst into fragments, which are scattered around the vicinity of the crater.

"That bolides of larger dimension could exist...do exist...it would be absurd to deny, even *a priori*, and without having had irrefutable proof before your eyes in that island. We do not know the entire surface of the Earth, especially the ocean beds, must vaster that the land surface, where four fifths of bolides must be swallowed up, nor all the possibilities of intersidereal space.

Certain regions of space must be much richer than others in vagabond materials, and the appearance of the moon suffices to make us admit it, if one believes the recent hypothesis that attributes our satellite's craters—so strangely similar to shell-craters—to the arrival of a host of bolides.

"Must we expect a celestial bombardment of the same sort someday, of which the bolide that has formed Island N is only the advance messenger? It's quite possible, and the future will tell us—or our successors. In any case, there can be no doubt about this fact: a fragment of a heavenly body, a block of iron and gold several kilometers in diameter, was circulating on the fifth of September last—a week ago—in the same region of space as the Earth. That block fell into the Atlantic Ocean, at an oblique trajectory, heading from east to west—a circumstance that considerably aggravated the effects of the aerial and marine waves over Newfoundland and the American coast, which were, in any case, situated much closer to the point of impact than the Old World.

"The fall of that mass, Messieurs, was witnessed by human eyes, and if you had not been hypnotized, like everyone else, by the anecdotal news of the tempest"—the mineralogist thus qualified the loss of a hundred and fifty ships and several hundred thousand human lives!—"you would have attached more importance, on the sixth to the radio messages sent by three ships that had escaped the tidal wave and noted the appearance of an exceedingly bright bolide of an apparent diameter twice that of the full moon, which they had seen fall beyond the horizon in broad daylight an hour or two before the arrival of the devastating wave.

"Messieurs, you are now informed; I shall not abuse your attention any longer—but if the Commandant will authorize me to do it, I shall ask Monsieur Madec to send a message for me to the Académie des Sciences to take note of and announce the communication that I shall immediately begin to draft regarding the Atlantic bolide...alias island N."

"Île Fer-et-or!" Lefébure put in, humorously.

Hurrahs saluted that impromptu baptism.

"Yes! Yes!"

"That's it!"

"Île Féréor! Île Féréor!"

The vibrant voice of the corvette captain demanded silence. "Île Féréor—so be it; the name is fine and harmonious,[13] but we alone will employ it, for the time being. As for you, Monsieur Gripert, I beg you not to budge. Monsieur Madec has strict orders, and I renew them here publicly, to keep the nature, as well as the exact position, of the island secret. The discovery of the island and its taking into possession by us—yes, the government of the Republic will be informed of that this evening; but you know that the League of Nations has not yet made a decision as to the attribution of the island. Announce by radio that it is made of gold—even in encrypted language? Bah! We know what secret codes are sometimes worth, with all the possible leaks at the min-

---

[13] The crew's contraction of Lefébure's *Fer-et-or* [iron-and-gold] to *Féréor* does, indeed, make it more harmonious, but it also carries an additional implication, undoubtedly intentional on the part of the author, by virtue of modifying the pronunciation of the first syllable. *Fée* means enchantress, or fairy, so the island's new name carries a phonetic implication of "fairy gold" that is entirely suited to the novel's fairy-tale aspects.

istry and ever-watchful espionage. That would be to risk a check at the League of Nations, and attract a horde of gold-seekers here."

"They'd be here in no time," the Commander said, supportively. "Like you, Captain, I'm of the opinion that we should keep the secret. In any case, our right of first occupation is incontestable. France..."

"France has, in this island, a unique opportunity to reestablish its finances. It's up to us to take advantage of it before it's too late. Who knows what the future holds in store for us? The exploitation must begin tomorrow."

"Fortunately, we have the equipment!" said the Commander.

There was no need to say any more; although it was not official, the true goal of the expedition was not a mystery to anyone aboard, and Lefébure, who had discovered its nature, had revealed it to me and to the others two days before.

Hazard had served the government of the Republic well is causing it to chose the *Erebus II*, because it was readily to depart and fully equipped for a polar expedition. In reality, Commander Barcot, covered with glory but financially ruined by his previous voyages, had only obtained subsidies from the financier Jean-Paul Rivier by agreeing to add to his scientific objectives other aims of a practical order, to which the cargo of sulfur was merely an accessory. According to certain indications obtained in the course of the preceding voyage, a gold-bearing deposit existed south of the volcano Terror, in the vicinity of the eight-second parallel. That is why the *Erebus II* had embarked four mining engineers in addition to its scientific personnel, and why the holds had been loaded, before Lefébure's perspicacious eyes, with an entire apparatus for mining exploitation: huts, explosives, a conveyor belt, diggers, rails, Decauville locomotives and wagons...

When he had seen, with a knowing smile for everyone, that everyone was in the know, Commander Barcot added: "Messieurs, we're about to do better than enrich our backer, to whom I had resigned myself in order to obtain the means of returning to the Pole. We're going to save our county's credit, and reestablish the fortune of France. Tomorrow we begin taking aboard the yellow nuggets of Île Féréor!"

VI. Celestial Gold

The weather had improved overnight. By dawn, the rain had stopped, but black clouds, chased by the northeast wind, were still attached to the summit of the snowy peak.

Undertaken at first light, the circumnavigation of Île Féréor revealed more of its geological structure to us and permitted us to find a disembarkation site in the western face.

The ferrous part of the bolide, visible above the ocean surface like a pedestal on which the auriferous cone was set, was neither level nor all of a piece. One might have thought that two gigantic slabs of iron had been stuck together at their ends, with opposing slopes, as if their junction, or hinge, had been prized apart by the weight of the cone—with the result that the black cliffs, several hundred meters high on the southern side, at which we had arrived, declined gradually until they disappeared beneath the waves at the location of the "hinge." They rose up beyond, to the north, in a symmetrical slope, but in the interval a breach opened, about ninety meters wide and two hundred deep: a kind of basin of calm water, sheltered from the wind, prolonged by a ravine about half a kilometer long, which ended at the base of the peak itself.

In this V-shaped opening, the steep blood-red slope appeared to be much closer to us than it had the previous evening, beneath the clouds that hid its snowy part. There was no mistaking the fact that yellow pebbles of all sizes were encrusted like flints in that makeshift cliff.

"Nuggets!" said Gripert, in a slightly-hushed voice, pointing them out to us.

No one replied. An anguish gripped the throats of the ship's officers, assembled on the upper deck, and it was in silence that the commands were uttered and the maneuvers carried out.

Not without difficulty, utilizing the fissures and projections that the two iron shores presented at this point, the immobilization of the *Erebus II* was contrived by means of four mooring-ropes, which protected it from drifting in the current and the waves. The starboard side of the vessel was scarcely three meters from the edge of the cliff, which was shaped like a quay, and an initial communication with the ground was established with the aid of a gangplank, while awaiting the setting-up of the conveyor-belt for the transportation of materials.

A crew of ten men, equipped with pickaxes and spades, disembarked first, and the bosun took them on reconnaissance, while the four engineers, Gripert and I followed by the two commanders, went over the gangplank in our turn.

A disorderly scene ensued, however. At the end of the creek, at the entrance to the ravine, a red stream, like the one in the gorge the previous day, was rolling its nuggets over a miry thalweg of gold chloride, which plastered the hinge like a mudslide from the peak. Having arrived there, the sailors threw their tools away and broke ranks in order to collect the gold.

Seeing that, their comrades still aboard the ship, along with the other officers, loudly demanded to go ashore too. We called a halt, anxiously—but Lefébure, stationed at the head of the gangplank, fired his revolver, threatening to blow out the brains of the first one who stepped on to it. He succeeded in containing them and sending them back to their posts.

We resumed our march, and Commander Barcot severely reprimanded the men occupied in heaping up nuggets at the edge of the muddy stream. He succeeded in making them understand that the real deposit was further on, at the top of the ravine, in the red wall in which the nuggets seemed to be stuck like the almonds in a fantastic bar of nougat.

Rallied and dragged away by the bosun, the sailors picked up their picks and spades and launched themselves forward at the double, their heels making a tremendous racket on the iron ground.

We "civilized" individuals affected a more casual and moderate manner—but I confess that I felt greatly disturbed. A continual tickling sensation was irritating my throat with an absurd desire to laugh or cry; I could already see myself as the master of unprecedented wealth, and I dedicated it to Frédérique...

The engineers excited one another with cubic measurements and estimates of percentages in chloride and pure gold. Cubic kilometers and millions of tons leapt to their lips; all four of them were debating with the aid of grand gestures, like drunkards.

Captain de Silfrage and Commander Barcot walked in silence, gravely, their features contracted and jaws clenched in a determined and triumphant rictus. The former, holding fast to his idea of the previous day, had brought his flag with him, whose shaft he was finally able to plant profoundly in the layer of gold chloride mud in the middle of the thalweg.

The most disinterested of us, probably, was Gripert. The prodigious golden alp was no more interesting to him than the landscape of iron that the two slopes displayed immensely to the right and left, in a black and hideous desolation that was lost in the mist in the distance. The mineralogist embraced "his" bolide with his gaze, with a satisfied proprietorial smile, and while moving forward, he made notes for his future paper.

During that march along the wall, on the sloping edge of the red torrent, an embarrassment, every time we looked at one another, caused us to turn our gazes away, invincibly attracted by the gold, as if by a theatrical performance that was simultaneously indecent and tempting. We tried in vain to adopt an "innocent" appearance.

When we reached the foot of the peak, however, although the sight of such a mass of gold, in excluding any fancy of egotistical possession, reduced the intoxication of gold to its pure state, so to speak, all of us, without exception, experienced the need to pick up a nugget—just one, but a big one—and pocket it as a souvenir.

We had, in any case, only to bend down. Under the action of the rain, and even that of the saline air, the rocks of gold chloride were disintegrating into a pasty magma; a bed of nuggets was already deposited at the foot of the wall, in the hollow formed by the fusion of their matrix, exactly like pebbles at the foot of a cliff.

By virtue of a sort of modesty, before putting it in our jacket pocket, we each held our nuggets of gold in one hand at the end of an outstretched arm, feeling its several kilos of weight with a muscular astonishment—and we touched it in secret, smooth and cold, impregnating it, in a way, with the potential virtue of gold, irradiating within us a kind of illusion, of symbolically possessing all the gold in the mountain that loomed up in front of us.

Among the sailors, instinct was given free rein. The immensity of the deposit did not inspire any disdain in them for the "vile metal." It merely spared them the disputes and squabbles that would otherwise surely have broken out. They threw themselves into it wholeheartedly. With grunts of animal joy, litanies of blasphemies and outbursts of crazed laughter, or with a silent rage and a frenetic determination, they picked up the largest nuggets—some of them weighed seventy or eighty kilos—and, holding their burdens with both hands against their chests, ran off to deposit them a little further away, on their personal piles.

It required a forceful intervention by the two leaders to bring the ten crewmen back and persuade them and their comrades to organize the work in a less primitive fashion. I even suspect the bosun of having speculated on the avidity of the men by suggesting to them—an idea of dubious regularity, but effective—that they would not tire themselves out so rapidly if they used the mining equipment, and that they would not lose out thereby, if they were careful to divert a few tons of gold and store it in the crew's quarters for their individual benefit.

By the afternoon, the exploitation was in full swing. Under the cliff, an electric crane was picking up the nuggets dug out by the excavator and loading the miniature wagons of the decauville. The latter, released in series on the descending slope, arrived at the edge of the "quay," where they tipped their load on to the conveyor-belt. With every passing minute, half a ton of nuggets poured like a cataract into the forward hold of the *Erebus II*.

It was, of course, necessary to make room there—but the mining equipment was at the very back, and in order to reach it the barrels of sulfur had had to be dis-embarked first. It would have been quicker to throw them in the sea, but—by virtue of a scruple of honesty that seemed out of place to us—the Commander would not permit that, and had them arranged in an orderly manner on the shore.

That gave me a first opportunity to exercise my doctoral skills and inaugurate the infirmary. Two men were injured by the fall of a barrel poorly secured to the crane's hooks; one of them had a sprained ankle, the other a large scalp-wound.

Night fell while I was completing their treatment, but the activity of the improvised miners did not slow down. A night shift, made up of volunteers, continued the work by the light of the ship's searchlights and acetylene lamps set up along the ravine, all the way to the point of attack.

We were at dinner. Through the portholes I could see the shadows agitating in the beams of white light magically illuminating the snow that had begun to fall. The wagons were rolling noisily down the iron slope; distant appeals could be heard, along with the whistle-blasts of the locomotive taking up the empty trains, the hum of machinery and the dull impact of loads of gold emptied into the hold.

"Two millions francs' worth of gold a minute, Messieurs!" proclaimed de Silfrage, who had just pushed his plate of saffron-rice away in order to scribble a calculation on the tablecloth. "Once her holds are full, the *Erebus II* will carry away more than eight billion...gold francs, that is. And if all goes well, in less than three days, that gold will be heading for Cherbourg...and the Banque de France!"

VII. In Secret

The memory of Frédérique Kohbuler had certainly preoccupied me during the journey, and my hours of solitude were spent dreaming about her—but only my hours of solitude; at other times, her dear image vanished from my mind. Why, then, after arriving at Île Féréor—whether I was aboard the *Erebus II*, moored in the inlet, or on the iron ground, between the gray ocean and the unspeakable desolation of that ferrous landscape, before the red mass drowned in the flutter of the snow and the ravine filled with the tumultuous din of the factory—did the ideal presence suddenly acquire a new intensity, and impose itself upon me continuously, in "superimposition," to use an evocative cinematic term, over my every waking moment?

Was the proximity of the gold, in the same way that it exasperated the vile passions of the sailors, giving greater relief and force to my intimate aspirations in respect of the person who would be the happiness of my life, by appearing to offer me, by means of the great adventure, the wealth and prestige that would complete me assurance of her love?

Was it the evident impossibility of enjoying those riches and happiness on my own that made me yearn for her presence more violently and evoke her memory in continuous fashion...just as once before, against the backdrop of the Edenic landscapes of the Côte d'Azur, I had been driven to the point of anguish by the desire to share that excess of beauty with a sibling soul?

Was it, on the contrary, the impression of exile imposed by the very nature of the bolide—the obscure sentiment of contemplating, in the ferocious activity of the workers taking apart that fallen star, a forbidden spectacle, abhorrent to the intrinsic harmony of the Cosmos?

I leave the problem to those more expert than me in matters of psychology—but the fact remains that for those three days, even in the hours when my occupations were at their most absorbing and the gravity of the situation ought to have taken complete possession of me, the image of Frédérique inscribed itself in filigree in all my thoughts. While caring for my invalids in the infirmary, while chatting with the officers or my scientific colleagues in the warm atmosphere of the wardroom, as well as in carrying out hard and unaccustomed labor—about which you will read in due course—in the snow, or in mounting guard on the poop-deck, I thought about her with anguished aspiration.

Far from blessing the stroke of luck that had spared me the long polar expedition and reduced my absence from Paris to a matter of weeks, I could only see one thing: Frédérique was unaware of the imminence of my return. Like everyone else, she thought that I was on my way to the Antarctic.

The prohibition on sending her any message tormented me, and, in spite of all my hopes for the future, spoiled the present for me—and it was with a sort of personal rancor that I saw, as I passed the wireless cabin, the operator Madec huddled over his crackling apparatus, making it stridulate like a giant cricket. It was forbidden to transmit private communications, which might have alerted the public to the true location of the *Erebus II*. Yes, I was jealous of the messages that the ship's antenna launched toward Europe—toward Paris—twenty times a day.

Back there, in Geneva, the delegates of the nations were busy debating the fate of our island. They still believed it, on the basis of the *Champlain*'s report, to be a rock lost in the north Atlantic, a sterile mass of volcanic ash and scoria; and, in ignorance of its value—or, more accurately, the apparent certainty of its lack of value—were preparing to dispose of it "in the spirit of Locarno."[14] There was talk of internationalizing it, of making it a port of call and fuel stop for aircraft.

On the evening of the fifteenth, the corvette captain and the Commander had notified the Ministry and Jean-Paul Rivier, in code, that they had taken possession of the island. The two leaders insisted, in covert terms, on the importance of the island, and the vital necessity of its attribution to France, even at the cost of sacrifices. In addition, the naval officer urgently requested the sending of a destroyer and a transport ship.

After an entire day of quibbling, the request was granted. The two ships *Espadon* and *Cornouaille* would depart from Brest on the eighteenth or nineteenth. That was the limit of the government's audacity, however; the news broadcast to the world from the Eiffel Tower did not breathe a word about the taking of possession. The President of the Council awaited events, keeping that

---

[14] The Locarno treaties of 1925 negotiated at the League of Nations were supposed to settle the borders of post-war Europe and normalize relations with the German Weimar Republic, but were widely regarded at the time as an unholy mess of unsatisfactory compromises; viewed in retrospect, they were the first instances of a policy of appeasement that eventually had the opposite result to that intended, helping to precipitate World War II. Varlet's cynical sarcasm in respect of "the spirit of Locarno" was thus entirely justified.

card up his sleeve, in order to play it, if necessary, as a decisive trump, in the negotiations in Geneva.

It was an admissible tactic—but a few hours delay or advance in our arrival in Paris might have an incalculable effect on those very negotiations, for the French government could not comprehend the true importance of the island while the results of our exploration were not known in detail...detail that de Silfrage dared not confide to the Hertzian waves.

On the one hand, it was necessary that the world be unaware of the riches of Île Féréor, until the League of Nations had reached its decision. On the other hand, the negotiations would not be conducted by France with all the desired activity—renouncing, if necessary, one of our colonies in exchange for the island, the captain said—unless the government knew about those riches.

That is why we trembled at the thought that a ship might pass within sight of the island and make a landing there. That is why we had to complete loading the cargo and make ready to sail as soon as possible, without even waiting for the arrival of the two ships that were expected.

With regard to the inopportune visit, the snow, which resumed falling on the afternoon of the fifteenth, gave us a measure of temporary security, by reducing visibility at sea. A ship would have to pass within two miles in order to perceived the silhouette of the peak. With regard to celerity, all went well. The work progressed at a constant rhythm; it was completed within the anticipated interval of three days.

The fury with which the sailors worked did not diminish. On the other hand, however, symptoms of demoralization increased. Whereas, among our "civilized" selves, the initial intoxication was transformed into a patriotic fervor and a desire for intensive exploitation, the proximity of the gold seemed to aggravate its deleterious effect on our men. With somber and surly expressions, muddy and sweaty in spite of the snow, they no longer obeyed any orders but those of the engineers concerning the extraction of the gold, refusing to participate in any other task. Thus, for the erection of the huts designed to lodge the part of the mission that would remain on the island, we—I mean the officers and scientists— were obliged to set to work ourselves, and I was obliged to spend the entire morning of the sixteenth under the snow, opening boxes and screwing together the planks of the dismantled huts.. My hands were grazed and full of blisters for several days.

On the sixteenth, the midday meal was not ready; the cook, the waiters and the steward had abandoned their post to go and join the gold-diggers. We had to take tins from the stores, whose contents we consumed in anxious silence. From time to time, when louder outbursts of voices reached us from outside, we interrupted ourselves and mechanically patted the butts of the revolvers strapped to our thighs.

The probable plan of the crew was to abandon us on the island and set sail with the cargo of gold for a country where the customs and the authorities appeared to be more easily bought than in Europe: Chile, Ecuador or some other South American republic. And their frenzied labor was explained by the anticipated division that they would make of their future booty. In fact, the bosun, who remained faithful to his duty, told us that they had formed a syndicate and appointed inspectors charged with counting the wagons furnished by each crew.

The vigilance of the Commander and the rest of us, however, prevented this plan from being put into execution. The rebellion did not even become manifest. The men were too well aware of their impotence; there were forty of them and only seventeen of us, to be sure, but we held all the firearms, and a machine-gun set up on the poop transformed the ship into a veritable entrenched camp.

On the evening of the seventeenth, under a load of two thousand tons of nuggets, the flotation-line was brushing sea-level. The holds, however, seemed half-empty, thanks to the density of the gold, and the Commander had to appeal to reason in order to determine preparation for sailing the following morning, without heaping the available space with a further provision of gold.

There could be no question of setting sail for Europe and leaving the island and equipment unmanned, even under the safeguard of the French flag and an official declaration of its possession, enclosed, in accordance with custom, in a sealed tinplate box. Part of the personnel would remain on the island, at least until the arrival of the destroyer, in order to continue the extraction and form a stock of nuggets ready to embark on the transport vessel that was accompanying the warship.

The latter role was attributed to the corvette captain, the four engineers, Gripart—who had not finished studying "his" bolide—and all the scientists, plus Lefébure and the second lieutenant, who would be in command, and fifteen crewmen. How should the latter be chosen, though? In the state of indiscipline prevailing among the sailors, there could be no question of designating them by order.

The bosun, having been consulted, suggested that he ask for volunteers, and half an hour later he came back with fourteen names: ten sailors, the carpenter the steward and two waiters. How had he convinced them? Had he held out the hope of taking possession of the motor-launch and setting forth with a more modest but more easily negotiable cargo of gold? It's possible—at any rate, we were then able to drew up a complete list of those leaving: eight sailors, the eighteen mechanics and stokers, the storeman and the cook, with a general staff consisting of the first lieutenant, promoted to first mate, the four technical officers, the wireless operator and the bosun, promoted to the functions of first lieutenant, plus Commander Barcot and me.

It was nine o'clock in the evening when these arrangements were finally completed and communicated to the interested parties—for you must not imagine that we were all installed like good bourgeois around the wardroom table, smoking our pipes and enjoying a last glass of *fino* before going to bed! A state of siege reigned aboard the vessel, as I have said, and the night-shift was still at work on land. For those two reasons, the officers of duty were missing, along with the engineers directing the extraction, the scientists guarding the gang-plank and the poop and the wireless operator Madec, who no longer left the radio cabin since an attempt had been made to sabotage his apparatus. There was, in consequence, no one in the wardroom but the Commander and the Captain, the second mate, two mechanics, Gripert and myself—all harassed by sleepless nights, for we were almost constantly on our feet and had hardly slept since the threat of revolt had emerged.

Nevertheless, the prospect of soon seeing an end to the nightmare rendered us a measure of cheerfulness. Once the decision was made, it was like a release. Only the naval officer retained his frown.

"What's wrong, de Silfrage?" the Commander asked him. "You seem worried. Is it staying here that displeases you? You're under no obligation to do so, and your mission..."

"I consider that my place is on the island, where I shall maintain order until the arrival of the destroyer. As for my report to the Ministry, Commander, you will see that it reaches its destination. No, that's not what's worrying me—it's that we're at the mercy of an inopportune visit. It only requires a ship to pass within sight..."

"Obviously, there's a risk," said Barcot, "but it's unavoidable. If we could at least camouflage the mine..."

"Or cover up the stockpiles of gold, which are too visible at a distance with the aid of binoculars," I suggested.

"That's what comes of having to deal with a bolide," Gripart sniggered, "instead of a volcanic island."

Contrary to his habit, the loquacious Lefébure had not yet said anything. He was smoking his old brier-pipe, slightly to one side, and smiling to himself, seemingly very amused by some idea of his own. When Gripart had made his comment, he raised his head.

"A volcanic island? Bah! It would be sufficient to simulate a small eruption."

"What?"

"What do you mean?"

"Explain!"

No one understood—but enlightenment dawned on me. I remembered having seen Lefébure on several occasions, meditating in front of the barrels of sulfur stacked on the bank.

"Bravo, Robert!" I exclaimed. "That's it—you've got it. Yes—the smoke of an artificial eruption!"

70

Invited to explain, the first mate went on: "What's the objective, in sum? To gain time—a fortnight, a month, until the moment that island N is awarded to France by the worthy League of Nations. As the very existence of the island remains in doubt, and its exact position is unknown, there's little chance of another expedition coming to search for it, especially where it is—which is to say, much further north than is thought, and outside the usual traffic routes. So, if we have to put off two or three ships passing by chance, from now until the decision is made in Geneva, that will do the trick. And hide what? Not the existence of the island—these sheer cliffs and the snow-capped cone are scarcely attractive—but the only true landing-point, and our mine...

"Well, Commander, I'll take responsibility for that, especially if we have to deal with people who aren't overly curious and in a hurry—like the captain of a transatlantic liner, for instance. We have the sulfur..."

By now, everyone had cottoned on, but Lefébure, carried away by his subject, continued: "Those barrels, those blessed barrels of sulfur, about which we have all joked, and which you, Commander, have cursed as the dishonor of your vessel...well, they'll serve us well, and as we have no aircraft, we'd pay ten times their weight in gold to get hold of them. Given the price of gold in these parts, I might even say a hundred times.

"It's simple. At the water's edge, all around the inlet, you dispose a cordon of twenty open barrels covered by tarpaulins, and if a ship comes, you take of the tarpaulins and set fire to them. In three minutes, the creek will be filled with beautiful white smoke, which will simulate perfectly, up to and including the odor, a volcanic eruption. Behind that camouflage, neither seen nor suspected, the mine will remain unknown—and in order to deprive the boat in question of any desire to make a closer approach, nothing prevents us from letting off a few cheddite cartridges.[15] I'll bet you a round of orange curacaos at the Café de la Paix, when we get back to Paris, that the captain will steam away at top speed, for fear of catching a volcanic bomb on his funnel, or seeing the bottom of the ocean rise up beneath him and leave him high and dry on a peak like this one."

The idea was adopted enthusiastically; and, thanks to Lefébure's inventiveness, we were all more reassured, those departing as well as those staying, when the *Erebus II* cast off its moorings and put out to sea the following day, the eighteenth, before midday.

On land, the sailors gripped by gold fever did not even interrupt their work to watch the departure, and the rolling of the wagons, which were now discharging their gold into the stockpiles on the edge of the inlet, reached us like the distant and decreasing echo of the pulsation of our engines.

Standing on the quay, the group of our comrades remained visible for a few minutes, waving handkerchiefs, but soon melted, along with the snowy peak and the black cliffs, into the white flocculation of the snow.

Pitching and rolling on the long swell of the Atlantic, the *Erebus II* headed west-south-west, at its maximum sped of eighteen knots, directly toward Cherbourg.

---

[15] In the 1920s cheddite was a chlorate-based explosive named after the town of Chedde in the Haute-Savoie, where it was manufactured; it was mostly used in France in quarrying, but was subsequently employed during World War II in the manufacture of improvised hand-grenades. After 1970 the name was redefined to refer to a slightly different compound used as a primer in shotgun cartridges.

VIII. Father and Daughter

Claridge's Hotel, third floor above the Avenue; the apartment of Professor Hans Kohbuler and his daughter.

Frédérique-Elsa is alone in the study-drawing-room. Filtered through a net curtain whose pattern features a flight of ducks, the sullen light of the gray afternoon is no longer sufficient for her; she has just switched on the bulb beneath the turquoise porcelain shade that illuminates the American desk over which she is leaning, hard at work.

Framed by her blonde curls, her vertically-furrowed forehead, blue eyes and black eyebrows denote intellectual power combined with a certain indecision of character. Only the former is in operation at present, and not even at full tension, for the young doctor of mathematical sciences is curling her carmine lip slightly. That moue indicates disdain for the insufficient difficulty of her task, which a vulgar decoder could do as well, once the key had been discovered.

It is the key in question that she is consulting periodically, in a little red morocco-bound notebook…a kind of manuscript dictionary. After each page consulted, her fountain pen inscribes another French word between the lines of a piece of paper that features a short paragraph formed of baroque words that are not in any language, but which a initiate would recognize as a conventional code designed to ensure the secrecy of dispatches.

In the end, she sets down the notebook and the pen, and rereads between the lines of the document her translation "in clear."

Erebus II...Erebus II... Situation grave. Cannot wait for arrival of promised destroyer and transport ship. Commander, officers and doctor returning with vessel. You will have account of my mission in six or seven days. Meanwhile, urgent you obtain the attribution, as soon as possible, of island N to France, even at the cost of great sacrifice.

DE SILFRAGE.

The decipherer of the cryptogram raises her eyes to the clock-calendar held out to her by a bronze statuette of a nymph, and observes that it is fifteen hundred hours on the eighteenth of September. The vertical pleat of intellectuality on her forehead relaxes; she smiles, with a melancholy that is both tender and anxious, and then takes a little wallet from her handbag, placed on the desk. From that she takes a newspaper-clipping; it is the photograph of the *Erebus II* taken in Marseilles by the representative of the *Excelsior*. Among the officers it is possible to make out the shaven face of Dr. Marquin, in conversation with the first mate.

It is at him that Frédérique-Elsa looks: him, the frank and honest man in whom she has conceived an inexplicable interest...the man she loves, it is now certain, and the love of whom will turn her soul, and perhaps her life, upside-down...

But she shivers suddenly, and darts an apprehensive glance toward the door that leads to her father's room. Behind the curtain, the dull sound of footsteps is perceptible, striding back and forth on the thick carpet.

Her father? No. The man that she designates by that title, out of habit, but beside whom she feels so weak, so alone, so abandoned...the man whom she sees very differently now...feeling closer to the mother whom he has killed with his implacable tyranny.

Dr. Hans Kohbuler, whose double life no longer has any mystery for her...officially Swiss, and a honorary professor, a world-renowned scientist and originator of medical discoveries, in communication with important people in all the countries of Europe, which he frequents in the casual manner of habit and wealth; in reality, German, the secret head of economic espionage in France... that is the father for whom she has been playing the role of secretary-cryptographer for two years.

Why does that work inspire such repugnance in her today?

Until now, technical interest has sustained her. A doctor in mathematical sciences at nineteen, absorbed by the exercise of her precocious and marvelous intelligence, she believed herself permanently free of patriotic prejudices, and worked, like all the great chiefs of secret services, solely for the joy of successfully solving difficult problems, with perfect indifference to the consequences for one nation or another. Moral conventions? Verity here, error elsewhere! She has seen so many countries, crossed so many frontiers, lived under so many different skies, since her childhood and the revelation of her extraordinary mathematical aptitudes! In that rootless international existence, devoid of ties and only having the anonymous decor of palaces for a home, she had become a insensitive monster, a sort of angel of pure intelligence, whose conversation had, the previous year, extracted a cry of admiration from Einstein—an angel of heavens beyond good and evil, a stranger to the normal concerns of humanity, living in a sphere in which mental intoxication replaces and inhibits all other passions.

It is for that reason that she has submitted without revolt to the sly ascendancy of that pseudo-father—she knows, her mother having told her on her deathbed, that he is not her progenitor—and it is for that reason that she has previously accepted without protest the work of assisting him, always as a cryptographer, in the affair of the false Banque de France banknotes that has been going on successfully for four months, inundating Europe with thousand-franc bills forged in the villa with the concrete cellars that the professor owns in Audresselles, near Wimereaux, printed on the same paper as the Banque, with an ink identical to the true ones, on presses imitative of the Banque's, down to the last screw.

Given that, why this repugnance today?

She has always shrugged her shoulders at the stupidities of love; she is elegant and beautiful, because she is very much a woman, that Amazon of pure speculation, but she has ignored her heart and rejected the homages that have pursued her in society. However, since she has seen Dr. Marquin at the Jolliots in Wimereaux, a secret fiber has quivered within her. She is in love; it is impossible to doubt it. A new soul has been born within her, invasive and despotic: a loving and sensitive soul; that of her mother—"the Frenchwoman," as Kohbuler calls her...

Yes, a Frenchwoman, and in love, that is what Frédérique-Elsa has surely become, as well!

And for a few days, since she has devoted herself, still the docile secretary, to deciphering the coded dispatches intended for the Ministry of Marine and captured by her father's clandestine antenna, she has experienced a reluctance unknown until now, a veritable distress, in discovering secrets whose divulgence might harm a country that was her mother's. But she also feels a secret joy is having news of Dr. Marquin…knowing that he has not departed for the Pole…that he is sailing for France…that perhaps she will soon see him again…

In the next room, the footsteps approach the door. Frédérique makes a gesture, as if to destroy the document—but what good would that do? She renounces it, and limits herself to hiding the cutting from *Excelsior*.

Kohbuler comes in, and speaks to her in his guttural French. "Well, Elsa"—he never calls her Frédérique, out of hatred for her dead mother—"what about the dispatch? You've taken your time!"

He studies his daughter with his malachite-green eyes, with a mixture of possessive tenderness and anxiety. He senses, obscurely, that she is getting away from him, that she would disappoint his hopes if he made a wrong move—and even he, the pitiless manipulator of men and international events, hesitates before certain secret cogs of the psychic mechanism, of which he has not yet dared to make use.

She hands the piece of paper to him, silently.

"Good. That's perfect. But what can they have discovered on this island that's so important? And we still lack the geographical location! It was a good idea of mine to put one of our men on the *Erebus II*—it was that story of the so-called scientific goals of the expedition that put me off. That Marquin is more artful than he seems—or perhaps even he didn't know the truth. But that cruise had another purpose than the scientific, that's obvious. Another six days? The League of Nations won't pronounce a judgment before then, and we can delay its decision if necessary. But to make sacrifices in order to obtain the island? Hmm! We need to know what it's about before getting involved. Messages have escaped us, undoubtedly, which specified it. They must have them at the Ministry, but agent K12 has been burned, for the moment, and his successor hasn't yet been able to introduce himself in his stead. Rivier's also up to date, of course. We need to make Rivier talk. You're going to find him, Elsa, and use any possible means...any. You can say, by way of introduction, that you're interested in Dr. Marquin."

Kohbuler has pronounced the last words with an affectation of cheerful assurance, but he sees clearly that his ascendancy over his daughter is counterbalanced by new sentiments, and that the beginnings of rebellion have been born in his daughter's soul.

The latter stands up straight, seems to struggle against her habitual submission, and concludes, in a deferential tone, but one in which a firm resolve vibrates: "Father, I regret to tell you that you're making an error—a mistake—in proposing this enquiry to me. You're talking to your daughter, your secretary-cryptographer, not a worldly collaborator in the Service—Lotta Schumbach, Gregoria Lotescu or someone like them. That's what you need for the special task you mention. Personally, I've only given my intelligence to the Service...any anyway, I don't have the professional aptitudes of those ladies. Sending me to Monsieur Rivier, therefore, would be infringing the rules of Taylorism[16] and the division of labor. Each to her specialty."

"Elsa," says Kohbuler, with a false joviality, "you're scaring me. I thought for a moment that you were suffering an attack of that vulgar and conventional morality from which I've invested so much case in liber-

---

[16] The organizational philosophy popularized by Frederick Winslow Taylor's highly influential *Principles of Scientific Management* (1911).

ating you since your late mother attempted to inculcate it in you. Thank God it's not that. You have, at any rate, a dangerous propensity for independence...to avoid the necessities of the Service. More might be demanded of you than the utilization of your analytical talents.

"In the present case, however, I don't want to compel you. We'll wait for Marquin to arrive. He won't fail to come to see you, and we'll get the truth out of him. That will mean a delay of about a week. No matter! I'll take care of it by making sure that the negotiations in Geneva drag on—a little watering of the delegates...

"In that case, we'll leave tomorrow for Audresselles. That animal Gédéon always bungles things. I should have stayed out there, as before, to keep an eye on the printing of the banknotes. The latest batch of paper isn't in conformity with the specimens. It doesn't take the ink like the preceding batch. Either that or it's Gédéon who can't do it. Either way, the notes are unusable. I've just seen that, when I opened the parcel that came by mail. So, as I said, I have to go to Audresselles. You'll accompany me, of course; I need you out there as I do here.

"We won't be there more than a week, I hope—in order that we'll be able to receive Dr. Marquin the day after our return, if he visits us, as I assume he will. You won't refuse to see *him*, will you? At that imbecile Jolliot's place, he looked at you with such an expression...and you'll make him talk."

The malachite-green eyes drill into the blue eyes with black lashes. Once again, the professor exercises on his daughter the sovereign seductive force that sometimes accompanies unscrupulousness, and then makes great criminals, just as, allied with nobility of soul or virtue, it produces heroes and saints.

Frédérique-Elsa replied: "Al right; I'll see Dr. Marquin."

But Kohbuler comprehends that if he were to repeat, as he has a desire to do: "And you'll make him talk," she would reply frankly, "No." He does not reiterate that injunction, therefore, and limits himself to smiling benignly, as if he were duped by her reticence.

IX. To Paris

Thanks to the precautions taken, and incessant vigilance, the anticipated mutiny, when it became manifest on the third day of our journey, failed pitifully. By virtue of an acuity all the more meritorious because it came from Commander Barcot, a stickler for exact discipline, the latter had turned a blind eye to the two or three tons of nuggets stashed away in the crew's quarters by the sailors on board, who considered them to be their personal property, and their covetousness of the cargo in the hold was partly neutralized by the direct possession of those few hundred thousand francs'-worth of gold apiece. With that wealth, immeasurable to them, they glimpsed a limitless spree as soon as they arrived in port, and the hope of those delights, in those primitive minds, limited by a short temporal horizon, weakened the courage that they might otherwise have deployed in taking possession of the ship.

In addition, they lacked a leader. The Indochinese cook attempted to play that role, but the color of his skin worked against him in the minds of his accomplices, and prevented them from taking him seriously.

The whole affair was therefore limited to an attempt to take possession of the wheelhouse, the engine-room and the wireless station. A volley of machine-gun bullets, fired from the bridge by the Commander and his first mate, dispersed the four men armed with crowbars who attacked the helm; the chief engineer remained master of his domain; and in the third instance, the operator Madec, armed with his revolver, valiantly repelled the attack of another cohort. Unfortunately, a heavy projectile hurled by the assailants—an ax, I believe—struck the wireless apparatus squarely, and caused such damage that we were deprived of communications for the remainder of the voyage. The last radio message we received came from the destroyer *Espadon*, on its way to the island with the cargo-ship *Cornouaille*, which "crossed" us some two hundred kilometers to the south.

That was the only unfortunate result of the attempted revolt, however. A quarter of an hour after the blast of the whistle that launched the mutineers' assault, everything was back in order, and the crew, subdued, resumed normal service.

I ought to remark that, during those critical minutes, I happened to be in the infirmary, and that no violence was exercised against me. The mutineers limited themselves to locking me in for the time that the skirmish lasted. My special position as doctor and the perfect apparent serenity with which I carried out my functions with regard to the sick—as if I were making rounds in a hospital on land—had won me a particular indulgence on the part of the men, and a kind of respectful familiarity.

Their confidence permitted me to play a decisive role in safeguarding the secret that had to be maintained for an indeterminate lapse of time after the disembarkation regarding the mineral nature of the island and that of our cargo. A solemn oath taken, at the Commander's request, by myself and the officers, guaranteed our silence...but what about the sailors? As soon as we landed in Cherbourg, they would show off their nuggets and tell the whole story...

But for the superior interests of France, which dictated my conduct, I would have had some remorse for my conduct, for it was a kind of abuse of confidence on my part, but I thought I was acting for the best—and I hope I can end my life without having committed a worse sin!

The resource, suggested by Barcot, of having the men arrested as soon as they disembarked, on a charge of mutiny, seemed to me to be unlikely to be effective; dragging the sailors through the streets in the midst of a crowd of eager journalists offered a risk of grave indiscretion.

My familiarity with the storeman—a Northerner from Lille—with whom I sometimes went to the kitchen in the absence of the Indochinese cook, to chat for a few minutes, in order to hear the spicy accent of my native town again, permitted me to carry out my plan.

An adequate dose of morphine chlorohydrate mixed with the crew's soup on the last day, between eleven o'clock and noon as we were doubling the cape of the Hague...and when we entered the harbor at Cherbourg, all the men were snoring heavily, knocked out by the narcotic on the deck, where the Commander, once my coup was complete, had taken care to assemble them.

As for the stokers "down below," two of the officer engineers installed them as best they could on pillows of coal in the bunkers and took their place during the final minutes of the journey. The two others were needed up top, where no one else was left standing but the first lieutenant, the wireless operator, the Commander and me.

I still laugh when I remember the faces of the pilot and lieutenant of the vessel that accompanied us—for the semaphore had signaled our arrival—when they came aboard and saw the deck strewn with twenty recumbent bodies, which they took at first for corpses.

They looked at the six "survivors"—officers maneuvering a crewless ship—with an undisguised anxiety.

That was not the time for explanations, however. The Commander's first words to the lieutenant were: "What time is the Paris express?"

"Thirteen-thirty—in half an hour," replied the somewhat nonplussed naval officer.

On leaving Île Féréor we had planned to charter an aircraft from the Compagnie Aérienne by wireless on the eve of our arrival in Cherbourg—and that was the main reason for our choice of Cherbourg, because there is no airport at Brest—but the accident to our wireless apparatus had prevented that. To charter an aircraft now might perhaps take several hours. The express would get us to Paris just as quickly. We had to take advantage of it.

"We're just in time, then," Commander Barcot continued, addressing the naval officer. "Would you be so kind as to help my first lieutenant bring the ship into dock, and make sure that the orders I give you are observed. Transport all these lascars snoring hereabouts to the infirmary of the military prison and keep them there, incommunicado. Keep the officers aboard until I get back tomorrow. No communication with the city, especially with journalists. Understand? All this is extremely serious. It's a matter of national interest."

The naval lieutenant bowed. "I've received orders to put myself entirely at your disposal as soon as you arrived, Commander. The pilot will take your ship at half-speed as far as the entrance to the military harbor, where he'll take on reinforcements—a few State mariners—to complete the maneuver. If you wish, I'll take you ashore; we'll get there more rapidly in my launch. In ten minutes, we'll be on the quay in the commercial harbor, two hundred meters from the railway station."

"That's best," agreed the Commander. He turned to me, and added: "Doctor, you'll come with me, as agreed. You have your justificatory pebbles in your pocket? Good. Too bad about the baggage—we'll do without until tomorrow. Let's go!"

And, with a rapid adieu all round, Monsieur Barcot and I, with nothing but our waterproofs, leapt into the launch with the lieutenant, who cast off and sped away at fifteen knots, leaving the *Erebus II* far behind.

Monsieur Barcot took advantage of the short journey—Cherbourg's inevitable fine rain was falling from the uniformly gray coastal sky—to communicate to the naval officer the story that he was to put about concerning the premature return of our vessel—that by virtue of engine damage sustained at sea off the Azores, it had been decided to return to France for repairs. The officer similarly gave us the news of the last three days that was most important to us: in Geneva, the League of Nations was still deliberating, and the attribution of the island remained in suspense.

At 13.23, the Commander and I set foot on the quay and ran toward the station. The external clock marked twenty-six minutes past. Monsieur Barcot bounded to the ticket-office while I bought a handful of newspapers. The doors were being closed when we climbed on to the train.

Even after getting rid of our waterproofs, we stood out like a sore thumb in the sumptuous first-class compartment, upholstered in soft gray fabric, with our suntanned faces, our mariners' foulards and our old worn jackets still stained with gold chloride mud. I don't know what the old Englishwoman who was alone there took us for, but she hastened to decamp with her bags and baggage and go into the next one—which amused and pleased us, making it easier for us to talk.

But first, the papers! The *Matin*, the *Figaro*...

Subscription for the victims of the typhoon and tidal wave, tenth list... Gala performance at the Opéra, with Madame Ida Rubinstein and Messieurs Silvain, Grock and the Fratellinis, in Circé... *Goodrich-Leonard bout... Pound at 464... At the League of Nations...*

Here we are!

At the League of Nations, Island N. It appears that the original idea of internationalization will have to be abandoned, in order to envisage the solution of a mandate. That renewable mandate will be confided for a period of ten years to France, which will make Island N into a port of call for an air link to be established between Paris and New York...

"Well, that's a start; they haven't done too badly..."

"Hey, Commander, listen to this from the *Echo de Cherbourg*—this article in the latest news section:

"New island pinpointed by Danish ship. The doubts expressed by a number of newspapers regarding the existence of the volcanic island sighted by the Canadian Line's *Champlain* a few days after the volcanic eruption whose ravages are so familiar, are well-known. For these extreme skeptics, the island has only ever existed in the imagination of the captain and passengers of the *Champlain*. Others, more moderate, supposed that after a brief emergence, the island, constituted by scoria, had sunk beneath the waves again, as often happens to these unstable and ephemeral formations after a few days or a few months. It was to the latter viewpoint that we had finally rallied. Last week, in fact, the steamship *Weser*, of the Hamburg-Amerika Line, the first to make the crossing from Europe to America since the typhoon, was rerouted by governmental order to reconnoiter the new land. At the intersection of latitude and longitude identified by the *Champlain*, the *Weser* found no trace of the emergent island.

"This morning, however, a wireless message retransmitted by the Valencia station in Ireland has settled the matter definitively. Island N exists, but its position is considerably different from the one previously assigned to it. It is 150 miles—almost 300 kilometers—further north. A Danish steamer, the *Seeland*, commanded by Captain Saknussemm,[17] which ensures a monthly service in summer between the Greenland stations and Copenhagen, signals that it passed within view of island N yesterday, 23 September.

"It is a dark and bare shelf of lava surmounted by a snow-capped cone. Abundant vapors, evidently volcanic, are escaping from an accessory crater situated at the foot of the cone, almost at sea level on the south-west coast of the island. The captain of the *Seeland* set a course for that point, but a there was a series of detonations, and Monsieur Saknussemm, fearing that a further eruption might occur, veered away and put on full steam in order to get away from the dangerous region.

"We shall return to this news tomorrow, but we can say today that it confirms the thesis that we have always sustained. It is now evident that this volcanic terrain, doubtless bound for imminent disappearance, cannot be an advantageous acquisition. Even at the price of ten

---

[17] This adaptation of the name of the heroic explorer featured in *Voyage au Centre de la Terre* is one of two exceedingly oblique acknowledgements within the text of the debt owed by Varlet's novel to Jules Verne,

francs per hectare, which is two or three hundred francs for the entire island, it would be too dear—and if, by chance, the League of Nations were to decide to put island N up for auction, we hope that the delegate of France would abstain from meeting the reserve price."

"Excellent! Excellent!" exclaimed Monsieur Barcot. "Lefébure has done the trick, with his sulfur...but what a mug, that Danish captain!"

And he started laughing wholeheartedly.

I joined him, in chorus. The delight of the new joy dilated our chests. Although the exact position of the island had been determined, the damage was slight. "A shelf of lava and a volcanic cone..." It was scarcely probable that anyone would hasten to send ships here, after Captain Saknussemm's report! And we amused ourselves momentarily at the expense of the worthy Greenlanders fooled by Lefébure's ruse.

"And that reporter who wants to dissuade the government from buying Île Féréor!"

"It's a good thing that you'll be there, Commander, to rectify the Ministry's ideas."

"And you, Doctor, to tell your friend Jean Rivier that the *Erebus II*'s return has made him a billionaire eight times over...in gold...since he's the ship's backer!"

After the stop in Caen, the conversation lapsed. Exhausted by the fatigues of the previous days, Monsieur Barcot closed his eyes, dropped his pipe and went to sleep in his corner.

By contrast, overexcitement kept me awake, agitating me. I went out into the corridor to smoke, thinking about Frédérique. Was she in Paris? What would she say to me when I saw her? As a messenger of good tidings to Jean Rivier, I could obtain some enviable position from him, putting my fortune at the level at which I supposed that of Kohbuler and his daughter to be. I saw myself marrying the young doctor...

But what about the father? I tried to eliminate him from consideration, to treat him as a negligible quantity...but in vain. He persisted stubbornly, like a treacherous stone in the beautiful fruit of our love; every time I bit into the exquisite pulp, I found that stone between my teeth.

The train sped through the Norman countryside. It was no longer raining. Blue sky appeared between the clouds. Leaning out of an open window, I cooled my brow in the wind of our progress, and breathed in, seeking an evocation of the dear perfume, Remember, and the beloved face with the blonde hair in the Florentine bob...

I was dreaming, plunged into a kind of hypnosis by the smooth gallop of the express. The daylight was fading into dusk...

Suddenly, I recovered consciousness, on reading the name of a station as we sped through—*Mantes*—and, on a brick wall: *Paris 17 km.*

I went back to the compartment and woke Monsieur Barcot.

X. Finance and Politics

Paris Saint-Lazare. The illuminated hall. The bustle on the platform. The time—18.30—read on the clock. The tickets surrendered. The exit. Taxis hailed from the edge of the sidewalk...and in the first one, the Commander orders the driver: "Rue Saint-Florentine, Ministry of Marine."

I climbed into the other cab. "Avenue de Villiers, 80A." Jean Rivier's house.

The few minutes of the journey were swollen by a whole world of sensations: Paris; Paris in the evening, illuminated...

On the island and aboard *Erebus II* I had certainly been dynamized by the gold, but, being too close to it, I had been situated in the time ahead of me, the hours of high tension that the grandiose adventure in which I was participating would enable me to live. Cherbourg I had barely glimpsed, as a backcloth, totally preoccupied with the haste to get to the train. The hours on the express? A transitory atmosphere, separated, so to speak, from social communion...

This time, I was fully present, plugged in to Paris, in direct contact with the central circuit of civilization...the power-station of France: France, not as a verbal entity, but which I realized, by an explosive intuition, living in its hundreds of cities, great and small, in its thousands of villages, with its fields, its rivers, its mountains, more than twelve hours long by express train, and equally broad... Paris, the prototype, the synthesis, the supreme expression, the marvelous success of France,

charged me and saturated me, illuminating me with all
its potential.

Automobiles and pedestrians—the life of the city—
were circulating ardently, to the triumphant rhythm of
our accelerated era: the highest, in spite of everything,
that the terrestrial planet had ever known. The splendor
of the lighting, enlivening the masks of the crowd, set an
aureole of apotheosis over the functioning of the admirable machinery that is a twentieth-century capital.

It seemed to me to be monstrous to think that all
that beautiful activity, so generous and rich in effort, was
prey to the slow disruption of its monetary system—the
devaluation of the franc—that was corroding it like a
shameful disease, still invisible, but ready to explode in
hideous and incurable ravages...

But I would be its savior! I was bringing the reme-
dy: I would dissipate the insidious nightmare that, in
spite of the joyful appearances of civilized pomp, was
obsessing everyone, men and women alike, and sadden-
ing their dwellings, while they ceased to be, externally,
the witty and light-hearted Parisians galvanized by the
honor of depicting, for the world and for the Cosmos,
super-civilization.

And I twisted the straps of the taxi in both fists; I
put on a smile pursed by superhuman emotion, on feeling that I was, in that box on wheels, unknown to everyone, the instrument of their deliverance, the messenger
of financial reestablishment.

In the Avenue de Villiers, my marine waterproof
and my old hat initially obtained a rather cool reception,
but on hearing my name the porter became more human.
Even for that flunkey, ignorant of my mission, I was already someone of importance—for the telegraph must
have been busy since my departure from Cherbourg—

and the great financier Jean-Paul Rivier, who had returned from his bank in the Boulevard Haussmann half an hour earlier, was waiting for me…"impatiently," the servant added, with a hint of respect.

A lackey in maroon livery took me up a thickly-carpeted staircase, along a luminous corridor—a true art gallery, full of paintings and statues—and finally introduced me into a brightly-lit and simple study-library, where I found my friend at a desk, in conference with a telephonic apparatus.

He did not get up or interrupt himself, but on seeing me, his face, whose features were contracted by a battle-hardened determination, lit up with an affectionate smile. Once again, I admired the manipulator of millions, who knew how to keep intact the fiber of gratitude and amity at the height of his grandeur and in the midst of his bothersome occupations.

A few replies in a distant telephonic voice alternated with the banker's "Yes… No… Understood… Adieu." Then the latter hung up, leaned forward in his armchair and took my hand in both of his, with a warm and emphatic grip. His piercing brown eyes examined my maritime costume curiously.

"Dear old Antoine! Welcome—but what happened? We thought you were lost, body and possessions…no news of the *Erebus II* for three days! Finally, two hours ago, I had a telegram from the first mate at the bank. Barcot is in Paris too? In the same costume as you? It's very urgent, then? And your hasty departure from island N…and de Silfrage's insistence… There's something extraordinary, eh, that the wireless didn't reveal? Why wasn't it explained?"

At that formidable moment, of which I had formed such a dramatic idea in advance—the moment when my words would determine the salvation of France—I had arrived without impact, by insensible transitions, on the inclined plane of continuous reality. I was astonished to find myself so calm. I was almost amused, as if I were examining the scene as a spectator.

I repeated "Why?"—and I lifted up the flap of my waterproof in order to take a lump of gold as big as my fist from my overcoat pocket, weighing about three kilos, and put it in Rivier's hand.

Surprised by its mass, he weighed it in his hand. His businessman's mind penetrated the truth in an instant, as if he read it in me. His eyes lit up with an interior fire.

Laconically, he said: "On island N?"

"On Île Féréor—iron-and-gold, understand? A foundation of native iron, as in aeroliths...for that's what it is...and above it, a golden rock, a mountain nine hundred meters high. Pebbles like this." So saying I took three smaller nuggets from my other pocket, one after another and deposited them on the desk. "The hold of the *Erebus II* is full of them. Two thousand tons. Eight billion francs in gold."

I listened to myself pronouncing my sentences and executing my gestures, like a disinterested witness.

The magic words and the sight of the yellow pebbles, which still bore traces of gold chloride, merely caused the banker to frown. He scrutinized me attentively, studying my face. He could see that I was not mad, and that I was telling the truth.

"Tell!" he ordered.

In five minutes, with a clarity and precision that even astonished me, I brought him up to date with the details that our wireless messages had prudently kept silent.

"Unless you've all been victims of a collective hallucination...but there's nothing illusory about these nuggets..." He rolled them on the desktop with his fingertips, then continued: "Tell me, where's Barcot, at this moment?"

"At the Ministry of Marine, where he's gone to see the minister."

Hastily, Rivier consulted the directory, and picked up the telephone.

"Hello? Monsieur le Ministre? Jean-Paul Rivier here. Are you alone? Oh, with Commander Barcot! Perfect. He's told you? And he's shown you his nuggets? No, nothing else, thanks. We'll talk later...Oh, wait! When you've finished with Monsieur Barcot, send him to me."

Then, as if the enormity of the situation had suddenly revealed itself to him, he stood up, leaned toward me, and in a virile accolade, rubbed his clean-shaven cheeks against mine.

"Oh, my old comrade! You deserve a national reward, and you'll have one, without prejudice to the one I'll reserve for you myself. You've brought France the gold that she needs."

That was the only trace of excitement that in observed in the man who found that he was, for a few hours, the richest in the world—for, in spite of the official requisition of the *Erebus II*, which permitted the State to claim its share of the treasure, Jean-Paul Rivier still remained the ship's outfitter; half of the cargo was rightfully his: four billion in gold. But he also considered that such a sum was incompatible with private property, and destined the whole of it for France.

"That gold will serve to redeem the value of the franc...by the intermediary of my bank, on the one hand,

and with the cooperation of the Banque de France on the other. Let's see, it's seven o'clock...we'll get a bite to eat, and then: to work!"

In spite of the credulity that politicians and financiers display in certain domains, there could not be any question of undertaking anything without having exhibited—in default of the island, which was too distant—the cargo of the *Erebus II* to the two people destined to become Jean-Paul Rivier's necessary allies in his maneuver to raise the value of the franc: which is to say, the governor of the Banque de France and the President of the Council.

As with Rivier himself, the reiterated and mysterious messages from the naval captain had prepared them both for a considerable event, and they were delighted, an hour later, when I repeated my story in the banker's study and showed them the nuggets and photographs of the island, with the supplementary testimony of Commander Barcot. Nevertheless, their conviction was only provisional, and, in a way, conditional. I could see that clearly in the haste with which they accepted Rivier's offer to take them to cast a glance over the holds of the *Erebus II* in Cherbourg.

"The prospect of a night flight doesn't frighten you, Messieurs? Nor you, Commander? Nor you, of course, Antoine? Good. Just let me telephone Le Bourget, and I'll take all four of you to the airport in my auto."

At nine o'clock in the evening, we were at Le Bourget.

On the immense illuminated field, in the beam of a searchlight, a large airbus was just taking off as we arrived.

"Englishmen in a hurry to get back to London," the employee who was escorting us told us. "This way, Messieurs."

Shiny white in the electric light, its two propellers already roaring, a C. A. F. air-limousine was waiting for us, its cabin door open.

Monsieur Barcot and I were, of course, the only ones employing this ultra-modern form of transport for the first time, too costly hitherto for our modest means. The other three passengers, magnates of finance and power, had been familiar with it for a long time, and they installed themselves in the armchairs in the luxurious cabin as casually as in the saloon-car of a train.

Monsieur Barcot modestly took a back seat; he seemed intimidated, not by the aerial journey, but by the social quality of our companions. As for me, a natural independence of mind had always made me feel at ease with all kinds of people, and I thought, in addition, that the present circumstances more-or-less equalized all five of us...six, counting the pilot, enclosed in his glazed cockpit at the front. It was simple human respect that prevented me from exteriorizing my first impressions of aerial baptism.

By virtue of having been suppressed, those impressions left me with an ineradicable memory, in spite of my ulterior experiences.

What a sublime joy it is, from the second that one perceives, by the throb of the engines, that the apparatus has taken off, and that one is in flight! What a generous and triumphant intoxication it is to see, through the windows of the sealed cabin, the illuminated ground—all the fires of the landscape—diminishing, retreating further and further beneath one's feet! Oh, how I would have liked to be alone, in the open air of the night, in a uncovered cabin...to stand up, hair blowing in the wind of velocity, to bathe my outstretched hands in the sky, in the aerial typhoon of the propeller, and to cry out my enthusiasm as a human triumphant over gravity...my joy of living in this miraculous century in which humankind has acquired a power over matter previously reserved to the one Divinity!

But I kept that tumult of sensations enclosed within myself. My companions, sprawled in the supple tan leather armchairs, were lighting cigars or cigarettes and beginning to chat, quite calmly. They scarcely had any need to raise their voices in the cabin, where the monotonous sound of the engines was muffled. Even Monsieur Barcot stopped gazing at the immense luminous field of Paris, which was disappearing over the "starboard aft horizon," in order to listen to the conversation.

Soon, it took possession of me too, and from then on I was only fragmentarily conscious of our aerial flight—during course changes, for instance, when the nocturnal landscape seemed to swivel on its axis, and I felt an abrupt internal sensation of "intestines becoming unhooked," in the Commander's picturesque expression.

Naively, I imagined that the immediate utilization of the eight billion in gold would unite the votes of the three potentates, but I was soon disabused. Jean-Paul Rivier was alone in suggesting that means. Monsieur Hautôt, the governor of the Banque de France, wanted to proceed in stages. As for the President of the Council, he feared the consequences of the revaluation of the franc, and was in favor of a gradual and slow withdrawal of banknotes.

Layman as I was, the arguments of each in turn seemed to me to be decisive. I soon realized that the problem was exceedingly thorny.

"If you maintain the present quantity of banknotes in circulation," proclaimed Monsieur Germain-Lucas, in his southern accent, "France will find itself with an exaggerated volume of fiduciary money, like a once-obese slimmer whose clothes have become too large!"

"It's an inconvenience, I admit," conceded Monsieur Hautôt. "Exporting will become difficult, at first, and the fall in domestic prices will hinder commerce for a few weeks, or months—but we can reduce those inevitable inconveniences tactfully, over a reasonable period of time. Because of them, will you hesitate to cure the aforementioned obesity—to borrow your comparison?"

"A surgical operation is necessary, and urgently," proclaimed Rivier.

"Urgently? Hmm! We've been expecting the catastrophe next week for six years now, but we're still here—social life is still functioning."

"That can't last indefinitely. Look at the example of Germany..."

"It's not the same thing."

"It doesn't matter. Fortunately, this time, we're no longer entirely submissive, forced to operate at the pleasure of Messieurs the politicians. There are technical experts who have taken matters in hand, under their sole responsibility; you have only to support them, along with the country."

"Do surgeons operate on patients without asking their consent?"

"Would you like a plebiscite?"

"That's impossible, in the present state of things, as you know very well. We can't risk failure by virtue of this delay."

"What if the government vetoed the operation?"

"The plebiscite would take place of its own accord; the entire nation would disapprove; you'd be thrown out. Then, the Banque de France and the Banque Rivier would be free to act. Besides, the operation, as you call it—that is to say, putting the gold on the *Erebus II* into circulation—will only serve to accelerate things a little; the mere announcement that there's another eight billion in gold in the bank's vaults, and another cargo of equal value on the way, will suffice to restore parity between banknotes and gold."

"Restore parity between banknotes and gold! But you're going to cause an upheaval in the national economy, provoke catastrophes, ruin hundreds of thousands of Frenchmen!"

"What does it matter if we save France? If, by the reestablishment of the franc, life becomes easier and happier for the rest of the French? Our action ought to participate in natural law; it ought to be as great as nature, which takes account of species and sacrifices individuals."

I interrupted, modestly: "But don't you also fear, Messieurs, that the unlimited flood of gold that the deposit will soon pour over the world might end up diminishing, or even reducing to negligibility, the metallic value of gold?"

The three potentates looked at me pityingly. "That's obvious, old man," said Rivier, "and that's why I want to act immediately, and Monsieur Hautôt only wants to brake slightly. It's a matter of making France benefit from its priority...of wiping out her debts, of bringing about her financial recovery while gold is still worth something...or putting her back in her rightful place, at the head of the nations. It's of little importance that the value of gold will be annulled thereafter, for Europe and the entire world, and that we'll be forced to change the momentary standard—to adopt platinum, for example. As that inconvenience will be equal for all countries, France, while being subject to it, will keep the advantage that she will have taken..."

"In any case," Monsieur Germain-Lucas went on, "whether you operate quickly or slowly, by massive or gradual deflation, you're going to alert the League of Nations. It'll be necessary for you to confess the origin of all the gold that you're throwing on to the market."

"No," Rivier retorted. "Until the definitive attribution of the island—which can't be long delayed, because we'll hasten it by every means possible—the cargo of the *Erebus II* won't come into play. We'll pretend to be using the Banque's reserves."

"People will say that you're acting precipitately, and with deplorable frivolity. Suppose, then, that when the truth gets out—as it's bound to, sooner or later—the League of Nations goes back on its decision and takes the island off France, to internationalize it, let's say, and demands an indemnity from us for the usage we've made of it?"

"It won't be able to take back all the gold put into circulation in the interim. And that's one more reason for us to act rapidly. Your politics isn't bold enough, Monsieur President, and you're looking too far ahead. Haven't we learned, during the war and in the course of the years that followed, the relativity of human actions and the impossibility of knowing in advance what it would have been wise to do? Let's strive to do our best in the light of our present knowledge, and according to our conscience. The future will decide. Act first. Act—that's all we can do."

The pilot had made good time. By five to eleven the lights of Cherbourg were in view, and at eleven on the dot, as he had promised us, we disembarked on to the brightly-lit landing strip.

A naval officer was waiting for us beside a comfortable auto—the lieutenant from the afternoon, sent to meet us, to greet the President of the Council on the Admiral's behalf, and to facilitate our entry into the military harbor at that unusual hour.

The *Erebus II* was, in fact, well-guarded; we were stopped no less than three times by sentinels between the gate of the arsenal and the quay of the dock where she was moored. Two marines, with rifles on their shoulders, were watching over the ship, inundated by light from two pylons, whose hatches were hermetically sealed.

The mate and the five officers still aboard met us on the deck; then Commander Barcot, resuming possession of his vessel, wanted to take us to the wardroom first, in order to drink an honorary glass of port—but the Parisians had no desire to hang about, nor to listen to the mate make his report to Monsieur Barcot concerning the efficient execution of his orders: all the sailors in prison and incommunicado; the crew's quarters put under seal as well as the hatches; journalists sent packing, etc., etc.

"Commander," said Monsieur Germain-Lucas, getting up, "you'll excuse us, but if we want to get back to Paris tonight..."

"That's true, Messieurs. This way, please..."

And, framed by the two chiefs, each of whom had an electric torch, we advanced through the interior corridors of the ship to a closed bulkhead.

"This is aft hold number one," said Monsieur Barcot. "It's just been opened for you, Messieurs. Be careful on the iron ladder."

The beams of the torches lit up, two meters below, a confused mass of yellow pebbles stained with red, randomly heaped: the nuggets of Île Féréor.

Without a word, the three potentates of finance and politics, descended one after another on to that bed of golden shingle—but when they felt them grating beneath their feet, their emotion surfaced.

Rivier drew himself up to his full height, breathing out forcefully, and sent a few nuggets flying with the toe of his shoe, as if to verify the density of the layer.

The governor of the Banque de France embraced the hold with his gaze, with a prolonged giggle that resonated bizarrely in the sonorous shell, and which almost turned into a nervous crisis.

The President of the Council uttered a litany of oaths in Occitan, and started sketching out a dance...

After which, recovering their composure, those three men of great intellectual power—those three representatives of superior humanity, those three masters of civilization—bent down over the golden idol, with detached smiles, and each picked up a nugget with their slightly tremulous fingers...as a souvenir.

Commander Barcot, having accomplished his mission to Paris, remained on his ship, in order to watch over it himself until the day came when it was possible to unload it. As for me, before climbing back into the Admiral's car with the naval lieutenant, Messieurs Germain-Lucas, Hautôt and Rivier, I took advantage of my trip to the *Erebus II* to go to my cabin and get my valise.

At two o'clock in the morning, exactly five hours after our departure from Le Bourget, we disembarked from our aerial vehicle there.

XI. The Franc Rises Again

"You're staying with me," said Jean Rivier in the automobile that was taking us back to Paris, in a tone which did not admit any protest. "My wife and daughter are in Biarritz for another fortnight, but the service doesn't suffer from their absence; I hope you won't find it too poor—but get up early if you want to witness the historic day that you've brought about with your news."

I was treated as a privileged guest of the house, an honored relative. The house in the Avenue de Villiers was not immense, nor did it exhibit the garish luxury of the *nouveau riche*; Rivier had taste, and one felt at ease and comfortable in his home. My room had a medium-sized bed, with a canopy and a raised alcove, which reminded me of Louis XIV's bed at Versailles. Thanks to fatigue, I slept therein "like a king," and it required the reiterated appeals of the *valet de chambre* to make me get up at eight o'clock.

I found Rivier in the middle of breakfast, already opening telegrams.

"*Bonjour*, my dear quadruple billionaire!" I joked, in accordance with the entitlement of our old friendship.

The financier shook my hand over his dispatches, and then said with an indulgent irony: "Me, a billionaire? Do you think so, old chap? But that doesn't interest me. I wouldn't know what to do with it. I could live on a hundred sous a day. These billions, of which half belong to me, I shall give to France. And from this morning on, the Banque Rivier will hurl them into battle, as the Banque de France will do for its part, to raise the level of the franc. Do you want to watch? You've earned it."

"Certainly," I agreed. "But a layman like me won't understand any of it."

"I'll explain it to you."

And with the marvelous faculty of dividing his attention, which I had already admired in him at school, and which he had further developed by methodical exercise, he talked, without interrupting his eating or reading his dispatches.

"As you've seen, the governor of the Banque de France is, like me, a supporter of revaluation. For months, he's been preparing an offensive, only waiting for an opportunity in which it would be possible to support his effort. Everything's in place. So, since last night at two o'clock, as soon as he was assured of the existence of the gold at Cherbourg, he's unleashed an offensive in New York—where it was then eight o'clock in the morning,[18] as you know, because of the time difference. Preparation of artillery before the assault. In a few hours, the pound has gone down 25 points; at 460 yesterday evening, it stands at 435 this morning."

"But why haven't you acted sooner, if it's so easy?"

"That's a good one! Because, if we couldn't sustain the effort, that artificial rise of the franc would be followed by a reaction that would bring it back to a lower level than its departure-point...as it has one every time it's been attempted without making use of the Banque's reserves. This coup, however, can be undertaken on a large scale, and there's trouble brewing. Have you finished eating? Yes? Get your hat and coat, then, and let's be off."

---

[18] In fact, it would have been eight o'clock in the evening, New York being six hours behind Paris, not ahead of it.

Ten minutes later, the financier's Hispano deposited the two of us on the sidewalk of the Boulevard Haussmann, in the new section, outside the Banque Rivier et Cie.

That temple to the god Speculation—more modern and more powerful than the classical god Gold, who shares his sanctuaries—rivals the Crédit Lyonnais and the Société Générale, and deploys an even more modern sumptuousness. Its vestibule and its central rotunda are clad in Portoro marble, yellow with black veins, which makes the gleam stand out and give it a nobler distinction. The high windows, collaborating with the electric light of invisible lamps, create an atmosphere on inhuman serenity. There are none of those old grilles between the servants of the god and the public; they can look one another in the face. Only the priest of the banknotes, with his coffer, from which wads of bills emerge, is enclosed in a cage of transparent glass, where he officiates.

On senses that it is one of the sacred hearts of Paris—that people, in going in there, are more genuinely pious than when they go into a basilica; believers and unbelievers meet there is a common devotion, that of wealth.

By contrast, the Exchange Hall, not open to the public, but into which Rivier took me, after a brief pause in his office, has the bare simplicity of a substation distributing electric current. And indeed, as I was to learn, it is there that currency is distributed. On the wall, there are two dozen telephones, each surmounted by a bell or a buzzer of some sort, all sounding different notes, which are sufficient to identify the instrument in the brain of the "broker"—the leader of the orchestra—and to open by reflex in that polyglot brain the pigeon-hole of the corresponding idiom.

"This is Monsieur Harduin, our chief broker," said Rivier, introducing me to a plump, bald little man with a gray moustache, who was moving back and forth with an unexpected briskness in front of his instruments. "He speaks eighteen languages."

Like his employer, Monsieur Harduin possessed the faculty of exercising his attention in several domains at the same time. He bowed to me and listened to the banker's orders without interrupting his work. A solemn bell rang.

"That's London," Rivier whispered to me.

"Hello London!" proffered the broker, in English, into one of the twenty-four telephones. "Four twenty-five, you say? Too late...at twenty this morning."

Then hanging up and going to the next apparatus, which was tinkling an octave higher: "Hello Brussels," he said, in French. "Nothing to do about yesterday. I'm selling sterling at 420."

It was the turn of other clamors. Madrid, Florence...and corresponding languages.

A telegraphist irrupted, however, and threw a flood of blue and white forms on the table.

"America now," Rivier explained. The blues are wireless messages and the whites Cable and Western."

And while the broker listened, replied, read dispatches, made notes, put things in order, scribbled figures and flew back and forth, my friend continued to educate me.

"We have a dozen large banks in Paris allowed to trade currency, where the same thing is happening—which is to say that, at this moment, there are three hundred telephones in communication with foreign capitals, in the process of diffusing throughout the world the currencies that are in or out of favor."

"Hello Frankfort. Four hundred and twenty?"

"What—they aren't lowering it?" said Rivier.

"Frankfurt and Berlin are selling paper francs hand over fist these days, Monsieur," the broker replied. "I daren't..."

"They'll pay dearly to cover it, if they take it to term; it's impossible for them to have all the paper they're offering at their disposal—but it doesn't matter. Sell, and keep selling, pounds and dollars. I repeat that we're acting in concert with the Banque de France."

"You need to indicate a limit to me, though, Monsieur, for they're not selling on term, but for immediate settlement. We could be liable before noon for eighty or a hundred million francs in gold...which we'll have to buy back in gold, to meet the obligation. We don't have the gold, and neither does the Banque de France."

"We will have. I'm giving you carte blanche."

"Even if we get to a billion?"

"Even then—and more. Go!"

The broker looked at his employer, saw that he was serious, and rubbed his hands.

"Oh, in that case, Monsieur..."

And he resumed his maneuvers in front of the apparatus, with renewed conviction.

Following the law of communicating vessels, the flow of pounds and dollars poured out fictively by that curt, dry voice—as well as by the Banque de France a kilometer away—redirected the course. In two hours of that exercise, almost without my noticing Rivier's departure, the pound had fallen to 320.

At half past eleven, Jean-Paul came back in and tapped me on the shoulder.

"Now, if you want to see the second act, let's go have lunch in the vicinity of the Bourse. It's there that the aftermath of the battle will unfold."

I followed him back to his office to collect my coat—but before going out I asked his permission to make a telephone call.

"As many as you want, old man." And with one hand sorting out the papers, he used the other to push the apparatus across the desk to me.

"Élysée 29-81," I requested, and then: "Hello, Claridge's Hotel? I'd like to speak to Professor Hans Kohbuler...or, if he's not there, to Mademoiselle Kohbuler."

I intended to announce that I would visit then late that afternoon, but the metallic voice articulated in my ear: "Professor and Mademoiselle Kohbuler have been away from Paris for a week, but they've retained their apartment and will be returning any day. Shall I tell them that you called?"

"Yes."

I hung up, disappointed and annoyed—and was suddenly embarrassed to find a singular stare fixed upon me by my friend.

"Kohbuler?" he said "Do you know him?"

I attempted to adopt a casual manner. "Oh, I met him once...with his daughter...at the Jolliots." I felt as if I'd been caught out, like a guilty schoolboy interrogated by a teacher.

Rivier addressed an amicable gesture of protest to me with his hand. "It's all right, old man. Don't get excited. I'm not an examining magistrate interrogating you about citizen Kohbuler—and if you're interested in his daughter, you're not wring; it appears that she's a pretty thing, the little doctor, and as charming as she's irreproachable. She has much more merit than her father..."

"You can talk freely," I said, as he left the sentence suspended. "The father doesn't inspire any sympathy in me at all."

"Well, in that case, Antoine, listen, I'll tell you this in confidence, as an old friend. I've never met Kohbuler but people have mentioned him to me, not very favorably. Yes, someone highly placed in the Prefecture of Police, duty-bound to be discreet...so don't go overboard with regard to Mademoiselle Kohbuler too quickly, for her Papa, the so-called Swiss Professor, might be something else entirely. They're keeping an eye on him at the Prefecture. Travels a lot...too much. Stays at Claridge's like a Yankee billionaire, and spreads thousand-franc notes around as if they don't cost him anything."

I didn't simulate astonishment; I recalled the man's eyes, his Teutonic accent, and the indefinable antipathy that he had inspired in me.

"So much the worse for him," I replied. "Let them throw him in prison or deport him. That won't prevent me from marrying his daughter, if she wants to. She's not at risk, I hope?"

"No, I don't think so. But I've said too much. Hush, eh? Don't let Kohbuler know that he's under suspicion. You're a good enough Frenchman to understand, even if you're smitten with the demoiselle. But let's go to lunch! Quarter to twelve. We need to be at the Bourse for the opening bell, at twelve thirty."

The journey by car took almost as long as it would have done on foot, amid the hypertension clogging the arteries of central Paris. In the Place de la Bourse, we went to a restaurant full of brokers, where we had difficulty finding an empty table-end...

While we were served, hurriedly, I examined my neighbors. Their faces revealed an intense internal animation: a fever of anxiety or triumph; but apart from a few outbursts of numbers, the majority conserved their vocal cords, conversing in low voices, or eating in hasty silence.

"Tell me," I said, leaning toward the banker's ear, "are these people dealing in shares?"

My naivety made Jean-Paul smile.

"Dealing in shares? Oh yes, you imagine, like a true 'average Frenchman,' that stocks and shares are discussed publicly, whether one is under the peristyle of the Bourse or in the wings? Not at all. The second act is even less ostentatious that the first, as you'll see. I'll introduce you into the den where it's simmering gently."

The ritual bell rang. Rivier guided me through the bustling crowd obstructing the environs of the Palais de la Bourse and took me up to the second floor. The "den" was well-guarded; ushers stopped us several times, and my friend had to negotiate to obtain my admission.

In a banal room, ripolined in cream and garnished with a blackboard, a dozen individuals were gathered around a table, among whom I recognized the Banque Rivier's broker. They were exchanged numbers in low voices while riffling through notebooks, lists and—above all—dispatches that telegraphists entering at every moment rained down in front of them.

"The official areopage," Rivier whispered to me. "The chief brokers of the great banks of Paris. They've centralized the orders of the smaller ones. The clerk at the blackboard is noting the fluctuation of the results, which modify the new orders."

Every five minutes, the marker approached the table, picked up a figure, and went back to inscribe it, erasing the previous one. Beside him, another clerk was operating the keys of some sort of calculating machine.

Even to me, who did not understand the first thing about the Bourse, it was evident that the crisis was enormous, and I felt a shiver go through me at every figure indicating a further fall in the pound. In twenty minutes, in successive leaps of between five and ten francs, it had fallen from 300 to 275.

Rivier was triumphant, but apart from a brief smile of complicity darted at him by the brokers of the two allied banks, the Twelve maintained the phlegm of mathematicians in their concentrated activity. The moderate tone of their voices ended up revolting me.

"But these fellows don't feel anything," I whispered to Rivier. "They're automatons!"

"Layman that you are," he joked, "you can't comprehend the pure emotions of our transcendental algebra. It's a great spectacle you want, is it, gawker? So be it— let's go back down. But don't forget that the movement originates here. The man playing the keyboard, beside the marker, is transmitting the figures from the blackboard to the floor of the Exchange."

As soon as we were out of the den, a gust of noise greeted us…a vast rumor of raised voices that filled the corridors, coming from below. On the staircase, it became the buzz of a beehive in revolution. The peristyle, the wings, the parquet, all the speculative compartments of the Bourse, the external steps as well as the internal ones, communicating through all the openings, were uniting their clamors, which attained the paroxysm of their frenzy in the great central all, around the floor.

At first I stood there, stunned and bewildered, in the midst of that crowd of fanatics, who were shouting orders at one another at the top of their voices, all at the same time, with the volubility of morra[19] players, employing gestures when voices became impotent to pierce the tumult.

Here, there was genuine panic and rage, such as I had imagined, poured over vibrant human beings by the twelve Olympians on the second floor. All eyes went incessantly to the automatic displays installed around and above the floor, twenty centimeters from the ceiling, where white figures on black inscribed the official exchange rates. Every time the figures jumped, orders were exchange more vigorously, voices bursting out in hoarse and shrill yells.

"Pound at 260!" Apoplectic and sweating, or grinding teeth and drunk with rage, exhibiting all the animal deformations of impotent fury in the face of a cataclysm or the joy of an unexpected and unprecedented triumph can impose on human features, all around me the dealers in stocks were striving in vain to alleviate the movement of foreign shares, to maintain them on the slippery slope down which they were inevitably sliding, following the pound.

Already, Rivier scribbled to me in his notebook, for lack of the ability to make himself heard, *Royal Dutch has fallen from 190,000 to 110,000, Rio from 18,000 to 9000.* On the other hand, French shares were climbing: "family savings," rents and loans were recovering their former dignity...

---

[19] Morra was an ancient and exceedingly simple gambling game, the ultimate ancestor of all coin-tossing games and finger-display games, in which players usually shouted out their wagers at the same time as the tosses or displays were made, thus making it rather loud.

Meanwhile, Jean-Paul Rivier had been recognized. People already knew about the role his bank was playing, conjointly with the Banque de France, in the operation to revalue the franc. Glances of envy and admiration saluted him as he passed by—or venomous smiles anticipating the imminent reaction. But hostility predominated in the groups around us, and I perceived, in the midst of the pandemonium, fragments of evidently-hostile phrases hurled in Rivier's face, including such terms as *upheaval, catastrophe, ruin, scoundrel* and *pay dear*.

Could he not hear? Was he pretending, bravely, to ignore the threats? I invoked the malaise that the frightful crowd and the heat of the room were causing me to drag him toward the exit, and then on to the stairs, and then outside the gates and the densest crowds.

When it became possible for us to converse again, he laughed scornfully. "Upheaval? Catastrophe? So they say! Imbeciles! The reraising of the franc to its gold value—which I'm seeking and will obtain, by God!—is, on the contrary, the reestablishment of equilibrium...the normal state of affairs. Since the war, as the franc has been debased, we've been living in a topsy-turvy house...increasingly topsy-turvy, if I can use that expression. Well, I'm setting the house to rights. There are going to be people who break their backs, obviously—those who took the new situation to be definitive; those who clung to foreign currencies or took their capital elsewhere, and the profiteers who speculated on the aggravation of the fall in our currency. So much the worse for them. In compensation, the others, the great mass of Frenchmen, will congratulate themselves on no longer being constrained to perform deplorable acrobatics standing on their heads. Yes, there'll be some temporary inconvenience in recovering the legitimate basis, and then a new division of wealth, but it was inevitable sooner or later...and this will doubtless spare us a worse revolution..."

At that moment, one of the agitated individuals that I had noticed on the stairway howling insults at my friend emerged from the swarming and vociferating crowd that was overflowing the gates all around the monument and marched straight toward us with a grimly resolute expression.

"Are you really Rivier, the banker?" he demanded of my companion.

I tried to interpose myself between them, saying "Be careful, Jean-Paul"—but Rivier gently eased me away and faced up to the individual.

"Yes, that's me. So what?"

"It's you, wretch—you who have unleashed this movement, you who have made sterling fall like an ar-row...you who've ruined me, you bandit, villain, bas-tard!"

I saw the nickel of an American knuckleduster glit-tering on the fingers of the brandished hand and leapt forward, trying to hold it back—but I only succeeded in diverting it. The blow slid along the length of my arm, and the weapon struck me full in the epigastrum, above the solar plexus.

I tottered...saw in a fog the attacker overcome by witnesses...and fell unconscious into Jean-Paul Rivier's arms.

XII. Forger

Professor Hans Kohbuler has just returned to Claridge's with his daughter, beside himself, not knowing which way to turn.

The sudden rise in the franc took him by surprise, four days ago on the twenty-fifth, in his villa at Audresselles, where he was attempting to produce a series of perfect banknotes, exempt from the faults that would not permit those printed by the factotum Gédéon to be used without risk.

Kohbuler was not worried at first; he thought it one of those ephemeral spasms that had been repeated several times in the last seven or eight years, thanks to Morgan or other funds, and which had invariably produced an even steeper fall of the ordinate curve toward the zero point of the abscissa.

On the twenty-sixth, the rise was accentuated vertiginously—the pound fell to 90!—and he was irritated to see the results of his months-long campaign canceled out at a stroke. Reproachful messages arrived from Berlin and Frankfurt, and he had directed his own anger against the subaltern agents charged with spreading the apocryphal Banque de France bills.

On the twenty-seventh, when a question in the Chambre had provoked the response from Monsieur Germain-Lucas, President of the Council, that the Banque de France had resolved to throw all the gold in its reserves into the conflict, down to the last louis, he had thought that the French were insane. In a week…two days…twenty-four hours…that gold would be exhausted, and the franc would fall back into the depths of the abyss...

In the meantime, the pound continued to fall; that day, it closed at 30. And yet, according to the calculations of all the exchange markets centralized in Frankfurt, the famous metallic reserves had been swallowed up, and more. Even so, in all the markets of Europe and America, France had not ceased to offer gold, gold and more gold. It was a deluge, an inundation, an avalanche of gold, which absorbed and drowned the paltry efforts of foreign agents to sell paper francs.

And it is necessary to believe that there is still gold in France, for today, on the twenty-ninth, the last step has been taken; the implausible has been realized; the paper franc has resumed parity with gold; sterling is at 25.25!

Too bad! Doomed, in the estimation of his chiefs, the professor has resolved this morning to play his trump card and to distribute the batch of defective bills regardless.

Postal packages have been sent to his correspondents, stuffed with false banknotes, irreproachable or suspect—it no longer matters. And he has brought the remainder of the stock back to Paris in his suitcases: twenty pseudo-millions of paper francs.

Among all the hypotheses that he envisages and passes in review to explain the success of the "French fit of insanity," he has not thought of linking the return of the *Erebus II* with the seemingly-desperate maneuver by the Banque de France. He knows that the ship has returned to Cherbourg, but since it is waiting there, inert and disarmed, for orders to depart, he has lost interest in it.

In his preoccupation, he is even neglecting Dr. Marquin, of whose telephonic communication some days ago the hotel desk has notified him. The business of island N has retreated into the background, and he has read in the newspapers, almost with indifference, that the League of Nations will attribute to France tomorrow, by international treaty, the legal property of what he believes, since the message from the *Seeland*, to be a mass of volcanic rocks.

But Frédérique-Elsa has not forgotten. Having arrived in Paris two hours ago, she hopes…she expects—perhaps for that very afternoon, who knows?—the visit of the man she loves. Just as long as her father is absent when he comes!

The franc is maintaining parity, seemingly stabilized for good—and the professor, who has just received the latest news from the Bourse by telephone, hangs up the receiver furiously.

He will attempt his final maneuver, with the collaboration of the banker Heinrich Goldshield. He embraces his daughter, goes into his personal apartment—number 203—by the communicating door, which he closes and bolts. He stuffs his pockets with banknotes, and goes down the stairs, for he needs to walk in order to relax his nerves.

Half way between the second and first floors, he goes past the elevator, which is rising. Dr. Marquin!—a fleeting glimpse. Dr. Marquin, looking the other way, who has not seen him!

Struck by a sudden idea, Professor Hans Kohbuler pauses on the steps, turns back and climbs back up to the third floor. At the end of the corridor, the doctor's back is just disappearing, and the door of room 204 is closing behind him.

With a silent grimace, the professor stops outside the next door, 203, enters without making a noise, and goes straight to one of the telephones, whose receiver he raises to his hairy ears.

On the other end of the wire, in the drawing room of apartment 204, where Frédérique-Elsa and Dr. Marquin are conversing, a microphone is hidden in the rose of a brass ornament in the form of a chimera...

XIII. Amorous Indiscretion

Ordinarily, that blow from the fanatic's knuckle-duster would have knocked me out for four or five minutes, after which I would have resumed he normal course of my affairs without further distress, but I was in a condition of depleted resistance because of sleepless nights on the island, and then on the *Erebus II*, not to mention five hours on a train and four on an airplane when I had scarcely disembarked. All that accumulated fatigue degenerated, under the trauma of the blow, into a serious gastric crisis, which kept me in bed for three whole days.

It was a further opportunity for Jean-Paul to prove his friendship. Oratory extravagance was not his style, and he made no allusion to the accident except to say to me, once I had recovered consciousness, thanks to the attentions of the famous neuropathologist Raginski, to whom he had turned to ensure my immediate care: "I'm greatly indebted to you, old chap. That's the second time you've save my life, or as good as…I need an opportunity to settle up, don't I?

With what was for him an authentic devotion, however, he gave me hours of his time—hours more precious than ever during the crisis in which he was risking his fortune and the very existence of his bank. He had a horror of sick-rooms and the spectacle of illness, but he came three or four times a day to chat at my bedside, telling me the latest news.

"The pound's at 151…92…74," he announced. All's going well, and we're winning the battle, but the hardest part remains to be done, for in order to ensure that gold money is reestablished we need to buy back paper francs above par. Oh, if we could publish right away that we have eight billion in gold at Cherbourg and eight more on the way...because, by the way, I forgot to tell you that the destroyer and the transport vessel arrived at the island on the very day you disembarked in France. The destroyer is still there, but the transporter, loaded in double quick time, has already set sail. Not to mention that yesterday, two more cargo ships set sail from Brest."

On the evening of the twenty-fourth, as I was dining in my room, I learned that Jolliot had come to inquire about my health.

"He's been in Paris since yesterday. He read your name in the newspapers, after the attack in the Place de la Bourse. Not knowing whether his visit would be welcome, I told him that you'd go to see him once you were back on your feet. You'll go? Hold your tongue, then—he's a chatterbox, your friend; I sensed it right away."

By virtue of an excessive modesty—for Rivier had been straight with me and not tried to hide anything—I dared not ask him for permission to telephone Claridge's to ask whether the Kohbulers had returned from their trip. My first excursion in Paris, when I finally got up on the twenty-ninth, was to go there, by way of a convalescent stroll.

As if nature itself were participating in the celebration of the Resurrection of the Franc, a renewed warmth had spread over the capital as September came to an end. After three weeks of cold and rainy weather, the meteorological perturbation provoked by the fall of the bolide had brought about equally-unusual simulacrum of summer. For three days, the blue sky had had the ardor of June; overcoats and furs were abandoned, and lightly-clad female flesh was displayed to extent of the heart's desire.

Paris was joyful. A lightness, forgotten for a long time, impregnated the atmosphere, as in distant and happy times past. For years, I understood then, post-war anxiety and instability had been weighing upon us without our being aware of it; people had got used to it, adapted to it—but what had been taken, a few days earlier, for an everyday humor had been nothing but that chronic melancholy in which everyone had partaken.

Oh, it was very different that morning! A jubilation irradiated Paris, putting a new light into everyone's eyes. It reminded me invincibly of the Golden Age before the war.

In that Paris transfigured by thirteen years of mechanical progress and intensive civilization, I rediscovered my youth. Nothing but beaming faces on the sidewalk; nothing in the light air but optimistic remarks commenting on the invincible rise of the franc. I heard one shop-girl with a brazenly pretty face say to her companion, who was carrying an enormous hat-box: "You wonder, my girl, with the pound at 28 this morning, whether we can afford silk stockings!"

But that was nothing but juvenile bravado, a symptom of the general confidence—a confidence disappointed so many times, recovered at a stroke, full and smiling. The effect of the rise of the franc, as Rivier said, was entirely in the mind, limited to the satisfaction of knowing that, as before, paper was worth almost as much as gold. In the same way that every jolt in the franc's gradual fall had been deadened by the mechanism of commerce, the brutality of its decline absorbed, only raising the cost of living with a certain delay, it would take weeks, this time—perhaps months—for prices to adapt to the new value of the franc.

What joy to Claridge's to hear the reply: "Professor and Mademoiselle Kohbuler will return this afternoon."

I felt a need to go as far as sharing my delight with someone. Rivier was eating lunch out that day, I had no idea where. That left Jolliot. I took a taxi to his place—12A, Avenue de l'Observatoire—but he was in conference with an American theater-manager; I was only able to see him between two doors for five minutes.

"That swine didn't do too much damage, then? You look splendid. Yes, Cienne's here; she's dressing to go to the studio. But she's fed up with Panama, as I am; we're going to spend the winter in Los Angeles. But the deal we've been offered doesn't look so good any more, with this damned exchange rate—the dollar will be at par soon! What's got into your mate Rivier? They're crazy to move out the Banque's reserves, after having sworn that they were untouchable! What incoherence! What a mess! Where are we headed?"

He ended up interrogating me about my voyage, but as he had read the official version about the engine trouble off the Azores, he provided the questions and the answers, and when he had asked: "When are you leaving again?" and I had replied: "I don't know," I got away with being called "a washout as an explorer."

"Well, old chap," he concluded, "I have to get back to my Yank. But I'll see you again? When can you come to lunch? The day after tomorrow? Good—we'll talk then."

I had lunch alone in a student restaurant on the Boulevard Saint-Michel. The prices had not changed; the fixed-price menu that I had seen at one franc twenty-five before the war was still twenty-two francs fifty. Nowhere in the stores on the boulevard, which I then amused myself by passing in review, was any symptom of real lowering yet in evidence. On the windows of the Petite Samaritaine, it's true, slanting calico ribbons announced a 20% discount on all articles, but the reduction was purely fallacious.

I went back to Claridge's by way of a long walk along the Seine, trying to soothe my impatience by looking in the boxes of the booksellers, and then going up the Champs-Élysées in the shade of the plane-trees, which were still green. It was warm. The water-wagons were spraying the shiny roadway, along which automobiles were speeding rapidly. The waves of confidence and hope emitted by all the passers-by penetrated me, and my brain amplified them, like an ultra-sensitive resonator.

I was as excited as a student ringing the doorbell of his first mistress as I stepped into the elevator at Claridge's.

"The professor and Mademoiselle came in two hours ago..."

And the luxurious cage, its mahogany and nickel gleaming, that hoisted me up to the third floor of the palace, seemed to be bearing me up to Eden...

Frédérique! She it was who opened the door of number 204 to me, in an ultramarine blue dress, the same color as her gold-flecked eyes. Her! With her blonde hair in a Florentine bob, her frank smile and the perfume Remember forming an aureole around her, like an evocation of the sun on a beach and an infinite sea...

"Monsieur Marquin! My father's gone out, just a minute ago. He'll be sorry to have missed you..." But she seemed, on her own account, to be delighted. Not for a second did I fear that she might hesitate to let me in.

I pronounced the conventional formulae while following her into a study-drawing-room decorated in white lacquer with gold threads, and net curtains with the design of ducks in flight...

I was not a child; I was thirty-four years old, and had experience of feminine seduction—but what I experienced that day was completely unprecedented.

As in a glorious dream, an apotheosis of realized joy, in which a new love swept away my old life, leaving me brand new before her, and absolutely confident, I sat down in the armchair she indicated to me, and accepted a cigarette.

Her face stood out, fully illuminated, and I could not see anything but her.

The polite comments that were exchanged mechanically were of no importance to me. Gripped by a marvelous emotion, I followed the expressions passing over her mobile features...which transfigured her, causing her to put on successively, from one minute to the next, the thousand and one faces of my most cherished dreams of old...the harem of beauty that fortunate love is able to discover in the Chosen One...

We chatted, by way of social reflex, but another exchange of thoughts, infinitely more serious and emotional, was effected between us...as if the waves of a fluid and inarticulate language—the primordial language of souls—were bathing us in an atmosphere of reciprocal comprehension, connecting the essential and secret magnetisms of our being...

I did not make a gesture toward her; I did not even want to take her by the hand. Those effluvia created an atmosphere of sacred drama that was sufficient in itself.

Was she afraid of seeing me anticipate future joys? Or, warned by her subtle feminine instinct, did she understand that we had exhausted the beauty of the moment, and it could only decline?

I was woken up, so to speak, by a direct question: "Would you like to tell me about your voyage, my friend? Let's take advantage of being alone."

Her face, as if haloed by superhuman light, revealed the utmost depths of her limpid and fraternal soul. No secrecy could exist between us. My oath of silence, made to Commander Barcot, did not concern her, the sister soul rediscovered...the complementary half of my being, the one that vibrated in perfect harmony with mine.

I told her everything: the voyage of the *Erebus II*, the exploitation of Île Féréor; the mutiny; my flight from Paris to Cherbourg in company with the magnates...

An anxious expression invaded her features. "Lower your voice, my dear," she ordered.

And, drawing her armchair closer, she leaned her elbow on the arm of mine, her ear extended toward my mouth. The perfume of her hair came to me in waves. The satiny beach of her bare shoulder gave me vertigo. I closed my eyes momentarily.

"And you were sworn to secrecy!" she murmured, in a voice that was almost inaudible. "And you're an honest man! With what confidence you honor me, my friend!" All of a sudden, she added: "But what if I were a spy?"

She looked me in full in the face, at such close range that I could feel the pure warm current of her breath. She had such a strange expression that I fell silent, shivering, anguished by the memory of Rivier's insinuations on the subject of Kohbuler.

But confidence flooded back within me, greater still, and submerged me like a tidal wave. "Even if you were what you say, Frédérique, I sense that you would not betray me."

She smiled, both dolorously an ecstatically. "Oh! You sense that! Thank you." And in the nudity of her words, simple but spoken with an emphatic gravity, there was the most perfect declaration of love, the absolute and definitive gift of her life.

The muffled shock of a door closing in the next room caused her to start anxiously. "My father's back! Don't let him see you, Antoine! Go away, quickly."

"I'll do as you say, without seeking to understand, Frédérique. When will I see you again?"

"Tomorrow evening, if you wish, after dinner, at nine o'clock. I'll try to be alone."

And in the shadow of the vestibule, we exchanged our first hasty and anxious kiss.

XIV. The Triumph of the Franc

I had not been in Paris—for good reasons—in November 1918, when the Armistice was agreed, but I have
some slight mistrust of the current assertion that those
who were not lucky enough to be in Paris on the historic
day when the franc reached Paris could only form an
approximate idea of it by recalling the day of the Armistice.

The scale of human emotions does not vary much,
of course, and they only have a limited series of words
and actions, always the same, for their expression. The
triumphant joy was analogous in both cases, but there
were essential differences between the end of the war
and the victory of the franc, for which reason there were
more than nuances between the kinds of delight manifested on the two occasions. The second celebrated a
bland victory, which put an end to years of malaise, not
years of slaughter. Moreover, it lacked something of the
clarity and conclusiveness of the armistice—the signing
of the treaty between the German and allied plenipoten-
tiaries. It lacked soldiers to be embraced and carried in
triumph. The franc triumphed, but without its enemies
having capitulated; a counter-offensive remained possible.

In sum, the price of things, which remained immov-
able, contributed to leaving opinion, at first, slightly surprised, as if wrong-footed, without knowing where to pin
its future certainty.

It was in that state in which I found the capital as I
came out of Claridge's, but in the course of the following hours, which I spent wandering around Paris on my

127

own—because Jen-Paul Rivier was dining with Monsieur Germain-Lucas, and I did not care, effervescent as I was after by conversation with Frédérique, to dine alone beneath the "gilded paneling" of the house in the Avenue de Villiers, served by flunkeys as grave and severe as judges—the kind of dissatisfaction that underlay that victory faded away to the point of disappearing.

The great news, repeated by everyone, cried out to anyone—the pound finally at parity at the close of the Bourse—filled Paris with a clucking of joyful voices and was inscribed in the headlines of the newspapers. On store-fronts, strings of white or colored light-bulbs added to the habitual luxury of illumination as bright as daylight; on the terraces of the cafés, which were overflowing, orchestras played the Marseillaise and the Madelon, and street-hawkers sang new songs, composed by some unknown bard, celebrating the victory of the franc...

On the Boulevard de la Madeleine, I saw the traffic gradually easing, and I had not yet arrived at the Opéra when it had ceased almost completely; the buses were going back to the depot, the taxis to the garage. It was a general strike of rejoicing that Paris granted itself that evening, and the boulevards were soon surrendered to pedestrians alone, whose flood filled them, their feet kicking up the dust of fine holiday evenings, in the odor of fireworks that were being let off here and there. Then there were the open-air dances, which I found in full swing all the way from the Boulevard Bonne-Nouvelle to the Place de la République, where an entire brass band, perched on the pedestal of the giant statue, was projecting the rhythmic gaiety of its instruments all around.

The police had disappeared, or were taking part in the rejoicing; a few agitators waving placards demanding "death to the monopolists" were surrounded, merrily manhandled and forced to join the farandole that had already swept up an English family getting out of an autocar, who were squealing, thinking that the Great Day had come...

For a few hours, Paris was a Utopia, on a planet of merriment and amiable ease, where everyone had he facile generosity of opulence...

Which is what it would have been, if it had been possible to reveal to the public the existence of the gold of the *Erebus II* and Île Féréor!

Not for an instant, all evening, did my conscience reproach me for my indiscretion. Caught up in the currents of the tramping crowd, or carried away by the chain of the dance, I wanted to raise my arms and shout: "Oh, brave people, if you only knew what I know! What I can't tell you, today or tomorrow, but which you'll doubtless be told the day after tomorrow, if the convention is signed tomorrow in Geneva attributing island N to us. If you only knew!"

I contained myself, not always without difficulty. I was slightly intoxicated...like all of Paris...like all of France.

I got up late the next day; Rivier had already left for the bank. I had breakfast on my own, and went to Jolliot's, making the last part of the journey on foot, from the Place Saint-Michel to the Avenue de l'Observatoire.

A gay Paris, luminous beneath a blue October sky—a matinal Paris—was mocking itself for its enthusiasm of the previous evening, as if to spare itself too cruel a disillusionment if the future Cockayne were to draw away once again...

As it was too soon to go up to Jolliot's, I sat down for half an hour in the Jardin du Petit-Luxembourg, irritated in advance by all the hours that still separated me from the one in which I would see Frédérique again.

I found Lucienne Jolliot alone in the drawing room; her husband was late, as usual. It was necessary for me to suffer the star's conversation—an exceedingly boring experience, for the marvelous cinema actress had the least photogenic vocabulary. I didn't know what further details to invent with regard to the *Erebus II* and the Azores, when the door of the vestibule opened violently and slammed shut, and the director burst into the room like a blast of wind.

Without saying hello, he threw a *Paris-Midi* on to the table, wide open. "Great gods! They've had us, the Boches! I've said so before, that it can't go on! They need to be reined in! Island N...Île Féréor? They've put one over on us! Right under our noses!"

Without paying any heed to these incoherent exclamations, I swiftly scanned the headlines, which gave me gooseflesh.

GERMAN REVELATIONS. ISLAND N IS A GOLDEN ROCK. DECISION SUSPENDED IN GENEVA.

And I read:

This morning's Berlin newspapers have published information that, if true, will have the gravest consequences for us. It is the story told by an ex-sailor on the Erebus II, *who was, it seems, a German journalist, a correspondent of the* Berliner Zeitung. *According to this account, the premature return of Commander Barcot's ship is connected in the closest possible fashion with the revaluation of the franc and the insistence of the French government on being attributed the famous island N. In other words, the* Erebus II *set a course on leaving Marseilles, not toward the South Pole, but to toward the North Atlantic, where it made a landing on island N.*

Contrary to generally-admitted opinion, apparently corroborated by the testimony of the captain of the Seeland, *island N, far from being volcanic in origin, is an enormous bolide, a giant aerolith, whose fall on September fifth caused the meteorological upheavals and damage that are well-known. The geologists of the Barcot expedition ascertained that the bolide is partly constituted of iron and partly is an exceedingly rich gold mineral, including numerous nuggets of pure gold— hence the name Île Féréor. An agent of the French government, clandestinely embarked at Marseilles on the* Erebus II, *took possession of the bolide-island in the name of our country.*

Still according to the reporter of the Berliner Zeitung, *half the crew remained behind to exploit the deposit, under the direction of specialist engineers; in the meantime, having embarked one or two tons of gold, as proof of the discovery. Commander Barcot returned to the port of Cherbourg. There, the fake sailor, initially interned with his companions in the prison of the arsenal by the authorities, desirous of keeping the secret of Île Féréor, finally succeeded in avoiding surveillance and reaching Germany.*

We reproduce this information with all reservations, which the newspaper from beyond the Rhine follows with indignant commentaries. They denounce the 'duplicity' of our government, which has kept the discovery of the gold deposit secret and taken possession of it, intending to proclaim it the day after the League of Nations attributed island N and it wealth to France...

Joliot, leaning over my shoulder, read it aloud for his wife's benefit, shouting at me from time to time: "Come on, Antoine, respond! Is it true? If it's true, you must know!"

I was horribly embarrassed. I replied with vague grunts, pretending to be absorbed in reading the next paragraph:

A question will be asked in the Chambre this afternoon. Monsieur Zerbuco, the spokesman for the extreme socialist group, will demand a clear declaration from the government regarding the politics followed in this circumstance. In the meantime, we can only reserve our opinion with regard to the veracity of the German claim, although it must be said in support of the arguments invoked on the far side of the Rhine that they do not lack plausibility.

First of all, the financial maneuver of the Banque de France, throwing all the gold in its cellars—previously considered intangible and sacred—into battle, out of the blue, cannot be explained unless the aforesaid bank knew that the unlimited deposits of the Golden Rock were behind it, which imminent arrivals would put at its disposal.

Secondly, the haste and insistence of the French government, described beyond the Rhine as imperialist politics sustained by the vilest deceit, in claiming possession of island N would hardly be justified if the island were no more than a simple shelf of lava, useful at the most to serve as a refueling stop of the aerobuses of a Paris-New York service.

The fury of the Teutonic journalists is somewhat overblown, but from the patriotic viewpoint, if this information is true—which, for our part, we are tempted to believe—it must be regretted that it has emerged at the last moment, to disturb the negotiations in Geneva, for it is all too evident that the convention attributing island N to France will not be signed today, as announced.

We must also deplore the economic consequences of this premature revelation for our money. In fact, this island, this Golden Rock, which a fortunate hazard and the valiant initiative of our navy had given to France as a kind of material compensation for the evils of the recent war, will doubtless be taken off us by the League of Nations. In the case of it being internationalized, as is probable, the bold but reckless maneuver of the Banque will only have served to deprive us of our reserves. The massive influx of gold that it had the right to expect will not take place, and the franc, after a few days of recovery, will plunge lower than ever by virtue of the abolition of the metallic backing for our banknotes. Germany is triumphant at this prospect, and predicts for us all the evils suffered there by virtue of inflation. ...

I read, and kept reading, in order to have the time to master myself and conceal my disturbance. Distress gripped me by the throat. Frédérique! Could it be her? For I had not given credence for one minute to the fable of the seaman-reporter. There were certain details that a crewman could not know, and in the tenor of the story I recognized the exact terms that I had used myself with Frédérique. That so-called interview was nothing but my conversation of the previous day, copied down and scarcely disguised.

I was a traitor, I spite of myself; by virtue of my indiscretion, I had caused France an irreparable injury. But what about Frédérique? The letters danced before my eyes; my attention had gaps, for it was necessary to multiply it, in order simultaneously to seize the meaning of what I was reading, drive away the problem of

Frédérique—no! impossible! not her!—and, eventually, reply to Jolliot.

He was harassing me: "Well, old man? Well? Answer me, damn it! Is it true? You know, since you've be there, since you've seen this island N—this Golden Rock. And you said nothing about it, the day before yesterday?"

What could I say? Was the government going to deny it, try to dismiss it as a lie? What good would it do? It was impossible now to stifle the scandal. There was no way that Geneva would award the mandate for island N to France...

I ended up admitting it, while invoking, to justify my silence two days before, the necessary secrecy...

"Yes, obviously, you were forbidden to speak," the film-director went on. "Professional secrecy. But even so, it's not very polite. With an old friend—with me! You know me well enough to know that I'm as mute as the grave!"

He was exasperating me. Even the star, contrary to her habit of playing a decorative and mute part, was putting her oar in. I was on the brink of exploding.

Throughout the meal I was under torture. A fever of remorse was gnawing away at me, with a desire to run to Frédérique, to reassure my faith in her by the honesty of her face, to proclaim my certainty of her innocence, perhaps to discover the truth of the trap to which I had fallen victim...and in the meantime, my pitiless chatterbox of a director was bombarding me with his inept suppositions, insisting that the government ought to declare war on Germany...

Invoking the necessity of offering my support to Rivier in the grave circumstances, I was finally able to escape. My mental torture seemed easier to bear once I was alone and in the midst of an anonymous crowd.

Where should I go? To Frédérique? Now, though, I feared finding myself in her presence...because of the subconscious dread of finding that she was guilty? Because of the horror of encountering her father, the evident traitor? At any rate, I forbade myself to make my visit before the appointed hour.

The splendor of the sun appeared to me to be a bitter irony, given my suffering. The horse-chestnut trees on the avenue and the trees of the Petit-Luxembourg were full of chirping sparrows, and blue sky reigned over the scene of the gardens.

I went down the Boulevard Saint-Michel. There was anxiety in the air. Groups of foreign students at the street-corners were holding forth in guttural tongues and waving canes indignantly. I bent my back, as if they were meant for me, as if I were the object of their disapproval—the man who had perhaps ruined France, and had, at any rate, deprived her of an inestimable windfall...

And yet, no! I was not running any risk of discovery. Neither Rivier nor anyone else would suspect me, since the story was attributed to a seaman-reporter. With what objective? In order to spread suspicion in France? As a bluff, to demonstrate the omniscience of German espionage?

Persecuted by the gazes that took stock of me, but having a horror of being alone in a taxi, I took a bus to the Place de l'Opéra and went along the boulevards, heading east, mingling with the crowd in a desire to bolt out my personality, to disperse it, to lose it in the anonymous social atmosphere.

On the terraces of the cafés, as crowded as in mid-summer, there was nothing to be seen but anxious expressions and unfolded newspapers. On the sidewalks, the gaiety of previous days had disappeared. Even the prostitutes, parading their lamentable bodies in garish costumes, too new or over-decorated, were limiting themselves to exchanging news of the Bourse with one another. Since nine o'clock in the morning the franc had failed to maintain parity; the pound was gaining ground. It had reached 42.

At the corner of the Rue Richelieu, I hesitated over heading toward the Bourse, and then continued straight ahead.

People were crushed against the red façade of *Le Matin* to read the latest news. As on days of riot, a rumor of voices dominated the mechanical noise of automobile traffic.

Suddenly, the great daily's newly-installed loudspeaker projected these stentorian words over the crowd: "Ten minutes ago. In the Chambre, questioned by Monsieur Zerbuco regarding the allegations in the Berlin newspapers, Monsieur Germain-Lucas, the President of the Council, made a speech justifying the politics of the government. In a fine burst of eloquence, and with an unexpected audacity, he declared: 'Yes, Île Féréor exists. Yes, it contains gold in immense quantities. Yes, the expedition of the *Erebus II* took possession of it in the name of our country a fortnight ago. And since then— something that the German newspapers did not report— the *Erebus II* has brought back its first cargo of gold to Cherbourg. It will be in Paris tomorrow...'"

All along the boulevard a religious silence had fallen. The crowds on the sidewalks came to a standstill. Buses, taxis and cars had stopped, as far as the eye could see. Even the policemen with the white batons forgot to operate the sonorous and luminous signals at the cross-roads.

The loudspeaker continued: "Parisians, people of France, remain calm! The fate of the franc is assured. France does not intend any imperialism. If the League of Nations refuses France, in spite of its right of first occu-pancy, the mandate of the island, France will bow to its decision, but France considers herself justly authorized to continue its exploitation until then, and to reap the just fruits of its discovery, which will permit her to repair the financial damage inflicted by the war...

"Parisians, people of France, in addition to the *Erebus II*, three other vessels are already sailing toward our ports, similarly laden with nuggets. The Banque of France is assured, imminently, of a new reserve of thirty billion gold francs. You have heard correctly, and I repeat: thirty billion in gold francs!"

The loudspeaker fell silent, and cheers burst forth from ten thousand throats, an ovation to gold, reinforced by horns, klaxons and alarms of every kind.

Then the traffic resumed, with its familiar hubbub, going to spread the news throughout Paris.

Pride straightened me up. I no longer felt guilty. Thanks to the firm reaction of Monsieur Germain-Lucas to the grievances of the German press, my imprudence would not have the disastrous consequences that I had initially dreaded. It had only hastened a declaration that was bound to be made sooner or later, and which would certainly have caused the League of Nations to annul the international treaty of attribution to France, if it had been signed...

To complete my reassurance, I turned around and went to the Place de la Bourse. In spite of the closing bell, a dense crowd around the gates of the monument was prolonging transactions. The news of the firm governmental attitude—that superb and unexpected audacity, inspired by the power of gold, in all likelihood, thrown down like a challenge to the world—had caused the market to bounce back. In a matter of minutes, the franc had not only recovered from its drop, but, transported by the surge, had surpassed parity.

As I arrived to the corner of the Rue Notre-Dame-des-Victoires, the song of the *Marseillaise* bust forth, intoned by a crowd of stockbrokers, heads bare, and an old investment clerk in a threadbare woolen jacket said to me, with tears of joy: "Twenty-three seventy-five, Monsieur! Oh, the Boches have got it wrong, believing that they could knock us down with their premature revelation. On the contrary, they've inspired the true politics of frankness and audacity. 23.75! There are still fine days for France! Sterling is one franc twenty-five above parity. The paper franc is worth more than the gold franc!"

XV. The League of Nations

In Geneva, in the headquarters of the League of Nations, there is a general hue and cry, and Monsieur de la Meilleraie of France deserves some credit for continuing to stand his ground before his colleagues.

A great crisis of altruistic and sublime virtue is raising all the delegates toward the summit of disinterest, and from up there, they are judging France's actions severely.

Here they are, at tea-time, in the great smoking room of the left wing, with which everyone is familiar, at least by way of photographs and the cinema. The oak-beam ceiling and the Gobelins tapestries give it a grave and official atmosphere, but the bay windows are open on the perspective of a lake as blue as a stretch of the Mediterranean. There are seagulls here, as in Nice. The sun, already low and oblique, is reminiscent of a theater projector. Without a certain ingrate and sullen element in the beauty of the landscape, one could believe that one is on the Côte d'Azur. The grounds have palm trees—in tubs, it is true—agaves, Peruvian candle-trees and bougainvilleas in flower, as in the gardens of Monte Carlo. Is not the Palais des Nations, too, a casino, where the chips laid down are replaced by the interests of peoples? A casino? Or a theater of society? An International Guignol.

The time fixed for the signing of the treaty attributing island N to France is fast approaching. The delegates know that it will not be signed, and that nothing will be pronounced in today's session but vain speeches. The president, Hieronymus Maeseyck of the Netherlands, will deplore the new facts that prevent the signature and put the matter back in question. He will propose the internationalization of the island as a "basis for discussion." Hollow formulae will serve as a temporary mask of fictitious bargaining for the eyes of the world, until it has stopped listening and everything can be settled by diplomacy.

One might think that one is in the hall of a club—let us say an English one—at tea-time. There are women, admittedly—stenographers, secretaries, journalists and telegraphists—scattered among the groups; but are not all these correct and detached men socialites talking about sports? What a sport, in fact, this is! The game does not deceive anyone, but it is necessary to follow the rules of play. The majority put on fixed smiles. Others, more skillful, force their features to express sentiments opposite to those that animate them. A few—the supreme ruse!—are frank and clear; they are assumed to be Machiavellian.

They are chatting in twos and threes, coming and going, changing groups as if fluttering randomly.

Herr Durkheim of Germany—a corpulent giant with a sandpapered cranium—is the most sought-after. It is his nation that has discovered the covert foul and blown the whistle on it. He is sanctimonious and benign, full of hypocritical virtue. Germany will do anything to receive the mandate of the island instead of France, the unwarranted usurper. The normal right of the first occupant cannot apply in this circumstance; the bolide is not *res nullius*;[20] it is a gift offered by the divinity to all humankind, and all people have, in principle, a right to it—but they cannot exercise it themselves; it requires a unique

---

[20] "Nobody's property."

mandate. Thus, why not give Germany the mandate to the tiny island, in exchange for its lost colonies?

"Yes, why not?" opine, one by one, over their varied beverages, the delegates of Austria, Bulgaria, Hungary, Denmark, Norway and others who are hoping for a slice of the cake. Even Signor de Sussi of Italy does not say no; he is drinking his iced orangeade through a straw, meditatively.

Monsieur de la Meilleraie, who is courting Messieurs Etterbeck of Belgium and Wronski of Poland is only too glad see the brick-red monocled face of Sir Arthur Gray of England—a perfect gentleman—coming toward him. Sir Arthur, who was once scornful of the flaccid politics of France, had been gripped by a new respect on seeing her capable of playing this neat trick on the nations and supporting her gesture proudly. He talks to Monsieur de Meillerie about a possible understanding; France can keep its ill-gotten gold, and even continue to exploit the bolide...on condition that it shares the property—the word "mandate" will be used, for form's sake—fifty-fifty with England.

Monsieur de la Meilleraie perceives all the merit of the plan. He knows that, even with the support of Belgium and Poland—not to mention Czechoslovakia, Rumania and Yugoslavia—France cannot resist the covetousness of all the other nations, even divided between themselves. With England for an ally, on the other hand...

And Belgium bravely offers a piece of the Congo, in exchange for a part in the projected syndicate.

But here comes T. M. Ferrick of the United States—not a delegate, but an observer, although the difference is immaterial, weaving through the groups in his overflowing socks, an *enfant terrible* with a fine

Yankee insouciance, to put his feet in the platter. His government has just cabled him as follows:

The bolide has fallen to the west of the fortieth degree of west longitude from the Greenwich meridian— which is to say, nearer to America than to Europe, and, in consequence, in United States waters, Canada being discounted by virtue of the generalized Monroe doctrine; therefore, the bolide belongs to the United States.

Q.E.D. As a gesture of consolation, France can keep the gold she has already taken and its war debts will be written off. Besides which, the United States will not exploit the gold of Île Féréor; they are uniquely concerned with the iron. They have enough gold for their needs, and do not want the price of gold to drop by virtue of an excessive superabundance.

But who can take America seriously, gravely wounded by the cyclone, no longer having more than twenty seaworthy ships in its Atlantic ports? And the dreadnoughts that remain—those dreadnoughts with the bizarre wrought iron turrets—are in the Pacific, where it is convenient to leave them, for is there not Japan to consider?

Here, Japan, honorable Japan, is Baron Kaki, always polite, extremely polite—too polite. Honorable Japan affirms that it has no interest in this bolide. It would certainly have the right, like everyone else—is not the Lord Mikado the Son of Heaven, and did not the bolide fall from the heavens?—but has no use for the gold, since Japan is on the silver standard! Whatever is decided, Japan will say yes, very politely, and remain very wise in its own coinage.

Should they really believe Baron Kaki? Is there not some hidden agenda in his brain, behind that smiling mask, so polite, forever polite, protesting his universal cordiality?

There are many other delegates too, but, being small fry, they are not playing the game.

While waiting for the session to start, the delegates kill time, denoting an inspiration by raising a foot—a madrigal, might one say, for one of those genteel scribes?—or scribbling a few lines with a pen on a note-book taken from a pocket, which they will have taken into the nearby code-room.

That is the corner of the Palais where all the official nonchalance re-enters the circuit of quivering worldly activity—for diplomacy is functioning at top speed and everyone is conferring with his government. The clerks in the code-room are worked to death. All the keys of the telegraphy section crackle like a major power station.

Each of those special wires transmits its messages incessantly in both direction, harassing the molecules of the metal—and at the other end of each wire departing from Geneva, humankind's artificial brain, out there in the nerve-center of each country, gold fever is increasing its temperature by the hour. The hypnotic bolide is shining on the horizon of all avarice.

XVI. Frédérique

If I had conserved any remorse regarding my indiscretion, I would have lost it while dining in the Avenue de Villiers with Jean-Paul and the governor of the Banque. Both were jubilant at the unexpected denouement brought to the situation.

"Still impossible to foresee the good and bad that will emerge from events," said Monsieur Hautôt, sticking his fork into an anchovy. "If the secrecy that we considered indispensable hadn't been broken, Germain-Lucas wouldn't have reacted that way; he would have continued the politics of his predecessors. Without that German seaman-reporter..."

"You believe that, then?"

"Why not? It's quite probable."

"Pooh! I telephoned Commander Barcot in Cherbourg this morning. No sailor has escaped from the military prison, so there's been a leak somewhere. The warders? The ship's officers?"

I was on tenterhooks—but my embarrassment did not last. The conversation soon chanced course. The two men of action that I had before me scarcely worried about the past, especially when it was irremediable, as in the present case, and there was not even a lesson to be learned therefrom. They were entirely occupied with the future, and the present, insofar as it was destined to produce the future.

According to then, a Franco-Britannic accord was certain. England would gladly form a kind of syndicate with France for the exploitation of the island, in which the friendly and allied nations would co-operate to the extent of their means. It was the only possible solution, the only one advantageous to France that had any chance of prevailing at the League of Nations.

Nevertheless, the relevant deliberations would take a few more days, and it was necessary to obtain the maximum profit from that interval.

No time had been lost thus far. A wireless message that afternoon announced the safe arrival at Île Féréor of the two transport vessels, the *Girondin* and the *Saint-Thomas*, that had left Brest on the same evening as our arrival in Cherbourg. They had begun to take on their cargoes.

By a fortunate coincidence, almost at the same time, the transporter *Cornouaille*, which Monsieur de Silfrage had contrived to have sent to the island with the destroyer *Espadon*, had just returned to Cherbourg with gold in its holds, and was moored alongside the *Erebus II*.

Secrecy no longer being necessary, the unloading of the two vessels had begun. The first truckloads of gold would arrive at the Banque the following afternoon. In order to be prepared for any eventuality, two more destroyers, the *Émeraude* and the *Béluga*, were preparing to sail for the island from Toulon that night.

That was all that I learned that evening. We were only on the cheese, but the clock was already showing five to nine, and impatience was urging me to go and see Frédérique. I excused myself, pleading an indispensable and urgent meeting, and took my leave just as Monsieur Hautôt and my friend were broaching the subject of the study mission that it was necessary to send out as soon as possible, in the probable case that the negotiations with England would conclude in the formation of a Franco-Britannic condominium.

"Would it amuse you to be a part of that?" Rivier asked me, while accompanying me as far as the vestibule.

I was about to say no, because of Frédérique, but I changed my mind. After the treason that her father had committed in hr regard—I no longer had any doubt about that—who could tell whether she might not leave him...that she might agree to accompany me!

"You're very kind, Jean-Paul," I said, "but you've caught me off-guard. I need to think. Give me two hours."

"That's only fair. And if you have useful friends for whom you need to find a place—even the Jolliots—there'll be room for them in the plan..."

In the hall at Claridge's, the attitude of the porter seemed to me to be embarrassed; I thought that he gave me a strange look when he replied to me that Professor Hans Kohbuler was in his apartment. In addition, two individuals posted at the bottom of the staircase—men with bowler hats and large shoes, whom I would have taken, anywhere but in a palace, for agents of the Sûreté—looked me up and down.

Elevator...third floor corridor...room 204...

I was nonplussed on seeing appear, instead of Frédérique or her father, a fellow with a bushy red moustache. He too was in "in it."

The intuition of a catastrophe shot through me. The sentiment of my culpability reawakened—but I did not retreat.

"Professor Hans Kohbuler?"

"Here. Come in."

The man stood aside, and swiftly closed the door. Through the open door of the antechamber, in the brightly-lit drawing room, I saw Frédérique standing, in a jade green robe. She was livid.

I advanced into the apartment, and, once having crossed the threshold, instinctively turned my head.

Inside, to either side of the door, two more plain-clothes policemen examined me sardonically, and one of them ostentatiously clinked something metallic in his pocket, which could only be handcuffs.

Without paying any heed to the man—evidently a commissaire—installed at the American desk, I went straight to Frédérique and took hold of her hands.

"What's happening, Frédérique?"

"They came to arrest my father, an hour ago. He's committed suicide. And I..."

"Come on, Mademoiselle," the commissaire interjected, in a curt tone. "Enough chat. And you, Monsieur, will you tell me who you are, and what your relationship is with Hans Kohbuler."

I gave my name, and told the simple truth: that I had only met the professor once, at a friend's house.

The man relaxed, and consulted some papers. "That's all right. You can go. But you'll have to remain at the disposal of the law. The examining magistrate will summon you."

At that moment a policeman emerged from the next room and deposited a package on the desk beside other similar ones.

"Here's another ten wads of bills, Commissaire. I ought to tell you, too, that on putting my ear to one of the telephone receivers in there, I've just heard everything said in here. There's obviously a hidden microphone in here."

With his professional flair, the policeman's gaze followed the trajectory of beams of light beneath a gilded rod that dissimulated them, went straight to a wall-ornament in the shape of a chimera and introduced an inquisitive index-finger into the perforated mount.

"Here it is!"

My latent doubt on the subject of Frédérique had just vanished. As for her, I read a tragic bitterness in her dry but burning eyes—the shame of having had such a father. She even murmured: "The wretch!"

Meanwhile, at the name of Jean-Paul Rivier, which I invoked energetically, the commissaire moderated his tone. He became less aggressive, and a telephone call to the Avenue de Villiers, which he permitted me to make, rendered him entirely pliable once he had heard through the other receiver the great financier's voice reply to me in familiar terms and place himself entirely at my disposal.

It would not have taken much for the commissaire to do the same! He concluded: "Don't worry, Monsieur. You have time to act. My enquiries won't be finished before midnight, and Mademoiselle won't be sleeping in prison—I give you my word on that."

I abandoned Frédérique with less apprehension and ran to the Avenue de Villiers. Monsieur Hautôt had just left; Rivier was alone, and I was able to plead my beloved's cause freely.

Jean-Paul did not conceal the difficulty, even for him, of the service I was asking of him.

"The old rogue!" he said, at the name of Hans Kohbuler. "I warned you. Why didn't you confide in me? We might have been able to spare that amiable child from arrest, and you from anxiety. No matter; never let it be said that you invoked me in vain for your Dulcinea. I owe you that, and much more."

Gratitude was not a vain word for Rivier. He employed all his energy in having Frédérique liberated. The role of simple supernumerary played by Hans Kohbuler's daughter—a role rendered evident as soon as the enquiry began—permitted that favor without any risk of harm to the law. Kohbuler's death, moreover, by rendering a trial unnecessary, facilitated the intention that existed in high places to hush up the affair.

There were, however, administrative obstacles that even the all-powerful name of Rivier was incapable of removing immediately at that late hour. It was not until eight o'clock in the morning that Frédérique was able to leave the police station where she had spent the latter part of the night as a prisoner in the commissaire's office—on a reasonably comfortable horsehair divan, she assured me, while completing fixing her make-up in front of the mirror she carried in her handbag.

At any rate when I took her away triumphantly, followed by the sly and mocking gazes of the policemen on duty, she did not seem in the least distraught, and only the cease in her forehead hinted at the tragedy that she had just lived through.

We spent two hours walking around Paris, uplifted by a need to move freely in the midst of the anonymous crowd. Frédérique had taken my arm in a spontaneous gesture of affection, which was worth more than a long speech of thanks.

I was fearful of interrogating her sentiments; the expression in her eyes, as soon as she turned them away from me to think about the events of the previous evening, became hard and pitiless, and I could see that the death of Hans Kohbuler had not produced within her the frequent phenomenon of the "apotheosis" thanks to which a widow, for example, who has spent ten years of marriage cursing her spouse, forgets all her rancor as soon as he has ceased to live, no longer remembering any but the rare bearable moments, deifying the deceased in her memory.

Either I allowed her to see some surprise in spite of my efforts, or she experienced a need to confide in me, for she suddenly said to me: "Kohbuler was not my real father. My mother confessed that to me on her deathbed. It was of no importance to me to obey the man, as long as my skeptical youth, impassioned by science and pure intellectuality, knew no other sentiment than the joy of solving problems. Yes, it was unimportant to me, then, that I had to spend my life deciphering encrypted messages. I didn't desire anything of the future. My soul was asleep. It had not been born. It only began to live recently, when I met you at Wimereux, my dear Antoine. When I saw you, I felt my heart quiver for the first time, and the tender and generous soul of my mother reborn within me...

"Since then, I've only borne my subjection of Kohbuler's orders with difficulty; my mother's grief was reborn in me. Every day I detested a little more being the agent of Germany, which forced me to harm France, the country that I felt to be mine as well, since it was my mother's...since it was yours, my Antoine!

"Now, my past horrifies me. As you can see, I left Claridge's with my hundred-franc dress in my handbag. I should like to peel off my past, just as I'm now abandoning everything that was mine in the time when my will was put to his odious cause by Kohbuler. Oh, take me with you, my love! Take me far away, to some place where I can forget that I used to be Elsa Kohbuler, the daughter of that wretch. My real name has been soiled by him—but where can I go, alas? There isn't a capital in Europe to which he did not drag me in his wake, to help him in his machinations..."

Softly, I replied: "There's a very simple, perfectly legal, means to make you forget that name, my dear Frédérique. I'll marry you..."

She straightened up, stoically. "I'm yours, my love, entirely yours; make me your mistress. But your wife...no! You'd blush..."

With a tender violence, I put my hand over her mouth, and told her about the offer that Rivier had made to me the previous evening. Then I concluded: "It's agreed? I'll propose you as a candidate to my friend Jean-Paul. We'll be leaving in three or four days, I think. Doctor and Madame Marquin, of the Franco-Britannic Study Mission to Île Féréor..."

XVII. France's Fortune

The matter was settled. Rivier received Frédérique and me in his office in the Boulevard Haussmann, and everything was arranged in ten minutes. He promoted me on the spot to Commissaire-Delegate of the Banque Rivier et Cie.

"But I don't have any expertise in that area," I protested. "I'm only a doctor of medicine."

"You're my friend. I can have every confidence in you, and I know that you'll follow my instructions with precision and fidelity. It's a matter of agreeing with the English the monthly production of the gold. You'll have technicians as collaborators. For you, it will be sufficient to have common sense. Oh, the salary! Will sixty thousand a year be sufficient? Yes? Shh! Don't thank me—it's a matter of business. You can speak English, of course?"

"Yes."

"Good. That's settled. Let's pass on to Mademoiselle...no, to your wife, since you have the intention of marrying Mademoiselle Kohbuler, and marrying her right away...you're in agreement with that, aren't you, Mademoiselle? It will save you from an awkward situation aboard the *Ile-de-France*—for it's that fine liner that will be taking you...

"Let's see; the departure is fixed for the sixth, in five days. It's not possible to marry in France in such a short time, so you need to hop over to London by airplane and request the ministry of a clergyman. When are you going? It's all the same to you? Tomorrow, then. I'll book you seats with the Compagnie Aérienne. The bank will pay for the little excursion. With the recommendation I'll give you, you'll have special passports from the Ministry of Marine...so we'll say 'Madame Frédérique Marquin.' Can you speak English?"

Frédérique smiled. "I can speak English and six other languages fluently."

"All right—you'll be your husband's secretary. Same salary as Antoine—let's be feminists—sixty thousand...and all presentation expenses. You need to put on a good show for our British friends..."

The business was concluded.

Assured of the future, forgetful of the past, happy with the present, we've had a good lunch together, and now we're setting off along the boulevards, lost in our amorous conversation, to wait for the offices of the Ministry to open.

The new atmosphere of these historic days in Paris is in harmony with our fever; we have the illusion of being, no longer in Paris, but in the capital of some unknown, exotic, unfamiliar France. The physiognomy of objects and people seems to have been scrubbed, endowed with unprecedented radiant powers; their spectacle astonishes us; we seem to be looking for the first time at the façades of the buildings toward which we raise our heads.

We arrive at the Madeleine. As we go down the Rue Royale we're surprised to see traffic prohibited beyond the Faubourg Saint-Honoré, into which mounted policemen are redirecting the vehicles. On the Place de la Concorde, where a stationary crowd is beginning to assemble, cordons of municipal guards are reserving a large free corridor, which extends from the Champs-Élysées to the Rue de Rivoli, which had also been cleared.

That astonishes Frédérique—and me too, at first; then I understand.

"The gold from Cherbourg! The gold of Île Féréor! This is the route that the trucks will take, in triumph. We read it in the midday papers, which gave the itinerary of the convoy. Let's go into the Ministry; we'll be better placed."

In fact, the name of Jean-Paul Rivier appended to our request for a passport had us introduced into the office of a divisional chief—who was, moreover, a friend of Commander Barcot, and who stationed us at a first floor window overlooking the Place de la Concorde. Directly beneath us, on a stage, cinematographers were beginning to turn their apparatus.

Piercing the rumor of the expectant crowd, the bellowing of a loudspeaker drew nearer, and a metallic voice emerged from the Champs-Élysées, borne by two automobiles bristling with radio apparatus. "Hello, hello! The trucks of gold coming from Cherbourg are coming through the Arc de Triomphe. They're descending the Avenue...they'll be here in two minutes..."

And over the excited din of the crowd, mingled with amused laughter, the exceedingly modern sequel to the announcement is heard: "Hello, hello! The Phoebus lamp is the sun in your own home... Hello, hello! Drink nothing but Kichof Apéritif..."

The annunciatory vehicles have passed by and are drawing away along the Rue de Rivoli. In its turn, however, an acclamation swells, increases and arrives like a tidal wave...and the throb of aircraft engines, which revive momentarily the slight tremor of wartime air-raids. Up above, airplanes with military insignia are flying and circling, performing stunts. Lower down, above the trees of the Avenue, a yellow mass shining in the sunlight appears in the triumphant azure: a dirigible at the level of the innumerable riverside roofs glides towards us smoothly, decorated with flags, launching cries from loudspeakers in its turn.

Their apocalyptic voice is, however, drowned by the cyclonic howl of cheers—there might be as many as fifty thousand spectators in the square, dotted with moving heads on either side of the empty space—that goes up as the impressive cortege comes into view.

Three tanks, abreast across the width of the Avenue, are laminating the roadway with their caterpillar-tracks. The muzzles of 75-mm guns project from their flower-garlanded armor. Behind them, a platoon of Gardes Républicains on horseback, trumpeters at the head...

A combat deployment—but no Parisian is deceived by it. It is not a wary provision against any ridiculously improbable strike, some attempt of cinematic banditry to take possession of the billions, but a symbol: the clearly-expressed determination to defend the gold against external enemies.

The trumpets sound, and cause enthusiasm to resonate. Everyone in the crowd senses it: it is the end of dithering, incoherent politics, of the weakness and silly tricks that have brought the country to the brink of the abyss. Confidence has been reestablished from top to bottom with the recovery of the currency. Like some poor fellow who has been walking for a long time with his spine bent by misfortune, and who, suddenly been ballasted with gold by a stroke of good luck, stands up straight again with an unconstrained authority, the same politicians who were previously afflicted with paralysis and imbecility are standing up straight again, finally able to act and to govern.

Everyone in the crowd senses that, and cheers the horizon-blue helmets in battle-dress that are flanking the machine-gun carriers. "Cries of "Long live the army!" and "Long live France!" cleave the musical waves of triumphal marches, rumbling like a hurricane, while the military trucks of the air force file past, two by two. The gold is hidden beneath their tarpaulins, invisible but radiating its glorious effluvia.

"The return of the zaïmph!" Frédérique whispers to me.

Yes! Like her I was thinking of that scene from *Salammbô*, in which the Carthaginians, standing on the walls of their city, follow Matho with their eyes as he carries, with the veil of Tanit, the fortune of Carthage.[21] This is a kind of counterpart, at a distance of twenty centuries. Paris, packed all the way from the Étoile to the Banque, is acclaiming in the arrival of the gold trucks the return of France's fortune.

In the sky, the aircraft continue to circle like a flock of swallows. A second dirigible, this one a rigid steel-

---

[21] The reference is to Gustave Flaubert's sumptuous historical novel *Salammbô* (1862), set in Carthage in the wake of the first Punic War, in which the city's most important symbol, the zaïmph (supposedly the veil of the goddess Tanit) is stolen by the obsessively lustful mercenary leader Matho, but subsequently recovered by the eponymous priestess. The final chapter, which describes the victory celebrations following the crushing defeat of the rebel mercenaries by Hamilcar Barca, concludes with Matho's torture prior to his execution and Salammbô's death, emphasizing that those who have dared to touch the sacred veil are doomed; Varlet's decision to make that reference rather than likening the gold's advent to a conventional Roman triumph is, therefore, a further display of his sarcasm.

grey ex-zeppelin, the *Méditerranée*, floats above the trucks. The trucks pass by...and pass by...and the horizon-blues, the Gardes Républicains, the machine-gun carriers and other assault-vehicles...

It takes a good quarter of an hour, while the shouting never stops, directed with full lung-power at the gold, the gold, the gold...acclamations for the tarpaulin-covered trucks, as if for a column of gaudily-decked sovereigns...for the return of a victorious army...

We were going down the stairs of the Ministry when a jovial: "Hey, Antoine!" launched from above stopped me in my racks. I turned round with a start.

"Lefébure! Robert! You're here in Paris?"

The mariner, wearing civilian dress, with his right arm in a sling, came to join us.

"Yes, old chap, for an hour. Brought back as far as Versailles by the procession, under the protection of the tanks. But you're with Mademoiselle—I don't want..."

"Yes, yes, you can come with us, Robert...Frédérique, may I introduce my old friend Robert Lefébure, whom I've already mentioned to you. Robert, Frédérique, my wife... But say, your arm's in a sling. You're injured?"

"The wrist's slightly sprained. I'll tell you all about it—but let's go sit down somewhere and have a drink."

The crowd was dispersing slowly. Among its dense waves, we succeeded in reaching the Taverne Royale and finding a section of table and chairs right at the back.

"As you can well imagine, old man," Lefébure told us, "things got worse on the island after your departure. I was left as the only officer, along with de Silfrage, to keep the men in line—the scientists didn't count and the engineers had their hands full directing the exploitation.

We were preparing the cargo for the next ship—a stockpile of gold on the quay, ready to be taken away—but the fellows didn't want to take the trouble to wait. They already had enough for themselves, in their estimation. At the instigation of a chap named Le Moullec—you remember him, the big redhead?—my men loaded the motor-launch with gold…full to the brim…in order to run off with it. I was asleep in my dug-out. That fellow Gripert, who had seen what they were doing, came to warn me that they were already going aboard. I ran at top speed and tried to hold them back—I wounded two of them with my pistol—but nothing doing! They were furious. That was when I hurt my wrist—a blow from a gaffe. In brief, they stepped on the gas and shot off southwards.

"There was no one left but the four engineers, the four scientists, de Silfrage and me. It was up to the ten of us to carry on the exploitation as best we could. Not nice—but necessary, no? And we set to work, I can assure you, even Gripert.

"On the twenty-first there was the scare with the Danish boat. We'd spotted it quickly, fortunately, while it was still a long way out to sea of the northern tip of the island, and we had time to put my scheme into action—to set light to two dozen barrels sulfur lined up on the cliff—with the result that the idiots daren't come close to Port Erebus, the inlet where the mine is, because the wind was blowing that smoke at them like all the devils in hell. Add to that the racket of fifty cheddite cartridges. They thought the volcano was getting ready to blow and turned about in a hurry.

"On the twenty-second, two more ships—but they were flying the French flag and coming straight for us;

they were the ships de Silfrage had asked for, the destroyer *Espadon* and the cargo vessel *Cornouaille*.

"The lad commanding the *Espadon* made a lot of fuss about daring to dock. He was afraid of not having enough depth in the creek. But most of all, Antoine, the gobs on all those chaps! Excuse me, Madame, but your husband must have warned you that I'm a bit coarse. The faces of all those fellows, to seeing the stocks of gold heaped up for them! A pile of nuggets, pell-mell, just like a coal-bunker. And when I took them up to the face, at the bottom of the gold chloride cliff! They turned blue. But they were all navy men, the boys on the two boats, and discipline held up. They were put to work...

"There were a good three hundred of them, and in less than three days the cargo ship had taken on its load of nuggets and left. The destroyer stayed to guard the island. As I was no longer good for anything out there with my arm in a sling—and an officer without matelots to boot—I allowed myself to be repatriated by the *Cornouaille* with de Silfrage and three of the scientists. The engineers all opted to stay, and Gripert too.

"Yesterday morning we disembarked at Cherbourg. A wireless message had just been received from the *Espadon* announcing that two more cargo ships, the *Girondin* and the *Saint-Thomas*, had moored at Port Erebus. We'd also learned that some rat of a Boche claimed to have infiltrated himself into the crew of *Erebus II* and to have given the game away...but that's a lie. Commander Barcot immediately made enquiries at the military prison; not a single matelot was missing—of those, that is, that you had knocked out with your drug. A neat invention, I must admit, but they haven't all come round yet...

"By the way, do you know that the camp—Île Féréor—is sinking? They've had the wit to sent new and more rapid means of exploitation: electric dredgers and cables for aerial wagons to double up the decauville. Yes, the camp is rotting away, according to Gripert, who's studying its 'geological structure,' and it won't last much longer. The chloride rock is melting like sugar; at present the peak looks like an old saggy candle and there are incessant landslides at the point of attack. There's been no mention of it officially, but I was there six days ago and I tell you that the Golden Rock—since that's its name now—is coming apart at the seams and will end up collapsing on to the heads of the fellows at Port Erebus.

"At any rate, Antoine, you'll soon see for yourself—and you too, Madame—since I've just been told at the Ministry that you're both going to 'lay the foundations of a Franco-Britannic condominium.' That's how you pronounce it, isn't it? What's it all about? Tell me, will you—I'm not up to date..."

It was while paying the bill—Lefébure was leaving us to go to the Gare du Nord in order to meet his wife, who was arriving from Lille at seven p.m.—that I saw a *louis d'or* for the first time since August 1914. The waiter gave me two, along with notes, in the change for my hundred francs. The mere sight of one of those little yellow disks—one Napoléon III coin and one Republican dated 1897—impressed me more than all the nuggets piled up in the hold of the *Erebus II* at Cherbourg. Lefébure lingered for a moment and handled them with a fearful and tender respect, but Frédérique only manifested a mediocre curiosity. She had been too young in 1914, and scarcely remembered the Golden Age...

160

XVIII. In the Radiance of Gold

As sonorous and grandiose as the stroke of a gong emphasizing France's response to Germany's challenge, news of that triumphant entrance of the gold to Paris, with its military escort, its dirigibles and its tanks, spreads through the world.

By wire, from Paris, the electric news speeds through the cables alongside the railway lines, singing to towns great and small, provincial and foreign. By submarine cable it leaps from the continent to the islands.

From the antennae of the Tower, the pylons of Saint-Assise and the Croix-d'Hins, within a single second, it is offered as a rhythmic palpitation of the ether to all the receiving stations scattered over the world, simultaneously, at all the hours of the day, dusk and night that the time-zones distribute over the various countries.

Over the entire Earth, as if over a mere town, like a flock of butterflies released from an aircraft, it snows down. Over all the antennae of Europe, Africa and Asia Minor it declares the news in French. London hears it, Berlin hears it, and Brussels and Oslo, Helsingfors, Leningrad, Moscow, Rome, Vienna, Constantinople, Smyrna, Aleppo, Damascus, Madrid...

The retransmission stations pick it up, amplify it, translate it, and it soars, extended, over the entire globe, over sea and land, to the two Americas, Australia, the Southern Seas, Japan, China, Siberia, India, Afghanistan, Persia...

The newspapers of all countries capture it via the antennae on their buildings; it passes from loudspeakers to the ears of editors, radioactivating their brains; copied within five seconds—in French, in English, in Chinese, in Finnish, in Coptic, in Persian, in Tamil…three hundred language—commented upon, dressed up, ornamented with congruous headlines, there it is, composited, set up in type, in proof…and the presses roll, ten thousand, twenty thousand, thirty-six thousand copies and hour, and the sheets are in every hand…

And see, too, in towns and villages alike—in Bordeaux, Pantin, Cassis, Landerneau, Ronchin, Marseilles, Algiers; in Gibraltar, Clapham, Elsinore, Syracuse, the Escorial—in the smallest villages, everyone drinking avidly from the omnipresent spring of waves via the notary's luxury loop-aerial and ten-valve set, or the schoolteacher's improvised aerial and crystal set, as it is proclaimed everywhere, a simultaneous intoxication for the whole of humankind, all the way to the depths of the remotest regions…

Even in Tahiti, the little children, coming home from the missionary school or workroom crowned with red hibiscus flowers, are listening, on the loudspeaker in the cabin, to the retransmission from Noumea…

All humanity is thinking about Paris.

Ah, France! And Paris, that land of Cockayne! Envy in all its forms…naïve admiration and grim jealousy. Everyone sees the gold passing through the Arc de Triomphe, the gold unfurling in waves over Paris and France, the marvelous gold, the divine gold…

France has become the tabernacle of the world…

And the bolide too! The Golden Rock!

Since it is known to be on Earth, the entire world is in effervescence, like an anthill near to which a sheaf of wheat has been dropped. All human throats are dry with avarice. All the newspapers are full of "scientific" articles hacked out with a chisel and fake interviews with astronomers. All the newspapers are publishing that an American astronomer anticipates further falls of the same kind...

And in the evening, in the dark, over the entire Earth, in all the countries that see the Great Bar and the Pole Star, and in all those that see the Southern Cross and the Magellanic Clouds, all the people are palpitating with gold fever.

The people—which is to say, two billion human beings, white, black, yellow, red and bronze, who breathe, eat, live and fight over the ten thousand square degrees of the inhabited Earth—rich and poor alike, are palpitating with gold fever.

Bankers are saddened by all that excessive gold—which they do not have in their coffers. Factory workers are dreaming of their pay being multiplied tenfold, or a hundredfold, settled in bolide ingots. Housewives are calculating, sou by sou, passing their lives thereby, paying shopkeepers with a lighter heart this morning, in the hope that everything will go down when everyone has their share in the Golden Rock...

The miners of the South African Rand, those in Alaska on the edge of the frozen Yukon, those in Coolgardie beneath the Australian eucalypti and those in Guiana trembling with yellow fever beside the cayman-filled river, as they think about the Golden Rock, are all becoming discouraged and disgusted with their quotidian labor and the miserable gain of a few ounces of gold extracted from the amalgam of the sluices...

Gold fever!

In every country, inside the frontier lines dividing up terrestrial geography, that fundamental desire, interfering with patriotic egotism, is thinking about its realization by national possession of the gold.

In Berlin, a huge demonstration accumulates and descends Unter den Linden singing *Deutchland über alles*; people goose-stepping through cabbage-eating villages talk about going to Paris in search of the gold of Île Féréor.

In London, Edinburgh, Cardiff and Manchester, throughout the British Isles, John Bull, with his pipe of shag in his mouth gets on his high horse in front of his glass of gin at the pub counter: "Well! Those damned Frenchies! They think everything's permissible! But halt right there! Equal shares! The Mistress of the Seas is more than ever...*Rule Britannia!* It's for us that France has found this Île Féréor!"

In Dublin, in the guard-room, the militia of the Free State measure on the map the supposed distance of Île Féréor. "Ireland is the closest to it!"

In Madrid, Puerta del Sol, threadbare hidalgos gravely discuss this new and prodigious galleon: "Won't there be a few nuggets for the valiant Spaniards?"

"Our Latin brothers," say the lazzaroni of Chiaia, guzzling lasagna or fried calamari while Vesuvius fumes placidly in the violet sunset, "and our transatlantic brothers are pirates..."

"It's ours by right, that rock of iron and gold," people say in Chicago, New York and Saint-Louis...

"And why not ours?" thinks the half-breed docker in Rio de Janeiro, loading sacks of coffee on his back...

"Ah, we had a chance, once, to be French citizens," sighs the curly-haired Hova of Tananarive, the bronzed Hindu of Pondicherry, putting on his turban again after his ablutions, and the wretched man waxing shoes on the quays of Sfax...

And everywhere, people begin to talk about the act of violence that will probably be necessary to settle the question. They talk about it foolishly, with idle notions of present strengths and real possibilities...

All that talk is, to tell the truth, of scant importance. It is merely the degenerate phonographic reflection of opinions emitted by the newspapers, the newspapers that form opinion. There are governments to watch over the destiny of nations.

The one in Berlin senses that Germany is impotent before rampant France, supported by her gold. There are black troops on the Rhine; Cologne, Mayence, Karls-ruhe, ten large German cities would be bombarded, destroyed, at the first hostile gesture...and then there is England, which will be allied with France tomorrow, the two robbers ready to cheat Germany out of her share of the Golden Rock... Nothing to do on land, for the moment...at sea, it remains to be seen. For lack of ironclads there are the new submarines...and for a lightning strike on Paris or London, those two thousand aircraft in the Black Forest, and those Zeppelins in factories in Russia, Sweden and Holland, ready to rally at the first sign...

And just in case, Germany arms herself; secret factories are activated; gas is stockpiled, cannons and munitions...

People arm themselves everywhere on Earth, preparing—just in case—for war...

Scientists, in their laboratories, take fright momentarily. They think about the employment that will be made of their discoveries, hesitate...and go on, driven by the demon of modern science, by the implacable acceleration of progress, by the multiplied gush of discoveries, the benevolent and the harmful all mixed up...does one ever know which is which? One does not have the right to choose. The scientist limits himself to knowing, finding and delivering to humankind the secrets of nature—and the manner in which they are used... Too bad if it is the ferocious and barbaric instincts that want to use them!

Here are the new, monstrous products procreated by the incest of human genius with Mother Nature, who never anticipated them in this phase of planetary life...

Here are the explosives that evoke by the magic of chemical formulae the residual energy of creative chaos, hidden in the depth of heavenly bodies. Here, docile slaves of destructive humankind, are the cosmic forces that ought only to be deployed in the great conflicts of meteors. Here is the condensed electricity, in imitation of ball lightning, the deflagration of which produces four times the effect of an equal volume of dynamite. Here are new powders, asphyxiating gases, microbe-bearing shells. Here is the Ardent Ray...

All that will be used, perhaps imminently.

People are arming themselves on land. They are arming themselves even more actively at sea, for if there is a war for possession of the Golden Rock, it will be of paramount importance to be able to put a grappling-iron on it, to have a few ships within range of the bolide...

And from now on, the bolide attracts warships like a magnet, which are making ready to ail in every port. Portsmouth, La Spezzia, Cadiz, Kiel, Kronstadt and Odessa are unleashing their squadrons...and the sea foams beneath the bows of ironclads and torpedo-boats: the gray of the Channel, the blue of the Latin sea, the emerald of the Atlantic, the jade-green of the Baltic. The flags of nations flap, proudly, in the wind. Tons and tons of coal and oil and burned every minute, maintaining pressure in the boilers of a hundred ships steaming toward the Golden Rock...

Everyone will discover the island for themselves, even if it is not in the indicated location. It's the scent of gold, isn't it? And then again, will there not be squadrons all around it, their smoke perceptible in the sky for fifty miles around?

Pragmatic America begins the search. The aircraft-carrier *Lexington* was in the Gulf of Texas during the cyclone, protected by the Florida peninsula; it arrives first: 270 meters long, 33,000 tons, costing 45 million dollars—225 million gold francs. And as soon as it reaches the Grand Banks of Newfoundland, the four twenty-meter catapults launch the 72 aircraft on board in batches of four, one after another, which fan out as they fly off...

And as America, in a fever of avarice, allows herself to be taken in by the beaming smiles of Japan, in order to survey the seas more efficiently, she sends two Pacific aircraft-carriers to the Atlantic: the *Saratoga*, twin of the *Lexington*, and the *Langley*, a dwarf of 19,000 tons with only 34 aircraft...

But it is necessary to anticipate everything...and the Pacific coast, Hawaii and the Philippines are stripped of their squadrons, which head for Panama...

Japan does not budge. The bolide is unimportant to her, that's true...but in secret, the arsenals of Sasebo, Koure, Yokosuka, Muroran and Maidzuru are working day and night to ensure the glory of the empire on land, sea and air. It is now or never: with the American gone, what good are the British in Hong Kong and India, the Dutch gunboat at Batavia and the old French corvette guarding Indochina?

XIX. The Condominium Mission

Our journey to London? Bah! A hop over the Channel in an airplane. Not even two hours in either direction from Le Bourget to Croydon and Croydon to Le Bourget. Does that warrant description? For Frédérique, as familiar with air transport as international sleepers, it was pure banality, and even I was beginning to get used to it...

Our marriage? An episode of a quarter of an hour, in a lateral chapel of the old St. Martin's Church, on a gray and splenetic day.

There was nothing to stop us going back the same afternoon, but when I made that suggestion—we were just coming out on to Trafalgar Square in front of Nelson's Column—Frédérique said to me, in a coaxing tone: "Oh, my love, let's not leave yet. Wouldn't you like to spent the evening in London? Let's go see an English dance-hall...the Coliseum. I'm only familiar with official society balls."

"You, my love! You want to see a dance-hall?" I said, dubiously. "But you'll soon get bored if you aren't dancing with me..."

"And why won't I be dancing with you, Monsieur?" she said, narrowing her black lashes over her beautiful ultramarine eyes, full of charming insolence. "What do you take me for, my love? You imagine that I'm a wallflower because I have a doctorate and have been congratulated by Einstein? Don't worry—the pleasures of the mind have been sufficient for me until now, but, in the same way that I'm no stranger to literature, that hasn't prevented me from playing sport for hygienic purposes...as a duty to myself...in order not to be ignorant of anything. I can dance, and swim, and cycle, and drive an automobile, and play tennis, and everything. Perhaps, deep down, that was to prepare me to live, if the opportunity presented itself. Well, it's presented itself; you've given it to me, my love! You'll see—I have years of non-existence to catch up on..."

That evening, in the great London dance-hall, Frédérique revealed herself in an unexpected light, as the animator of our new life: supple and ardent for pleasure, exquisitely feminine in the modern fashion, more seductive than the most beautiful, by virtue of her marvelous intelligence. She "no longer recognized herself..."

"Well, darling, what do you say to that?" she whispered to me tenderly, at two o'clock in the morning, in the taxi taking us back to the Savoy. "Not too bad, eh, for a mathematician."

My only reply was an ecstatic kiss; with her held tightly against me, her soft warmth penetrating me, I was the king of the world...

The last two days that we spent in Paris went by in a whirlwind. In those days, a warm fever of pleasure expanded over France, and we participated in it delightedly; no atmosphere could have been more appropriate to our honeymoon.

That unbridled intoxication was due in part to the presence of the Bolide—as if the celestial visitor had brought to our planet the spores of a superhuman joy flourishing elsewhere in a world created purely for happiness. There was also the pride of having being transformed, in a matter of days, from a nation doomed to imminent bankruptcy into the richest people in the world.

What made it even more acute, however, I believe, was the muted presentiment of an enormous danger—wondering whether we might be living in the final days of civilized peace rendered the moments more precious, obliging us to extract the maximum enjoyment from them.

The newspapers, while praising the efficacy of the Franco-Britannic alliance in maintaining world peace, allowed menacing possibilities to be glimpsed: envious and frustrated Germany meditating some treacherous blow; America proclaiming its claims, not to the Bolide's gold—it was overflowing with that!—but to its iron...

American aircraft were flying over Île Féréor. Numerous Brazilian, Italian, Spanish and even Russian ships had been seen in its vicinity—and we certainly did not know everything; censorship of the news was in operation, and the regime of communiqués, as in the war, was inserting a kind of vague anxiety into that culminating frenzy to enjoy the lull.

Amidst the idleness of Paris, warlike spectacles suddenly appeared. Troops were seen marching through the city, led by bands; Senegalese battalions arriving at the Gare de Lyon were embarking at the Gare de l'Est to reinforce the troops on the Rhine. Every day, squadrons of aircraft were traversing the sky and dirigibles were circulating, as if on patrol. The searchlight on the Tower was scanning the nocturnal sky again, as if there were cause to fear an air raid.

A persistent rumor ran around that one of the two transport vessels, the *Girondin* or the *Saint-Thomas*, had been sunk by a submarine as it returned from the island—and Rivier, when I interrogated him, did not deny it.

But all these sights and this news did not disturb Frédérique and me, and only affected us, as it were, without our being aware of it, for we had very little time to reflect, or even to talk, so busy were those last two days.

On Rivier's advice, I had sold the few kilos of gold I had brought back from the island without further delay, and got 28,000 francs for them, to add to the 3000 of the last installment of my wages from the *Erebus II* and six months' advance on my new salary of 60,000 a year, matched by Frédérique. With that, in addition to a few items of jewelry bought during our trip to London, it was a matter of running around the stores for our equipment, our luggage, our wardrobe...suits and evening dresses in anticipation of celebrations on the *Ile-de-France*...

We got some use out of them in Paris, one evening at the Jolliots' and the next at Rivier's—for Madame Rivier and her daughter, back from Biarritz, were inaugurating their season by giving a ball "in the strictest intimacy" for fifty important people.

The departure of the *Ile-de-France* from Le Havre was fixed for 14.00 on the sixth of October. We left Paris at eight o'clock in the morning by the special train organized for the three hundred members of the French mission and the important people coming to watch the ceremony, including Rivier. The Jolliots were in our compartment, for at the first news of the mission, the star and the director had begged me to let them tag along.

Our ship was the most beautiful of the Compagnie Générale Transatlantique. Normally devoted to the Le Havre-Plymouth-New York service, the *Ile-de-France* weighs 40,000 tons. Launched in 1926, it is 241 meters long, 30 broad on the promenade deck, 21.50 inside, with a water draught of 9.75 meters. She is moved by four direct Parsons turbines producing 52,000 horsepower, the steam for which is provided by twelve oil-fired double boilers and eight single ones. She can embark 1740 passengers in her three classes and carries a crew of more than a thousand officers, sailors, stokers, waiters and employees of every sort—in sum, the population of a small sub-prefecture. For the voyage to Île Féréor, however, it was only departing from Le Havre with 125 first-class passengers: the French mission of the Condominium and a few Belgian, Polish, Rumanian, Czechoslovakian and Yugoslavian delegates. At Plymouth we would embark our English colleagues, only a little less numerous. In third class there was a company of colonial infantry, whose officers occupied second class, along with a hundred journalists and cinematographic reporters.

What a difference there is—entirely to the advantage of the later occasion—between my present departure and that of a month ago, surreptitious and adventurous, when I had set out alone, a petty doctor in the Barcot expedition, toward the unknown. This time there are two of us, two newly-weds, in possession of an enviable situation, departing for an expedition to which the eyes of the entire world are fixed, in the sumptuous glory of an official ceremony.

It is fourteen hundred hours. Presided over by Monsieur Germain-Lucas, the banquet at the Hôtel de Ville has been held, the speeches have been made. We are now embarked. Leaning on the rail of the first-class promenade deck, among our new colleagues, we are looking down from the height of a fifth floor on the quay where Rivier, his wife and daughter, on the official podium, are waving at us from afar...

Around them there are the band, the horizon-blue troops that are doing the honors, the innumerable crowd. On the lower decks, we can see by leaning over, the heads of the colonials, who are waving the flowers with which the ladies of the town have heaped them. The band is playing *Sambre-et-Meuse*; the bells of Le Havre are beginning to ring. Hydroplanes are soaring in the splendid October sky, circling the dirigible *Méditerranée*, which will escort us as far as the exit from the Channel.

From the ship's four funnels the white oil-smoke is spiraling into the sky; the bells of the bridge are launching orders to the engine-room. A long blast of the siren fills the air; it's the signal for departure. The sirens of all the boats in the harbor respond. The band plays the Marseillaise; the members of the crowd take off their hats and wave handkerchiefs... and while the cannon of La Hève fire a twenty-one gun salute, the monumental *Ile-de-France* draws away from the quay, gliding over the yellow waters of the Seine estuary, at a speed of eighteen knots, rapidly distancing us from the Lilliputian host of flag-decked tugs laden with curiosity-seekers, which follow us briefly. Two destroyers precede us, as scouts.

It was a genuine honeymoon trip, for us, for although we were both delegates of the Banque Rivier et Cie, charged with watching over enormous interests, our task remained putative on the Ile-de-France. The principal aim of our mission was to divide up Île Féréor, to share it out in syndicate between the nations, under the guardianship of the Condominium—and it was necessary for us to be on the spot to assess that. We had no map of the island, no plans—nothing but the photographs brought back by the *Erebus II* and the *Cornouaille*, prints of which were passed from hand to hand in the vast first-class saloon, where we were trying to make everyone's acquaintance after dinner.

Our naval escort increased significantly before leaving European waters. Firstly, off Cherbourg at about eighteen hundred hours, two battleships, the *Paris* and the *Porthos*, came to flank us, accompanied by the *Erebus II* herself, which took up a position on our port side, like a minuscule boat—and Lefébure shouted a joyful *bonjour* at me through a loudhailer. Then, at twenty-three hundred hours, we stopped in Plymouth harbor to receive the English delegates, under the intersecting searchlights of warships, two of which—the *Trafalgar* and the *King Edward II*—joined our convoy.

The following day, we had left European waters. The dirigible had turned back, and our fleet was advancing in orderly formation, the destroyers in the van and the battleships on the flanks. For three days we did not allow ourselves to think about that argonautical expedition sailing triumphantly to the conquest of the Golden Rock. Every evening, at sunset, we admired the magical spectacle. Trailing their long wakes of foam over the green extent, sparkling with red reflections, the eight ships seemed to be heading straight toward the red globe of the disappearing sun...

And thus it was that, on the seventh, we had the opportunity to see that rare and prestigious phenomenon, the "green ray."[22]

Our journey was partly spent in breathing the sea air and strolling back and forth along the two hectometers of the promenade deck. We gladly exchanged a few words with the other strollers, French or English, but

---

[22] As featured in Jules Verne's love story *Le Rayon vert* (1882; tr. as *The Green Ray*).

without letting them take possession of us. I confess that even had a slight dread of being harassed by the exuberant Jolliot, but although he was officially part of the mission, he obtained greater pleasure in second class with the journalists and cameramen. The star, tormented by sea-sickness in spite of the calmness of the sea, remained invisible throughout the crossing.

Immediately after sunset we went down to the saloon to take tea while listening to the news, after which there was dinner, and the evening was completed by two or three hours of dancing, most frequently to the trains of a cowboy jazz band borrowed from second class to add spice to our orchestra, which we deemed to be to old-fashioned.

The news.

We were abundantly provided with it by the loud-speakers in the saloons and dining-room. Six wireless operators working shifts two at a time, were constantly on duty at the ship's antennae, receiving mostly from Saint-Assise in Melun—50 kilowatts—which retransmitted the news from the Tower. Signals from the island, disentangled from long-wave signals of every kind, in all languages, with which they were mingled, coming from dozens of ships en route, like us, for the sector of the ocean, finally reached us direct from the evening of the eighth onwards.

After the American reconnaissance aircraft, the island had received the visit of ships baring the star-spangled banner: the aircraft-carrier *Lexington*, four long-range torpedo-boats and three cargo vessels. As they had not headed for Port Erebus the French destroyers allowed them to pass by and land four kilometers away on the southern cost of the island, where they had disembarked machinery and an army of Japanese coolies, who dug into the iron cliff with oxyacetylene torches, as into a safe...

On the ninth—we were due to reach the island the following day—two hydroplanes launched from the *Porthos* were able to fly over the island on reconnaissance and bring back photographs and films, immediately developed and projected that evening on the screen in the saloon.

Vision: we are looking down vertically from two thousand meters above sea level at waves feathered by solar reflections, rocked by the gentle pendular movement of aerial displacement. Ships, like the backs of aquatic beetles, on most of which small round turrets stand out, with the thin barrels of cannon. There's the long American aircraft-carrier, its upper deck bare for two-thirds of its length, it catapult-platform...and six other ships, also American, deployed in a crescent around the southern part of the island, where fissures stripe the edge of the cliff...

The entire island, from the vertical angle, looks like a relief-map; its form is somewhat reminiscent of a shoe, narrower in its median part, where the Golden Rock makes a granitic stain, eaten away on its flanks by streams. The stain is further diminished toward the north, as if the peak posed on the iron pedestal constituted the toe of the shoe.

It is toward the heel—to maintain the analogy—that the Americans have landed. Something like a shiny notch can be distinguished, carved into the height of the gorge when the first reconnaissance from the *Erebus II* landed. An ant-hill-like activity already reigns there: minuscule dots are moving around machines, and puffs of white smoke mark the explosion of mines in the process of eating away the mass of iron along the fissures of cleavage.

Among the two hundred spectators of the film there was a cry of indignation when two further white explosions were produced before our eyes—but in the air, not on the ground, Shrapnel bursts beneath the objective lens, evidently fired at the aircraft.

We understand then why the observer is circling at such an altitude, at a rather inconvenient distance.

Moreover, the observer himself—Monsieur de Silfrage—beings speaking at that moment, and tells us by megaphone that he has been ordered to withdraw.

Will the tolerance of allowing the Americans to land on the island hasten conflict instead of avoiding it? Will the game won in Europe thanks to the Franco-Britannic alliance be rejoined, this time with canon-fire, around the bolide? Is the statement from New York issued by the loudspeaker immediately after the cinema session—that the Pacific fleet is in the process of passing through the Panama Canal and will head for Île Féréor—an intimidation or an ultimatum? Its arrival can be expected in five or six days—and what then?

The danger is understood in Europe. Saint-Assise transmits a message saying that the Vatican station has addressed an encyclical from the Sovereign Pontiff to Christianity. The pope adjures his spiritual children to beware of the forces of Evil that are sowing dissent among them. He exhorts them to peace, union against the infidels.

The infidels! Translation: yellow people; the Japanese.

In spite of the unanimous silence of the Hertzian waves regarding the actions and deeds of the rival race, we believe we can sense it, separated from us by the thickness of the planet, meditating some evil coup, thanks to this American imprudence. The United States are presenting themselves to us as competitors, and we feel less intimacy than indignation in their regard; the thirst for gold—for this exploitation of the iron is merely a bluff, or a beginning—is making them neglect their duty as champions of white civilization in the face of the yellow, irreducible enemies beneath their progressivist make-up. The true guarantee of peace in the Far East was the American fleet, far more the few units maintained by France in Indochina and England in India. Will even formidable Singapore, the lock set upon massive treasures in the Strait of Malacca, hold firm before a Japanese shock attack?

But serious thoughts can be left until tomorrow! The cords of the instruments and cowboy jazz are calling us to the great saloon, and there will be dancing until three o'clock in the morning on the *Ile-de-France*, en route for the Golden Rock.

XX. Adieu, Baskets!

The blare of the Ile-de-France's sirens, to which the various howls of its convoy and other vessels reply—a formidable herd of machine-beasts of the Industrial Age—dragged Frédérique and me us from our bunks. After switching on the electric light and dressing in haste, we ran to the elevator and went up to the promenade deck.

In the pale October dawn, our flotilla was slowing down as it arrived among ships with red, white and green lights, and searchlight-beams.

Two kilometers ahead of us, a kind of luminous town rose up above the waves, in a mist of vapor and smoke blurring the silhouette of the island.

"Port Erebus!" de Silfrage told me.

A great deal of work had been done since the departure of the *Erebus II*! Where we had left a single excavator and a decauville, there was a veritable factory-city, seething with activity. The racket of machines reached us clearly, borne by the surface of the sea, in an interval of silence, with the impact of loads of gold, extracted from a mountainous stock shining vaguely beneath the arms of machines and poured into the holds of two moored cargo vessels.

The daylight brightened; we drew closer. I uttered an exclamation, and seized Frédérique's arm, when my gaze finally discerned the silhouette of the Golden Rock outlined in black against the gray background of the sky. And even though I considered the expression as pure rhetoric, which had never had any living reality for me, even before the most amazing spectacle, I will say that "I rubbed my eyes"—for the silhouette of the peak was transformed!

I saw it again in my memory, that pointed peak, white with snow at the top, red at the base, but shaped as an almost-regular cone...

Now, there was no longer any trace of snow, except at the summit, whose altitude had diminished by a third. The southern slope was cut vertically, and everywhere on the flanks there were large streaks of auriferous mud. It really was the "sagging candle" that Lefébure had mentioned to us.

The Ile-de-France, saluted by artillery salvos, came to a halt five hundred meters from the shore, a little way inside the blockade line formed by the ships that had arrived previously, which were now joined by the *Porthos*, the *Paris*, the *Trafalgar* and the *King Edward VII*. The *Erebus II* advanced as far as the harbor entrance, and immediately landed its personnel.

For us, the staff of the Mission—the only ones authorized to leave the ship that day—methodical work was about to commence with our initial descent on to the island. In view of the spirit of joyfulness that reigned among us, however, it ought not to exclude amusement. Jolliot and a few other fun-lovers organized a picnic. Thanks to the stewards, the two hundred and forty "representatives of the Condominium" were issued with provisions: canned preserves, terrines of *foie gras*, bottles of champagne, and we gathered in sympathetic groups. Jolliot was carrying a miniature camera, a kind of baby Pathé. The English all had Kodaks. Frédérique and I, still on honeymoon, with all the riches of the present and the future, neglected those avaricious precautions against future forgetfulness...

The motor launch, as large as a small tug, was big enough to take us all ashore in two trips. We were in the first party, which left at eleven o'clock.

The inlet was full of a demonic din. The confusion of machines with huge arms perched on their stilts of metal beams was reminiscent of the vision of the Martians that Wells evokes for us in *The War of the Worlds*. We disembarked at the entrance to the inlet, where the agitation and clutter were less intense.

On the shore I recognized Lefébure, who was waving to us. A little further away, flanked by two armed Senegalese, the engineer charged with piloting our group hailed us, waving a small flag: "This way! Come alongside!"

We had not all disembarked yet when the guide was already beginning to draw the group away, announcing through a megaphone: "Come, on Mesdames et Messieurs...Ladies and Gentlemen...line up along the rails to the right, and don't walk on the track—watch out for the trains! Pay attention, too, when you pass under the overhead cables—mud falls from the skips. Stop! Here, first of all, is nugget-bunker number one. It's a reserve, containing approximately..."

In the front rank of the group, Kodak's were clicking; Jolliot was beginning to operate his baby Pathé. The star was uncertain as to where to put her feet in the red chloride mud that was making the iron ground sticky—but Lefébure took possession of Frédérique and me.

"Come on, then! You don't need to paddle through all that. I'll show you something far more curious." And he drew us toward the huts situated to the right of the iron slope.

Half-way there, he brought us to a halt.

"Oh!" said Frédérique. "How the ground shakes! One can still feel the trepidation of the machines here."

The mariner smiled enigmatically.

"Good—you can feel it. That's already something—and you, Antoine, don't you notice something else? Look at the creek."

Only then did the double transformation leap to my eyes. The ravine that once prolonged the inlet was now a true fjord, the waters of which came to bathe the very base of the peak sliced into by the excavation. Furthermore, the breadth of the sheet of water between the two "quays" had increased considerably; whereas the *Erebus II* had once found it narrow, as in a floating dock, the two 6000-ton cargo ships that were moored there today, one to the right and one to the left, only occupied a third of its width.

"Damn!" I said, simply.

"How can the disaggregation of the peak possibly produce that effect?" asked Frédérique.

"I told you in Paris, didn't I?" Lefébure went on. "Île Féréor is clearing off. But let's go up to Gripert's place. He'll give you the explanation you want, Madame."

We resumed the ascent, and found Gripert in a sort of hangar, in the process of observing a white cross placed on the other shore of the inlet through a telescope. He was genuinely pleased to see me again, and looked at Frédérique approvingly in her capacity as a doctor of science. "It's accelerating, you know," he said to Lefébure. The rate of separation has doubled since I last saw you."

"Doubled! Do you hear, Antoine? But that's right—you need an explanation first. Tell our friends what's happening, Gripert—they aren't up to date."

Gripert shrugged his shoulders disdainfully. "Can you feel the tremor in the ground, Madame? And you, Doctor?"

"Yes—Lefébure's already pointed it out to us."

It was evident here that the muted and continuous trepidation that was agitating the mass of the bolide was not coming from the machines; we were more than five hundred meters from the mine-face where the excavators were at work, and no less distant from the quay where the decauville trains were rolling and the tractors, conveyor belts and elevators were roaring.

"It's obvious, isn't it? A child couldn't mistake the fact that the island's in the process of breaking up? In spite of that, no one wants to believe me, and the Académie hasn't yet published my communication related to the geological structure of the island. No matter— this is it. According to my latest research, the island is formed of two enormous blocks of iron, cemented together by the pudding-stone of chloride and nuggets filling the vertical fracture represented by the Port Erebus cutting. It's necessary to believe that the bolide came from a planet entirely devoid of water, where the chloride was able to subsist for many millennia without contact with it. At any rate, since it fell into the ocean, that chloride cement has begin to dissolve, and you can see that the thalweg of the ravine has disappeared.

"That wouldn't matter if the two fragments of the island were firmly set on the ocean bed, but the measurement of the gravitational field that I've been able to make with my improvised instruments have permitted me to determine the form of the immersed sections and the thickness of their masses. The two blocks are each tapered toward the base, and are resting on the bed on their tips. While they remain welded together, the assemblage remains upright—but take away the cement, and the peak that forms the key to the vault, and the two pyramids will each fall sideways, under the water...

"Now, I repeat, the cement has been dissolving like sugar for five weeks, and there's no longer anything between the two blocks, all the way to the ocean bed, but water."

"But Monsieur Gripert," Frédérique put in, "there remains, as you've just said, the key to the vault—the peak itself. It might still last for months..."

"No. It's visibly eroded, profoundly disaggregated. Its equilibrium is getting less and less stable—and might perhaps collapse *en masse* at any minute on the northern part of the island, which would complete the dislocation. A slightly larger landslide would suffice...and they're happening every day; two workmen were killed yesterday at the face. Even at the present rate, the dislocation is proceeding apace. The southern block of the island is gradually drawing away, in a slow slide. Here, judge for yourselves. This is the collimator lens by means of which I'm tracking the progress made..."

He rectified the aim of the instrument and Frédérique, Lefébure and I took turns to put our eyes to the ocular for a few seconds. Slowly, but with an undeniable motion, the needle was rising, the white cross of the reference-point being displaced behind the thread of the reticule.

"The angular movement," Gripert went on, "which is to say, the rotation of the two blocks around their theoretical axis, situated on the ocean bed, is accelerating rapidly. Until yesterday evening, there was only half a minute of arc, and the separation was increasing by about a meter an hour. When I saw you this morning, Lefébure, it was three-quarters of a minute of arc. Now it's reached a minute and a half...which is three meters of separation per hour."

"A catastrophe's imminent, then?" Lefébure queried. "How many days do you think...?"

"It's only a matter of hours."

"But we need to evacuate the island!" Frédérique exclaimed, just as I was about to say the same thing.

Gripert shrugged his shoulders. "The engineers don't want to hear it."

"Even so," my wife replied, "we don't have the right to risk the lives of all these poor people...three or four hundred workers...the crews of the two cargo vessels...."

"What do you expect? Reasons of State..."

At that moment, the Ile-de-France's launch disembarked the second cohort of excursionists. The first, having completed the tour of Port Erebus, was spreading out over the slopes. The Jolliots had spotted us and were coming toward us.

"If Reasons of State prevent the evacuation of the workers, nothing obliges us to leave the Condominium people here. We need to warn them..."

"To start a panic?" I objected. "No—impossible. Not directly."

"I'll go warn Commander Barcot," Lefébure decided. "He's a man of action. He'll know what to do. Would you care to go with me, Madame, and you, Antoine? I'll put you aboard the Ile-de-France."

"Do you want to, Frédérique?"

"No. That would be cowardly. We'll leave with the others. Here's the Jolliots—they've seen us. We can't avoid them."

"What about you, Gripert?"

"Me? Never in this life! I haven't yet witnessed the dislocation of an island, much less a bolide-island. I'm staying until the last moment."

"As you please. But above all, not a word to the others about the danger."

And Lefébure went down the slope at a rapid pace toward the *Erebus II*'s dinghy.

The Jolliots joined us, the director enthused by his tour and sweating under the double weight of his camera and his basket of provisions, the star declaring that she was dying of hunger.

The picnic! That hour of secret anguish in which it was necessary for us to simulate enjoyment, eat and swill champagne in imitations of the other groups disseminated over the iron slopes, beneath a jolly sky of milky clouds.

Fortunately, barbed wire forbade access to the dangerous regions situated to the north of the peak, where landslides were heaping up a talus of debris at the foot of the vertical cliff whose summit was even overhanging.

The last passengers from the launch had completed their tour of Port Erebus and were searching in their turn for a place to settle down. How did they have the insouciance to eat their *foie gras* and drink their champagne, on the quivering ground that was about to give way beneath them?

Frédérique was suffering visibly. She had something akin to a physical presentiment of the catastrophe, and her eyes only quit the peak of the Golden Rock to dart apprehensive glances at me. In that atmosphere, Jolliot's jokes fell very flat.

Suddenly, stopping in mid-sentence, my wife's eyes widened with stupor and fear, and I turned round mechanically, while a rumble resounded and a stronger quake shook the ground.

The overhanging crest of the peak had just collapsed, toward the north, less than a kilometer away from us, pouring its materials over the iron plain from on high.

Cries went up from all the groups; people got up indecisively, ready to flee—but as they were unaware of the supreme menace of that collapse, and it was not renewed, the excursionists gradually reassured themselves...

In Port Erebus the machines were functioning, the trains rolling along their tracks, the aerial skips filing along their taut cables, the loads of gold resounding in the holds of the two cargo ships...

We finished the champagne. A further quarter of an hour of anxiety. Frédérique and I were watching out for the tremors in the ground, which did not seem to have increased. Had Gripert been mistaken? What was Lefébure doing?

Ah! Finally! *The Erebus II*'s dinghy, returning from its visit to the Ile-de-France, and Lefébure and Commander Barcot disembarking at Port Erebus, accompanied by a dozen colonial infantry soldiers.

And almost immediately, the shrill siren of the launch launches its appeal, repeated three times—the agreed signal to return to the shop.

"Eh? What do they want us to do?" Joliot exclaimed. "We were told that the return would be at seventeen hundred...it's scarcely fourteen hundred..."

"We haven't even finished eating," said the star, who was digging into tinned pineapples."

"Too bad—let them whistle. The others aren't budging either. Let's stay here."

But that circumstance had been anticipated. The soldiers launched themselves up the slope at the double toward the picnicking groups, in order to force them to break camp. By their gestures, it was obvious that the lunchers were furious at being brought back *manu militari.*

Lefébure arrived breathlessly and whispered to me: "The slippage is getting worse. We've reached fifty centimeters a minute."

A hundred of the more docile excursionists had reached he launch. It was overflowing when we reached the quay, where Commander Barcot was striving by voice and gesture to hasten the laggards. As they arrived, they interrogated one another anxiously, questioning the commander.

"Stay calm," the latter relied. "You've been called back to the ship, that's all. Wait for the launch."

A further incident increased the disturbance, however. In the depths of Port Erebus, this time, a series of landslides followed one after another, which swept over the mine-face like curtains of red mud.

Work stopped. There was a panicked stampede, in spite of the remonstrations of the engineers. The workers ran to take refuge in the two cargo ships. One of them was equipped with Diesel engines, which started up immediately as it made ready to sail without further delay. The funnel of the other began to smoke vigorously.

The members of the Commission became agitated, taking fright. Like me, they could see with the naked eye that the other side of the creek was drawing away. The rip was accentuating under water. The ground shook, like the metal plates of a boiler under pressure. In the distance, auriferous masses continued to tumble down from the peak. An overhead cable broke, hurling its skips away. One of them fell on the deck of the first cargo ship, which was then passing in front of us, making its exit from the creek, with its deck crowded with howling men. The excursionists joined in the chorus.

"Calm down! Calm down!" repeated Monsieur Barcot. "Don't worry. Here comes the launch."

"Twenty-five centimeters a second!" howled Gripert, who was struggling in the hands of two soldiers commissioned with embarking him by force. "Twenty-five centimeters a second!" he repeated, relentlessly, furious at having been dragged away from his instruments.

"Gag him!" ordered Monsieur Barcot.

From the peak, the landslides were pouring down in ever-greater profusion. Boulders were rolling as far as the bridge of the second cargo vessel, which was having difficulty casting off its moorings. At sea, the alarm had been raised; the *Ile-de-France* had been set in motion and was slowly drawing away, along with the other sips.

"We're doomed! They're abandoning us! We're all going to die!" cried the women, wringing their hands.

"Every man for himself!" brayed the men, shoving their way to the launch, which was coming alongside.

"The first man who jumps the queue will have his brains blown out!" proclaimed Monsieur Barcot. "Lefébure, keep a weather-eye open! Four men on guard at the gangplank, and everyone goes over one by one!"

"What about you, Commander?"

"Lefébure and I will stay to get the engineers into the *Erebus II*'s dinghy. Embark! Embark! The troopers now! Get moving! Full speed ahead!"

And with its engine sputtering, our vessel headed out to sea, shaken by the eddies that the submarine aspiration of the moving walls was hollowing out in the water of the inlet.

Up above, the peak was visibly disintegrating, the rain of debris was running incessantly over its walls. The second overhead cable snapped in its turn; the conveyor belt was overturned...

"Faster!" shouted the officer at the helm. "Full ignition!"

In the launch, the members of the Mission, astounded, had fallen silent. On the starboard bench, an English lady who had fainted was trailing her hand in the water. Frédérique was huddling close to me.

Anxiously, we followed the maneuvering of the second cargo vessel, which was now detached from the quay and had set off to flee. Alas, it did not have time. The whole of the remaining summit of the Golden Rock—millions of tons of chloride and nuggets—collapsed with a thunderous roar, covering the rear of the cargo vessel with its mass. The vessel was upended for two seconds, hurling its human insects into the water, projecting its bowsprit into the air and exposing the underside of its hull, painted with red lead and plastered with wrack.

"Watch out for the shock wave! Hold on tight!"

The marine wave surging from the inlet picked up in *Erebus II*'s dinghy as it passed, submerging and carrying away in its furious wake the dozen men who were ready to embark thereon: the engineers, Lefébure, Commander Barcot...

Then it reached us, lifted us up, drenched us, as we screamed in fright, and tossed us about madly...but the engine kept sputtering, and we continue to speed toward the *Ile-de-France*, which was drawing away—fleeing with desperate slowness the accursed land prey to the catastrophe.

We were a kilometer from Port Erebus when it happened.

It was completed in two stages and lasted some sixty seconds—thus enabling us to gain another four hundred meters.

Up above, the decapitated and completely disaggregated peak finished its collapse, and spread out in a quasi-fluid sheet over the northern part of the island. The latter swayed beneath the overload and sank beneath the ocean, slowly and progressively, so gently that it hardly left an eddy.

The southern section remained intact, and it was possible to believe, for a moment, that it might subsist; its iron cliffs still offered their illusory aspect of a shore solidly anchored to the ocean bed...

There is a minute of intense suspense, while our launch bounds over the waves at top speed, with the precipitate clatter of the engine. Frédérique has grabbed my wrist and I can feel her fingernails digging into my flesh.

We gaze at the long black and regular frieze of the iron cliff, which extends over four kilometers, all the way to the American establishment, where smoke and ships close to the shore mark the location...and it is from that point that a spray of foam springs up, at the same time as the line of the crest outlined on the horizon tilts, shifting as if by some theatrical trick...

With an enormous anguish, we understand that it is the end for those hundreds, those thousands of living beings out there...and at the same time, egotistical hope is magnified; we congratulate ourselves on being safe from that destruction...

The surface of the island brushes the surface, like a sinister black reef. It is sinking, sinking...

It disappears.

Because of the enormous suction, in the place where Île Féréor had been a few moments before, fifteen hundred meters away from us, before our eyes, an almighty tempest explodes, in a sudden upheaval of tormented waves and aspirating whirlpools...

A massive swell is launched in our direction. Clinging to the side of the boat with one hand, while the other clutches Frédérique's torso—where I can hear the heart hammering beneath my fingers—I turn away from the liquid alp in order to look into her eyes, those dear eyes, before the supreme engulfment...

Drowned!

A giant force absorbs us, rips my hand away from the rim, and for an indefinite lapse of horror I feel myself being dragged down into the water, drunk in by the abyss, in the turbulent viridity that is stirring me in its giant eddies. I have not let go of Frédérique, and amid the conflict of superhuman forces, my vertiginous soul concentrates exclusively on that grip...

Asphyxia comes...the mental kaleidoscope that precedes death...

But no! It's no longer downwards but upwards that I am being hurled, still with the same violence...the chaotic viridity brightens...and we break the surface, coughing, spluttering...resurrected!

Ah! Air! Blissful air, respired into full lungs! While swimming, half-blinded by the saline water, in the undulant tumult...and the liberating ecstasy of feeling that my wife is also alive and swimming , swimming like me, ardently, in spite of the paralyzing hindrance of our garments...

But a mass, a cliff-face, obstructs the sky ahead of us...the flank of the *Ile-de-France*! Twenty meters away! And calls for help mingle, our voices coalescing...she with a great musical shout, me with a savage and furious hoarseness...

We've been seen, up above! A buoy plunges down, splashing me. I seize it, that resistant object, which sustains me. I shove it toward her; she grabs hold of it...and we wait to be fished out, breathless, painting, but saved—saved!

And I kiss that dear mouth, which, without the blind hazard of the eddies, a moment ago, would now be cold and inert, under water...

"Ahoy there! Hold hard!" shouts a voice close at hand.

"Bravo the lovers!" proffers another.

And raising my head, I utter a nervous burst of laughter. In the bow of the approaching, dancing boat is my friend Jolliot, kneeling on the edge, aiming his cinema camera at us, turning away, filming the scene of the rescue of the castaways...

XI. Deliverance

Like the head of a charmed snake, when the charmer's clarinet suddenly stops playing, all the avarice extended toward the vanished bolide immediately faded away.

It was nineteen hundred hours in Paris when the news began to appear on the luminous ribbon of the *Paris-Projecteur*. The passers-by, while walking, and those who were on their way home for dinner on the top deck of an autobus read:

...PÉRITIF...GOLDEN ROCK ENGULFED BY CATACLYSM...

And then, in the midst of the lights and the crowds, it is as if everyone were suddenly in a black desert, feeling a chill in the heart, and very poor...

But they would be joyful instead, the Parisians, if they only knew...and over there, beyond the Channel, the people of London...for that engulfment will enable them to sleep peacefully, in that beautiful calm night, in which Paris is haloed by a vast red aura...that night exceedingly propitious for air raids...

Orders have been countermanded. In the Black Forest, the two thousand four-engined bombers that were awaiting hour H, each with its four five-hundred-kilo hyperclastite missiles or its panathanatic gas, have been returned to their hangars...and the zeppelins already en route to the rendezvous at Taunus have turned round and are returning to their bases...

XXII. Epilogue

The European ships—including the first cargo vessel that had already emerged from the inlet—had had time to get far enough away from the island, and none of them had sunk or sustained serious damage. The eddies and whirlpools died down after ten minutes, and the dinghies exploring the waters of the disaster were able to pick up a few more survivors from the launch. No one from the second cargo vessel survived, however, nor any of the people still on the island—among others, Gripert, the heroic Commander Barcot and my old friend Lefébure.

The total number of victims remains unknown. Eighteen members of the Mission were lost; that is the only figure about which we can be precise.

On the American side, the losses were even more considerable. Too far from the peak to understand the gravity of the danger, and not having immediately obeyed the signals of alarm sent by radio from the *Ile-de-France*, they had, according to a wireless message from the Lexington, lost two cargo ships and a destroyer, plus the personnel of Iron City: several thousand individuals, including engineers, mariners and coolies.

With any object of rivalry abolished, we sent them our condolences, and the loudspeaker in the saloon relayed their thanks. As a sign of mourning, there was no dancing that evening. The joyful and frantic zest nourished by gold fever had lapsed. Everyone felt sad and at a loss, conversing with constraint and in hushed voices, as in a mortuary chamber.

With a common accord, the entire fleet spent the night in the place where the Golden Rock had been, as if waiting...for what?

At daybreak, two radio messages from America, twenty minutes apart, informed us of the advance of Japanese squadrons toward Hawaii, and that the Pacific fleet, not yet entirely in the Atlantic, had turned back and was moving through the Panama Canal in haste.

During that day, the twelfth of October, when the *Ile-de-France*, leaving the warships to observe, resumed its route to Le Havre, the fate of races and of white and yellow civilization hung in the balance...but Japan doubtless feared seeing the European fleet join forces with the Americans. The aggression was merely sketched out, without so much as a cannon-shot being fired. The Japanese squadrons returned to their bases after their so-called maneuvers.

The adventure had no other consequence than to make the whites conscious of their solidarity in the presence of a peril to which they had so far given little thought.

A chill reigned on the Ile-de-France nonetheless. People were ashamed, as if of a ridiculous escapade. The English and the French avoided coming together, the former aggregating in the winter garden and the latter the music room. By virtue of the suppression of its objective, the unanimity of our Mission had dissolved. Henceforth, the ships passengers were a fortuitous assembly of individuals who were merely waiting for the time to go our separate ways.

Before long, the problem of the future would be open again. A new situation would be sought—and how would the treatment of that one by arranged? Would the six months of advance we had achieved be retained?

Jolliot was expecting to make a lot of money with the films he had taken of the cataclysm, and he spent the crossing writing a screenplay in which the star had her role and Frédérique and I were featured clinging to our buoy, awaiting rescue...

As for the two of us, we were sure of obtaining a lucrative position from Rivier, but—and Frédérique was in entire agreement with me—I preferred to look for a practice somewhere in the Midi...the Midi that had once been too beautiful for me alone, but which from now on, with my wife, would be paradise...

Six months have gone by, and I am writing this in my villa at Cimiez, where I have opened a clinic, which my wife helps me to run, like the most skillful of nurses. Our participation in the story or Île Féréor ended with our disembarkation at Le Havre, and our life thereafter is of no interest to the public.

The Golden Rock—the bolide—was an insignificant episode in the planetary history of the Earth, which "digested" it within a month, but its "digestion" by humankind is not yet complete. France has become the richest country in the world; louis circulate there as before; other nations envy her more than ever. Nevertheless, in view of the exchange rate, which is presently unfavorable to them, Anglo-Saxon, German and American tourists have ceased to come here. They claim that their virtue forbids them to be led astray by the debauchery of Paris, in "the brothel of the modern Babylon."

THE THUNDER OF ZEUS

I was outside Castelvetrano when first light thinned out the opacity of the nebulous night. The footpath on the edge of the road became perceptible. Black vegetal silhouettes were outlined. And, in the reassurance of the visible march, it was as if I woke up, after the animal fixity of the instinct brought forth by the darkness. A warm breeze was blowing softly. Gradually, colors were revealed; white clouds frayed at the edges, confusedly; on the bank of the sunken road the baroque profiles of Indian fig-trees—bushes tormented into hirsute spatulas of coarse green bronze—alternated with the sheaves of blue zinc aloes, from which sprang frail lances topped with orange flowers. Peasants mounted on donkeys over-took me, draped in their shawls as if in chlamydes. Sometimes, a cart, high on its wheels, gaudily painted all the way to its shafts, jolted along at the leisurely trot of a mule caped in red leather, while the drowsy boy driver fell under the bench.

In spite of the places offered and the lure of spicy conversations, I was fearful of the bumpy aid of the crude indigenous vehicles and I continued on foot in the matinal alacrity. The daylight brightened; long rays of glory cleaved the amorphous layer of clouds; ultramarine patches opened up. The sun had risen.

The joy of the divine land of Sicily delighted me once again with its new and light intoxication. A sensa-tion of voluptuous heroism stirred broad communions with the familiar and benevolent soul of things. The amiable play of natural forces scratched out the mysticism of the North. I recognized the enveloping proximity of the immortal gods, and, thinking about the luminous eurhythmia of antique life, a great frisson gave me a momentary and precious intuition of that abolished grace and beauty.

Meanwhile, the countryside became distinct, flat and less fertile: a few islets of compact lemon-trees; the green dust of stunted olive-trees, mingled with the dark tufts of carobs—and sometimes, along a ditch, a screen of dry and noisy reeds. A moist wind rarefied the air in long gusts, beneath the dome of ashen cloud, which quickly closed up again; my pace slowed as breathing became more difficult.

The country became utterly desolate; the clotted black brush of the heather extended to the distant hills. A clump of eucalyptus, white whitened trunks beneath the jagged bark and limp, extenuated foliage, grew beside the crumbling walls of an abandoned farm.

The main road forked to the left and the path across the heath led directly toward the ruins displaying four isolated columns and vague tumuli on the horizon. Low dunes covered that area, infected with malaria and fever after ancient catastrophes, and the continual invasion of sand had driven broad pale moving banks through the new gravel, the crossing of which was made more painful by the insipid breeze, beneath the warm and flocculent velum of the sirocco.

A sacred horror emanated from the ruins. There was a prodigious chaos, incomparable with the bitter solitudes of Ségeste or the shores of Ostia, and more lugubrious still. The consecration of evident anathemas was imposed on that unique disaster. Risking the wreckage, I scaled the shapeless blocks and sat down in the gigantic groove of a broken column, from which the formidable ensemble was visible.

The stout Doric columns had fallen in a block, projecting their capitals, their bases crushes by the fall of the massive entablements; other scattered their unequal stubs; and those at the corners had spilled out their dislocated cylinders in titanic vertebral chains. The temples were unrecognizable; the marble beams had been shattered, naos,[23] friezes and frontons mingling their broken debris, and sections of architrave had staved in the triple steps cut into the rock like battering rams. There was not a single ridge that had not been chipped, slashed and hacked or a molding not bitten into by saws, and everywhere the stone was eroded, hollowed out and vermiculated by cavities in which green salamanders nested. Further away, other heaps overflowed the cyclopean walls of the Acropolis, the ravine of which opened an inverted delta over the glittering mercury of the Lybic Sea.

The strange character and the special malediction of those ruins penetrated me. Obstinate earthquakes had been requires, and inhuman determination. Neither war nor conflagration, and no assault by savage hordes, could have brought about that definitive and perfect subversion. Only the irritated violence of the gods could have cast down, crushed and leveled that vigorous architecture; then, with the vengeful monument abandoned to a land henceforth sterile and mephitic, the patient shroud of the secular sands had buried the remains, and the recent exhumation of archeological digs had not dimin-

---

[23] The naos of a temple is the inner sanctum, usually housing an idol.

ished the accursed solitude, far from railways, tourist itineraries and honeymoon voyages.

My meditation deepened, closing my eyelids to the density of the narcotized past. In luminous fragments, antique evocations appeared: profiles, against the sky, of sunlit temples, extensive walls; and the bright town; and the polychromatic streets, and the undulant and youthful rhythm of peplums and chlamydes. A sharpened and silent intuition projected, in living and fleeting colors, the thousand parcels of that history, animated by the presence of its debris—and that full comprehension of the plastic beauty initiated me to the joy of a harmonious and dionysiac existence: a full and graceful generosity of supple energies, by comparison with which our sad and complicated civilization appears a valetudinarian poverty and a pitiful senility.

Rendered lyrical by these evoked splendors, I restored the heaps of shapeless ruins to their legitimate maters: beneath the glory of the frontons and colonnades, in the depths of the temples, the Olympians of ivory and gold were enthroned amid clouds of perfumes. And with the attentive slowness of respect, the august and all powerful Majesty imposed itself: the marmoreal Face of Zeus.

In the distance, over the Acropolis, with hoarse cries, an eagle rose up vertically into the sky. And the sudden instinct of my recognition rose up with the bird toward the God, who thus acknowledged my tribute to Barbarism.

The complacency of an amiable torpor was pursuing the play of that illusion when I was awakened abruptly by a reverent greeting. The inevitable *custode delle rovine,*[24] with his red clay pipe in one hand and the other tugging at his silver-braided cap to offer me his services. The miserable and feverish face, which the over-waxed points of his black moustache tried in vague to reinvigorate, augmented the annoyance of the intrusion. I felt incapable of the energy necessary to reject the loquacious and tenacious harassment of an Italian cicerone. It was necessary to resign myself, to go down and follow the individual, who led me back to the road in order to observe the immutable itinerary of his demonstration.

He reminisced about "the excavations that had finally brought to light the debris of that town, of which even the veritable location had been forgotten"; he launched into a fantastic chronology of its first "kings"—but a noise, a rude buzz that was getting closer, made us turn round. A clear-cut silhouette appeared at the far end of the road: an automobile.

At the speed of an express train, the noisy machine, lacquered in vermilion, with a sharp spur between its locomotive headlights, bounced along, skidded in a swerve at top speed, and stopped dead in front of us with an exasperated gurgle of detonations. Amid the reek of benzene and oil, a giant completely armored in sealskin leapt out of the shuddering machine and, pulling off a kind of diver's helmet with his hairy hand—which unmasked his broad red bull-like face, set a long way above his huge boots—he roared in a stentorian voice, in English: "By Jove! One might think they were factory chimneys, those columns. Very curious indeed!"

---

[24] The author adds a footnote translating this phrase, which means "custodian of the ruins," but leaves some of the character's more obvious subsequent remarks in Italian.

Then he called to me: "Sir..."

I introduced myself.

"Charmed, Sir. Colonel William Klondyke, Chicago. What do you think of it, Sir? There's a famous capitolade of temples!"

And, his red and radiant beard gleaming like a copper-wire brush, he shook with satisfied laughter, the cyclopean spasms of which inflated the sealskin overcoat. Although the rictus of his bushy face immediately seemed odious, curiosity prevented me from abandoning him alone to the explanations of the custodian. I submitted meekly to his abrupt exordium.

William Klondyke turned back to the automobile, whose chauffeur, equipped with a set of tools, was checking the nuts and bolts. From the trunk he took a guide-book bound in bull's-blood shagreen, and a voluminous photographic apparatus, and he began comparing his text with the custodian's speech, and taking note of the viewpoints that were ratified by the resonance.

My instinctive animadversion was not based on the grotesquerie of his appearance; I devoted a profound seriousness to the assurance of his brutality, and by virtue of his arrival and conduct, I abominated the individual.

"This," said the cicerone, "is one of the largest temples that the Greeks ever built. It was 113 meters log and 54 wide." His expectation required the customary exclamations at the announcement of such figures.

With the metallic hoarseness of a phonograph, William Klondyke said: "And that's why they throw Antiquity at our heads! These people were civilized because they built temples! Well, it's not too bad—for the era. But let's be serious, Sir; compare their primitive building with modern construction: reinforced concrete, chrome steel, fiberglass, eh? They had marble and gilding. So what? All for décor, nothing serious, not a shadow of comfort. Look, these famous temples, in order to provide them with light, there was a hole in the ceiling, which also let the rain in. And don't talk to me about grandeur; a very ordinary railway station—Omaha's, for example—is worth half a dozen of them. Tell me, Sir, would they have been capable of building, not Brooklyn Bridge or a Big Wheel, but a Machine Hall? What would they put inside it, to start with? Gods? Yes, of course— their stupid anthropomorphic gods, for who they stupidly squandered their time in festivals and their produce in sacrifices. Do you want to know what I think? Well, these Greeks weren't practical people!"

He completed his vituperation with that vehement insult and sat down on an aluminum folding chair whose ingenious mechanism he had taken out of his pocket.

I have certainly been subjected some absurd conversations in my time, and the vile comments of tourists are familiar to me in their diversity, but I was unable to anticipate those enormous extravagances, and the bitterness of that tirade, which had no humor or wit in it, disconcerted my refutation.

I launched into a banal appeal to common sense. "For even in America, Monsieur, one concedes the ancients the role of the precursors—distant, I admit—of modern civilization, and even the most subversive thinkers can't deny the genius of equilibrium, harmony and proportion..."

He cut the foolish platitudes short. "Yes, Sir, I despise all those transcendentalists, those idealists. Imbecility, your Greek genius. What did it produce? In politics, anarchy and dementia: then again, Sparta, Syracuse and the rest, microscopic States that couldn't even unite, envious and peevish populations that spent their lives devouring one another. Their philosophy? A mess of contradictory and anti-scientific hypotheses; every one of Aristotle's affirmations is a howler; Diogenes was a crackpot, Plato a humbug. All artistes, I tell you!

"And not only were they not practical, they weren't moral. Their conception of Olympus ought to nail them to the pillory of history. A whorehouse, that Olympus! Godly debauchery! Their ignoble Zeus merited hard labor or the electric chair a hundred times over, and as for their Aphrodite..."

He ejaculated the most formidable blasphemies. His wild vehemence horrified me; I sensed that he was the fanatic devotee of some occult power, and his frenzy seemed to me to be a kind of posthumous revolt, a vengeful intrusion, into that divine necropolis, of some incompletely-crushed Titan.

Understanding the vanity of any response, the futility of any attempt to rein in that brutal and ferocious hatred, I suffered the confused terror of being implicated in the transcendent adventure of a forbidden spectacle.

Meanwhile, the cicerone, unaware of what was being said, sponged his brow—for the atmosphere was becoming stagnant and unbreathable—and, taking advantage of the pause, resumed his function. In a monotonous and inexpressive voice, he told the story of the siege by the Carthaginians, the pillage and the burning, the curse of the malaria sent to the region by the demon Jupiter—*il diavol Giove*—to which the city was condemned.

"For it is in this place, *Signor miel*, that Giove took refuge when our good savior Jesus Christ"—he crossed himself—"threw the pagan gods into the Inferno. And here he has conserved his power. When the monks, expelled by the Moors, came to establish themselves in the temples, which were still standing then, the demon Giove, offended by seeing them pray to God, made the stones crumble and slew them all—*li uccide tutti!* Today, he has his domain watched over by an eagle—and that is certain, Signori, for no other eagles have ever been seen on this coast. But that one was discovered in the diggings..."

A comminatory "Stop!" gagged the nonchalant speech of the nonplussed custodian.

"That's not in the guide-book," proclaimed William Klondyke, brandishing the volume, less scarlet than his apoplexy. He was foaming at the mouth. "As if it weren't enough, Sir, to be poisoned on every page by classical stupidities, without this imbecile boring us to death with apocryphal legends about that devil Zeus—that damned diabolical Zeus!" And again, he heaped his reproaches on the petrified cicerone, in Italian.

This invective against a folk-tale was not the absurd outburst of a loose-lipped maniac, nor was the relentlessness with which he attacked the episode of the eagle mere dementia. The very excess of brutality revealed more than the rancorous chicanery allowable in a modern individual; the man was in mysterious proximity to Antiquity; the organic depths of his being, his very essence, was rebelling against the Gods, and he was impugning the one and only Zeus with an impetuous and personal aggression.

"Show it to me, then, your eagle!"

Standing erect, his arms crossed, his massive stature displayed the provocation of obscure and mighty powers

By a *necessary* coincidence, for whose reply I was on the lookout, there was a raucous cry, and among the ruins, the eagle rose up with great wing-beats, in an ample revolution of regular spirals.

"*Eccolo!*" cried the cicerone, triumphantly.

I felt a pang of anguish.

A "Hah!" of ferocious joy drew back the giant's jowls over his fangs, and, disclosing the tragic completion of an infallible ambush, coughing up a magma of congestive blasphemies, he ran to the motor car.

"*E matto!*" interjected the bewildered custodian.

Yes, of course he was mad! Stirred by that surge, my anxiety blossomed, and in order to react more aptly, I blamed the atmosphere of my nervous irritation, prescient of extraordinarily grave events.

Heavy clouds, the color of sulfur and antimony, were welling up, completely filling the lurid sky. The cicerone offered me shelter, and even a meal, in his cabin over by the Acropolis. I accepted the opportune diversion; we took the sunken path that cut through the ravine...

Behind us, however, the staccato roar of the horrible automobile went up, and the ferocious blast of an imperative horn drive my companion back, shouting in vain to alert William Klondyke to the danger as he stood on the hood of his machine, moving off at top speed.

"*Piano! Piano! Signore, per Dio!*"

A terror gripped me, uncanny and absurd—not that it would crash on the way but, on the contrary, that it would reach the acropolis, where the eagle was soaring in circles.

It went forward, shuddering, veered across the bridge and launched into an exasperated climb. One final bound projected it on to the acropolis. Anguished, we waited. From a cyclopean wall surged a bust like some rude Hecatoncheire[25] emerging from Chaos. William Klondyke shouldered his rifle. There was a puff of smoke. Convulsively, the eagle spun...and the abrupt detonation echoed in the first rumble of thunder as the bird, beating its wings, fell...toward the man, immobile with his head raised and one hand on his weapon.

I trembled, impelled to run up there, to see...

The custodian was stammering incoherent lamentations; I grabbed him by the shoulder. At a run, in ten minutes, hearts betting in our throats, sweating and breathless, we reached the plateau.

A violet flash of lightning palpitated twice, blazing across the clouds—and a tragic scene overwhelmed us.

William Klondyke was sitting, his elbows on his knees and his chin in his hands, in front of the open door of a hut, hideously contemplating his acolyte, in the process of plucking the eagle. In the shadows, a pot-bellied stove was darting its crown of blue flame at the belly of an aluminum pot.

That cookery horrified me, like the sight of Carib Indians in the process of flaying an infant. The fearful hatred of sacrilege took hold of me. The custodian, strangled by panic terror, begged me to flee, but inertly, open-mouthed and fascinated.

The storm became more violent. Long serpentine ribbons of fire flared up, immense green flashes and violet lightning, dazzling me. The thunder was no longer discontinuous, and loud bombasts burst over the bass rumblings.

---

[25] A kind of giant ostensibly equipped with three hundred hands; the best-known, from available mythological sources, are Briareus and Gyges.

Unsteady, yielding to vertigo, I finally recoiled—but the instantaneous deflagration of blast of blinding sunlight drowned me in its thunderous explosion, a skyfall unleashing the definitive cataclysm of shattered crystal spheres.

Sidereal silence.

Crazy blue phosphenes filled my open eyes...

I glimpsed the hut, still there. I went forward.

The bitter reek of ozone was mingled with the odor of grilling. The gigantic nudity of William Klondyke appeared, charred, his face crushed. Four limp piles of rubber marked the location of the volatilized vehicle. The chauffeur's body was streaming and crackling, lying face down in a flaming pool of alcohol.

Of the Eagle, no sign.

The force and justice of the immortal Gods! The fulgurant power of Zeus, clearly manifest. The authentic Facts, transparent beneath the symbolism of their appearances.

I understood the significance of those things—and that I, an unworthy Barbarian, had witnessed the play of the eternal myths: a Titan struck down by a thunderbolt!

The rain began to fall in huge clattering drops. The storm, its role accomplished, was relaxing, releasing the superfluous clouds in a flood.

I took refuge in the custodian's cabin, where the latter was greedily chewing a wedge of gray bread. And under the roof, peppered by the deluge, I experimented mechanically with the comfort of goat's cheese that tasted like tallow.

When I perceived that the distraught man had lost all memory of the catastrophe, however, when he offered to resume the tour of the ruins, a sudden cowardice drained the life out of me. I was afraid of that breath of contagious dementia, and I fled, over the sandy road, with the obsession of that thunderbolt sent to punish— over and above analysis and examination—blasphemy and sacrilege.

On the main road, the Sciacca diligence caught up with me. Harassed by emotion, I huddled in a corner of the empty rattletrap, gazing absent-mindedly at the familiar Sicilian landscape filing past, the bronze-green Indian fig-trees, the zinc-blue aloes. And the odor of the moist earth came in through the open windows, with the perfume of lemon-trees, varnished by rain.

I was at Castelvetrano in time to catch the express, but its trepidation attacked, without dissolving, the somnambulistic haunting maintained by the red sumptuousness of the Apollinian sunset.

Finally, at Palermo, when I got back to the electric moons of the Via Macqueda, the jovial rumor of the Quattro Canti, the vesperal idlers on the sidewalks and the illuminated luxury of shop windows, I felt sheltered from the Gods.

It was only when I had washed and put on dry clothes, however, and was sitting at a bright table in the polyglot restaurant, from the moment that the waiter leaned his shiny bald head over me in order to point out a certain dish of fried calamari and anchovies on the menu, that I began to think rationally about that bizarre day in the sirocco, and gained a better appreciation of the absurd anachronism of this implausible story.

THE LAST SATYR

After an abrupt climb, blinded by a thicket, I came out into a dazzling clearing on a terrace emerging from the larch-wood that draped the upper slopes of Mont Antennamare. The lucid panorama of the Ionian and Tyrrhenian Seas presented the convexity of their miniature and supremely still fresco.

Beneath the ultramarine of an Angelico sky, the massive Calabras, dappled with snow, overlooked the peacock-blue estuary, where white Messina enclosed a crop of masts in the antique sickle of its harbor.

To the north, the lapis-lazuli sea widened abruptly, speckled with waves as white as a flock of seagulls, and it colossal slope extended as far as the sharp horizon, where the volcanic cones of the Liparian Islands were frayed at the summit by long streaks of vapor. From Cap Tindarsa, opalized in the distance, to the black clotted waves of the nearby forest, the bare mountains of the Pelorid chain stretched in azure-tinted, glaucous and ashen green planes. Their indolent profiles and bucolic flanks eternalized the sovereign landscape of sensual and divine Trinacria.

Mother of peaceful and luminous voluptuousness, another Greece, lasciviously anadyomene and burned by African suns, displaying on its beaches the nonchalant siesta of its rich cities, a luxurious sister of the spiritual Hellas, the sacred domain of animal deities, where their games, a long time after the death of Great Pan, were still exuberant in the liberty of the dionysiac forest... of which I dreamed.

To incite more precise visions, less panoramic syntheses, I sat down on the edge of the rocky terrace, took a copy of Theocritus from my pocket, and started to intone, in Greek, the fifth idyll.[26]

The sonority of the Doric syllables, the familiar spell of the verses, was evoking in the perspectives of my mind the enthusiasm of historic intuitions, when a sound of rustling branches disturbed me.

Brigands?

I started. At that grotesque supposition, however—blunderbusses and pointed hats—I shrugged my shoulders.

"Bah! Some animal."

And I resumed, more attentively than before, rhythmically intoning the verses, which lit up in evanescent imagery.

The noise was indubitable this time—the patter of footsteps, brisk and cautious.

I turned round.

A satyr!

More powerful than astonishment, an immeasurable curiosity kept me silent. I stared at the fabulous capriped who was contemplating me, with a suspicious and stupid expression, leaning on a staff.

Old age, the decrepitude of millennia, weighed down upon that survivor of a semi-divine race, the alert

---

[26] The poem by Theocritus, the great pioneer of Greek bucolic poetry, which is nowadays known as "Idyll V" features a song contest between the goatherd Comatas and a young shepherd, Lacon, the latter having accused the former of stealing his flute.

and petulant youth of which is commemorated in the marbles of our museums. Extending from his thin goat-like thighs, abundant red hair had invaded his torso and his overly long arms; a gray mane, from which projected chipped horns and scarred ears, hung in wisps over the snub-nosed face, in which a bestial degeneracy had added flesh to the once-anthropoid character—and in the atonal eyes with horizontal pupils there was a vague, confused sadness, the impotent horror of feeling the remaining drops of his ancient divinity drying up in his immortal veins.

We remained mute. To maintain a front, I finally slipped the Theocritus into my jacket pocket.

At that gesture, however, a grimace of infantile dolor twisted the thick slack lips of the silenus.

"No, no Signor! *Ancora!*" he stammered, putting his hairy fingers together and stamping his worn-out hooves.

I obliged his whim, and resumed declaiming the alternate replies of Comatas and Lacon,

A savage bleat cut off the tenth verse. The silenus sobbed, his neck retracted, rolling the green sclerotics of his upturned eyes, whose tears were matting the dense hair of his white beard.

The distraught brute's desolation wrung my heart. I drew closer to the poor lame god and patted him on the shoulder amicably.

He wiped his eyes with the back of his hand and sniffed loudly. An effort of intelligence contracted his pupils, and, with a crooked smile, he spoke, mingling Sicilian and Greek, with pauses and long amnesiac stutters, searching for words.

"Listen, stranger. Your voice has woken me up. I had almost lost my soul, and, as you see, I no longer

214

know the language of my youth. It's my youth that you're reading there—my divine youth—for I'm old, as you see! Old! Old!"

He leaned his chin to his hands, folded over the end of his stick, and he looked at me avidly, with the eyes of a whipped dog, not knowing how to untangle the confusion of his thoughts, knotted by the centuries.

I encouraged him to go on.

Then, assuring his gaze as to my sympathetic attention, he continued.

"Stranger, I shall try to tell you, for you are good, and in spite of your resemblance to the barbarians, the bearers of green umbrellas, who sometimes climb up here, perhaps you are a god. Perhaps you're immortal too?

"Oh, if you knew for how many centuries I have found no one who understands! The people of the region flee at my approach, or throw stones at me. Sometimes, when night falls, I take the risk of going to the farms; the servants mistake me for a smuggler and give me bread and cheese. But if they perceive my horns or touch my hair, they cry: 'To the devil!' and chase me away with pitchforks, and set the dogs on my hooves. I've almost been devoured ten times over. Everyone has forgotten the gods...

"Besides which, the gods have deserted Trinacria, or have fallen into ambushes. I believe there are still nymphs, in the town, but I dare not go there; it's an abode of unknown and terrible perils.

"So I remain a miserable, hunted wanderer in the mountains, alone—always alone. I have to spend long, often fruitless, nights lying in cactus hedges with thorns sharper than those of desire, watching out, on the edges of villages, for some peasant woman to pass by..."

215

He broke off, and, in a lower voice, as if for a shameful confidence: "Even that, that last furtive joy, escapes me—for a secret disease is corroding me, a divine malady, which came upon me after a young shepherd invited me into his cabin one winter night..."

And parting his hair bashfully, he showed me his breast and thighs, encrusted with coppery scabs.

"Do you think I can be cured?" he asked, humbly.

"In the town," I said, "there are savant therapies."

"Alas, this disease is sapping the strength that old age had left me. Soon, there will be no pleasure left to me but playing this flute, brought from the town by an obliging goatherd. He even taught me some tunes. Would you like to hear them?"

"Certainly," I acquiesced.

The fellow untangled from his breast, where it hung on a piece of dirty and twisted a blue ribbon, a thirteen-sou flute, which he put to his mouth with an assured modesty.

Abomination. "Viens, Poupoule," trembled its hideous refrain, followed by the Cake-Walk, and it was necessary for me to submit to "Tarara-boom-de-ay" before being able to stop the sinister performance, which the poor fallen god whistled frenziedly through his dented tin-plate tube.

"Good, good—have a rest!" I finally exclaimed.

The unfortunate was choking, his lips slate-colored by starvation.

"You're thirsty. Come on, drink!" And I handed him a capacious flask full of a dynamogenic mixture of rum, caffeine and cola.

He swallowed a redoubtable dose. His eyelids fluttered ad his eyes lit up. And, inflating his nostrils in a broad bestial and silly smile, he asked: "Is it Nectar?"

"Almost," I said. "Do you feel better?"

Making no reply, he picked up his stick—and, with his spine arched, his hams firm, his hooves rattling on the rock—which sounded hollow—he advanced to a point of the terrace overhanging the vertiginous wooded slope. There sticking his chest out, a sovereign silhouette against the sky, whose light added a gold plush to his ruddy pilosity, with a vigorous sling-shot action, he hurled the staff of his old age, no longer necessary, recklessly into the abyss

"Hee-ah!" he grunted, wildly, brandishing his fits toward the light. "Hee-ah!" And this thorax swelled, creaking like new leather. "Hee-ah!"

He turned toward me, his expression tumultuous, his lips gleaming, the color of crushed myrtle.

"Yes, Friend, you are a god! Give me the Nectar again!"

He grabbed the flask and gulped a large mouthful; then, snatching the tinplate flute from around his neck, he sent it flying, blue ribbon and all, over his shoulder.

"I remember. I'll make a syrinx. You'll see. How did I forget?"

He was speaking Greek now, in a deep and musical, slightly hoarse voice.

"Let's go!" And he dragged me away, by a path that led away from the end of the terrace, rapidly, imperatively and irresistibly.

We ran over the mountainsides, through the forest. Here and there, lukewarm blue holes cleaved the coolness of the foliage. Then, in the semi-obscurity of tunnels of verdure, a green fluorescence illuminated my companion's pupils. Every time they settled upon me, a spasm of vigor lifted me up; we galloped, frenetically, through the death-traps of that absurd path; we could, by

Hercules, have bounded over the tops of the larches and pines.

"You see! I remember. It was before the subversion of the luminous order of things. It was before the stupid Arabs, before the Christians, disparagers of life—in the times that simply were. In the torrid radiance of ancient Sicily, I was a god. In the days of the north wind, drunk on raw sunlight and the heady gusts, I looked down on the waves of the mountains. Their green and voluptuous soul filtered through all the pores of my soul—naked then, and beautiful!—and flowed in my young arteries. The universal heart beat in my breast. Listen. In the long summer nights, enraptured by the sirocco, I penetrated the essence of the Panic force. Hee-ah! I know again. I'll tell you—on the syrinx."

He fell silent, his hands clutching his pectoral muscles, his head tilted back in the rut of a dionysiac joy, savoring the inexpressible tumult of his enthusiasm, which was induced in me by contagion—me, the resuscitator of a god!

He went on. His somnambulistic feet kicked up pebbles, which rebounded from precipices. His mane became supple and aerated; his fleece, unmated now, floated like a garment, to the rhythm of his brisk gait, like a rapid dance led by interior harmonies.

We were going down, though. A valley appeared enclosed by undulating crests and girdled with umbrella-pines—and the great bottle-green sloops of the foothills extended down below in terraces of olive-trees, all the way to the red roof of a farmhouse.

Further way, in another sterile ravine, where the mountain was split by hectic landslides, the white threads of the highway appeared in the background. The

minuscule bells of an animal flock were tinkling, musical festoons in the silence.

The satyr's ears were pricked, his nostrils flared. He
was whistling through his incisors and he seized me by
the shoulders, pointing downwards with his hairy index-
finger.

"The goats! Do you see them? On the bare back of
the mountain, the black goats, like lice."

His breath jerky, trotting nimbly along the granite
spur, he drew me toward the herd, which was grazing the
herbage of the impracticable slopes near a bend in the
path.

Abruptly, the capriped let go of me and raced over
the landslides with exorbitant bounds. The little goatherd, barefoot and clad in goatskin trousers, started to
flee with vain agility, from the satyr's lightning pur-
suit—but the dog did not flinch, and the goats, chewing
the grass that was dangling in the beards, watched the
aegipan pass by placidly. He disappeared behind a mass
of rocks, where his victim had just taken refuge.

I galloped around the long bend in the road, breathlessly, anguished by the drama that was being perpetrat-
ed behind the hillock, from which the triumphant ono-
matopoeias of incoherent hymns soon emerged.

Five minutes later, instead of a catastrophe, I was
amazed to find a bucolic scene: on the knees of the
capriped, the little goatherd, still red-faced from running,
was fondling with his beard, chattering away, tugging
the two soft and downy appendages at the goatlike
neck—and the enraptured, ticklish god burst out laughing, in the pose of the drunken satyr of Pompeii...

But the child, frightened by the sight of me, suddenly, ran off.

Irritated by my stupid anxiety, I called out to the old aegipan: "Tell me, at least…"

"On the syrinx!" he cried. "On the syrinx! Come on!"

Ten paces further on, he pulled up a bunch of reeds with a single thrust, of which he chose the best ones. I handed him my penknife, and, while walking along, he shaped his pipes, the sonority which he tested as he went.

Then he fixed me with an ironic stare, sniggering in my face, brazenly. "He wasn't afraid of me, you know. He recognized me. You'll see, god-of-the-nectar: I'll tell you—on the syrinx. Eah! I'm still a god! From Drepane to Syracuse, Trinacria was ours. The country folk brought us offerings, and invoked us in their songs.

"On the sloping paths, in the rounded shadows of the umbrella-pines, I sat down with the young shepherds. I taught them new tunes on the flute; and I leaned over, running my fingers through their hair, which had the scent of fresh-cut grass, to see their red lips sliding over the mouthpiece of the pipes, which sometimes cut them and bloodied them with little salty droplets.

"In the long torrid middays of the late summer, when the landscapes quivered fluidly, lying in ambush beside the roads, I waited for the girls coming back from taking drinking-water to the harvesters—and in the ardent silence of the siesta, I caused the shrill cry of transfixed virginities to spurt forth.

"I lay in wait in the green daylight of the forests, at the time when the dainty hamadryads poked their heads out of the trees, cautiously parting their living sheaths of bark and leaping to the ground, supple green nudities. They too were mine.

"And the nymphs, as white and cool as the flesh of nenuphar lilies, who lay back in silence, their eyes closed, on the damp grass, cooing softly, like the gurgling murmur of the nearby stream...and then, alone, I leaned over the spring, to stick out my tongue at my reflection, still grimacing at their dive.

"I went along the edges of forests, sat down beside the sea at sunset, and combed the long hair of my thighs with my fingers, while night fell, sparkling with stars—until the lunar hours of the sirens.

"The sirens are all blue—do you know that? It's swathed in a nacreous squamous fur that they frolic with the fat tritons with lobsters' tails. Poor tritons! But it's naked, in their true azure bodies, that they love one another two by two, the sirens, in moonlit grottoes. Eah! I violated two sirens, stark naked, before the phosphorescent sea, on one equinoctial night.

"I'll tell you, on the syrinx..."

All of a sudden, he asked: "Have you any wax?"

"We can buy glue in the town, when we go to see the doctor."

A sudden terror immobilized him.

"No, no! Not the town! I'm cured!"

"As you wish. We'll ask for some wax at a farm."

Her excitement was fading away, however; his features crumpled, sweat moistening the thick wrinkles of his forehead. He tottered.

"You're tired," I said. "Have a rest."

The poor god sat down on a patch of pebbles. He crossed his legs and looked at his worn hooves with a sad smile. "What do you think? Do I need to have shoes fitted?"

His head swayed like those of people dozing in a railway carriage. I went to support him, but he stood up, abruptly tensed with grim resolution.

"The Nectar!"

This time, he drank the elixir to the last drop, and then threw the flask into a cactus hedge.

"Now, I'll tell you..."

Feverishly adjusting his syrinx, he tried it out—but for want of wax, the pipes came apart.

"So be it, god-of-the-nectar—let's go into the town."

We set off again. He walked with his neck stiff, his head held high, in a somber serenity, beneath the formidable weight of imminent Destiny. His voluble speech confused fragmentary tales, sometimes fulgurating with wild and grotesque visions.

"I was young and agile! I had races with the centaurs through the forests—centaur dung, mixed with pebbles, bouncing, like slingshots of the trunks of holm-oaks and carobs; the centaurs, without stopping, launched their arrows at the red eye of the sun, which peeped, polyphemically, between the eyelids of horizontal clouds—and the gallops of our dionysiac excursions ran all over Trinacria, from one sea to the other.

"I was young, and handsome! The fauns and the sileni..."

He became excited, in his stories in which ancient liberty was doubled by that of a satyr—and seeing him, his eyes crazed, dancing and whinnying hysterically, I began to dread the approach of the outskirts of the town, the first houses of which were coming into view.

Evidently, the half-liter of caffeine, rum and cola ingested by the god was putting too much strain on his integral youthfulness, and it was necessary, before anything else, to obtain some antidote from a pharmacist.

I buttoned my own overcoat over my companion's rhedibitory indecency.[27]

"To go into the town," I breathed, and I completed the plausible accoutrement—for a foreigner—with a pocket cap.

We passed through the customs post. The tax-collectors smiled benevolently at the "forester," whom they assumed to be an eccentric Englishman.

I pushed him into a deserted street, drawing him along rapidly.

Suddenly, though, a little girl in a red skirt and corset came around a corner with a bouquet of roses in her hand.

"*Un soldo, Signor, un soldo.*"

It was the catastrophe.

My satyr stopped dead and stopped in front of the little girl, who smiled at him. Then, suddenly, with an "Eah!" of frantic joy, he launched himself forward, snatching the bouquet in his teeth and the terrified girl in both arms.

I ran forward. He bit me, spitting out the roses, struggling—and, intoxicated, furious and epileptic, he escaped, carrying off the little girl, who was screaming loudly.

While, horrified, I left the implausible rape to take its course in the cowardly god's flight, dionysiac in spite of everything, two carabinieris emerged from a side-street, whose skillful trip brought the capriped down.

---

[27] Rhedibitory (*rhedibitoire* in French) means "demanding a refund," usually because a product is defective; its use here is eccentrically metaphorical.

It did not take long thereafter. The two avengers of outraged morality disengaged the weeping child and put the handcuffs on her odious abductor. He, heart-broken, decrepit, empty, fallen from the divine centuries—older than tobacco!—looked at me, stupidly and unreproachfully, and looked at the pipes of his syrinx, imperfect forever, scattered on the ground.

And, a ridiculous silhouette, with his flaccid overcoat and the cap dancing on his horns, my poor benighted satyr disappeared, while I repeated to myself the inept, but this time integral, sentence that would record his epitaph the following day, in the local newspapers: "Finally, the filthy satyr was taken to the police station."

MESSALINA

It was necessary for me to stay overnight in Toulon in order to catch, at seven o'clock in the morning, the wretched little steam train that serves Porquerolles and Port-Cros—the Îles d'Or that I wanted to see again, under the glorious midsummer sun, this time.

In the meantime, my evening started badly, on a terrace overlooking the port. The excessively beautiful sunset, over the harbor bristling with masts, the gypsy violins, the white-clad quasi-exotic crowd, had steeped me in the particular melancholy of idle hours while traveling—and in the sparse poetry of the dusk, evocative of ardent colonial serenities, I felt very far away, very much alone and out of place, before my aperitif.

I had Loti in my soul, and Farrère too.[28] Repelled by the attractions of the local casino or the cinemas, rendered blasé by the Old Port of Marseilles with regard to the picturesque qualities of warm streets, I yearned for impossible joys. I was ambitious to visit an opium den—rather foolishly, for I knew that that world was closed and inaccessible. To get into one without an introduction was a great deal more difficult than, for instance, hailing a seemingly sympathetic passer-by to engage him in conversation.

---

[28] Pierre Loti and "Claude Farrère" (Charles Bargone) were both famous for novels set in exotic locations. Varlet would also have known Farrère as the author of the celebratory *Fumée d'Opium* (1904; tr. as *Black Opium*) and several notable ventures in *roman scientifique*.

I was beginning to regret bitterly that the harsh certainty of wariness with regard to deception obliges civilized folk to such suspicion—and that the most intelligent are the most untouchable—when a woman brushed past me, in a subtle whiff of ether, and sat down at a table a little further away.

Pooh! A little ether-addicted whore—what was marvelous about that? Would she be any less stupid than her peers?

No matter; she interested me in spite of myself. Of the slender and sensitive type, predestined for delicate tastes, a pretty trinket to look at and doubtless also to handle, the fashionable white outfit brightened the youthful grace of her features and emphasized the charming down of her upper lip. The little whore wasn't like all the rest.

Anyway, her or another—just as long as I didn't feel so alone, in the voluptuousness of the all-too-lovely evening. A brief exchange of glances confirmed that she was free, that I didn't displease her—and, still in accordance with contradictory civilized custom, I moved to her table. She welcomed me with simplicity and I immediately put her at her ease, on the footing of discreet and natural familiarity that we men so gladly grant ourselves with "women of that sort."

I thus avoided pretentious affectations, the habitual counter to masculine arrogance. She did not even play the Parisienne. Her name was Odette, she was from a good Corsican family, and there was even a small inheritance waiting for her back there. But how could she raise the money for the journey? All her income went on clothes. So she liked "partying"? No, certainly not; she would have preferred something else—to set herself up as a milliner, for example—for the men were often so cruel and brutal. Drinking, moreover, scarcely suited her "constitution." "And that's bad, in our profession!" The slightest sleep-deprivation made her ill. Drugs? Oh, yes. A single pipe of opium, accepted on a dare, had made her sleep for forty-eight hours solid. Ether she sniffed occasionally from a flask, nothing much, "to settle her stomach"—and her "friend" complained, claiming that it made him ill.

Her voice was not unpleasant, but her torrential Corsican accent was combined with a barbaric, almost negro, syntax of words bristling with harsh dissonances. Such a contrast with her external appearance of a precious trinket, her subtle and refined animal lust, wrung my heart. Except that the naïve perfume of that savagery, enveloping the abject prejudices of her caste, slightly redeemed the lack of culture of her words and her stupidity.

A little port had got her three-quarters drunk, and I hoped for less platitudinous confidences when I took her to dinner.

There again, however, I was disappointed. Her curiosity and her pleasures were paltry or vulgar. All reading was a matter of indifference to her, except for miscellaneous facts and Fantômas, whose craziest and most inept adventures she related to me religiously. She had a horror of travel, which broke her habitual routine. About a sojourn in Tunis she was only able to tell me how repellent she found the city—that vision of the Thousand-and-One Nights!—so dirty and so treacherous for her high heels.

"Tunis, you see, is like Marseilles, except that the French there don't have any money. The Arabs will give you as many *douros* as you want and voilà! But they want everything for it, and that doesn't suit me. I had a friend who had a session with them; well, you wouldn't believe it, but she spilled her guts. I got back to Toulon right away!"

And she always came back to her story, probably apocryphal, of an inheritance in Corsica, where she dreamed of going back to get married—the people back there thought she was "in service"—and live her bourgeois ideal of a simple, tranquil life...

At ten o'clock, to avoid the dangerous "show" chapter, I made a direct allusion to the ultimate goal of our acquaintance, and agreed without haggling the first price quoted, while adding the sacramental promise: "I'll be very nice, you'll see!"

In the room at the station hotel, where I had left my suitcase, there was the eternal courtesan scene. The girl, having judged me to be a good fellow, if not a mug, didn't play up. She meekly allowed herself to be undressed, and, pleased to see me appreciating the quality of her frills, declared that I "wasn't that ham-fisted, for a man."

Entirely given over to the pleasure of handling her delicate underclothes and unveiling, beneath of moss of lace, youthful skin and pretty slender limbs, I gradually forgot my rancor, and the exact situation.

She was still in her chemise, standing amid her corolla of striped lingerie, gently massaging the imprints of her corset, when the professional trigger clicked,

"Give me my little present first."

Clumsy, spoiling the effect like that! No more illusion possible; you're just a wretched prostitute, to come out with that vile remark! Do you see in me the brutal coarseness of those who've "never paid a woman"? Will I, like them, take foul advantage of the law that leaves you without recourse, in view of our obscene pact, against the possibility of my refusing to pay and robbing you of a wage as legitimate in my eyes as paying for my beer of my coffee?

You're inflicting the ridicule upon me of going in my shirt-tails to rummage in the pocket of my trousers. And that further grievance is added to the disappointment of your stupidity. Oh, you really are all the same! No flair, no delicacy. Not one who knows her trade: a good merchant of illusions, making the most of her trashy goods, putting some grace into the flourish of spreading her legs and the rush of debauchery. Even if masculine boorishness justifies your surly sabotage to some extent, isn't it more than adequately paid for by the bitterly bargained louis?

Here, little imbecile, here it is, your louis! Bite it— it's good. And I'm buying a pig in a poke.

But you know only too well that there's no point in straining yourself; you know that an approximative botch of erotic functions will end, exactly like finely finished work, in the disgust of "animal triste" and the hasty decampment of the customer!

The girl had stuck her purse in her stocking, between the knee and the heel. But I forgot to take delivery. She was the one who had to wake me up from that incomprehensible whimsy, to play my ulterior role.

Passive, resigned, without even seeking to hide her indifference, she submitted to the task.

Afterwards, I expected the customary swindle. Doubtless she'd want to leave, after her hasty ablutions, if I didn't add a little supplement to the tariff already agreed, the whole night included. For she was only thinking, during the mechanical gestures, of the fabulous opportunity that might be passing by on the boulevard, which Lucie Ether or the little Mandarine whispers to her.[29]

Oh, I wouldn't have kept her! But with all her gaucherie and lack of awareness, she was as good as her word and, without hesitation, installed herself for the night.

In the secret hope of avoiding, with epidermal contact, the reiteration of "work," she put on her chemise "because of the cold"—it's roasting, and no breeze is coming in through the open window—and then, wrapped up at the back of the bed, against the wall, with her hair loose on the pillow, she became motionless.

I was alone, bitter and ironic, next to that sleeping flesh. My eyes wearied of following the shadows of the plane-trees on the ceiling cast by the street-lights in the square; the last sounds of footsteps died away, and nothing any longer remained to me in the silence but the whistling flight of swallows and the monotonous note of a cricket.

The whistle, the metallic rattle and the screeching brakes of an express train coming into the station woke me up. The locomotive came to a halt, wheezing in the darkness. Then there was the rumor of a crowd; talking loudly and walking briskly, the travelers were shaking themselves and dispersing; fiacres raced along the avenue.

The luminous dial of the station clock marked two o'clock. Beside me, the girl was still asleep. The black wisps of her hair partly hid her pale, crumpled, aged

---

[29] Lucie Ether and Mandarine are characters in Claude Farrère's novel *Les Petites alliées* (1910), whose adventures include a visit to an opium den.

child-like face, her nose pinched by a churlish existential weariness. She slept, her breath imperceptible, as if dead.

The door of the hotel banged; new arrivals climbed the stairs, invading the next room, where the bustle of unpacking began.

Malignity of fate! Why that particular room, with the hotel three-quarters empty? With that ridiculously sonorous partition wall, the traditional carelessness of my neighbors and their bumbling, I was in for an hour of enforced sleeplessness. What vestimentary complications can these people have to disentangle? What odious mania is driving them to prance back and forth instead of going to bed?

My only recourse was to employ the pastime that I had to hand.

Discreetly, in order not to demand my due, and to leave the game some grace, I attempted to stir that bestial and exhausted sleep, habitual in whores, who seem to be sleeping off the aftermath of an orgy. My caress explored the delicate leg, the boyish hip...

First she grunted, recoiling in annoyance; then professional instinct relaxed her muscles and disposed her submissive flesh for "work"—still asleep, arms extended, eyebrows furrowed.

Pooh! What insipid pleasure can be extracted from such passivity?

I abandoned the enterprise.

Besides, what was being said next door was taking a piquant turn, and my new neighbors, now vituperative, were about to take responsibility for my diversion.

"A second pillow, my girl! You can see, however, that there are two of us! Ah! And then you'll bring me a big, big jug of hot water—very, very hot!"

"Yes, Madame."

The imperative voice, lush and spicily sonorous, combined with a discreet Provençal accent and a slightly forced distinction, evoked for me a buxom and lascivious hussy, an arrogant hetaira.

As for her partner, the distracted monosyllables with which he greeted her passionate wheedling, until the chambermaid's return, gave me no clue as to is identity. In fact, were the bizarre acoustics that were conveying the slightest words to me so clearly no coming through some orifice?

I took careful stock of the partition.

In the sealed-up communicating door, a luminous point revealed the classic drilled hole. I looked through it, but could only see a black straw boater and a stupid dust-cover, hanging in the wardrobe. Since some traveler in a roguish mood had bored the eyehole, the bed had doubtless been moved.

Too bad; my imagination would supply the gesture and attitudes.

The expert courtesan—for the special terms of her ardor immediately set aside the hypothesis of a honeymoon voyage of a habituated couple, or even adultery—increased her efforts, less concern to arm herself up than to defrost her sulky lover.

The ass! Or, rather, what grave worries were absorbing him? His clipped and weary voice suggested a inveterate roué—but not aged, though, for the other praised in turn his beautiful bead, his beautiful arms, his beautiful chest, his "Herculean muscles." Yes...one of those semi-foreign semi-crooked lady-killers who hang around Nice and Monte Carlo, cleaned out by the green baize, thinking more about the failure of his martingale than the charms of his conquest.

The attraction of his physique compensated the latter for the absent gold; even after the delivery of the "big, big jug of hot water—very, very hot" had brought the psychological moment of the "little present," she didn't make the slightest allusion to it.

An affair of the heart, then? The whims of women! The irony of fate! To couple that boiling courtesan with a morose imbecile, a worthy pendant to the little brat who had thwarted me! While I, without any pretence to the contours of a Farnese torso,[30] would have given such a fine response to the impetuosity of the beauty, who was parading he glorious eroticism before an indifferent gaze there behind the partition!

Like me, she loved life, she knew the great game of Love—she didn't haggle!

And she was literate too! Her crude words—technical terms, after all—were relieved by allusions and images of whose refined condiment the vulgar minds of the meretricious were invariably unaware.

"You're my beautiful male," she proclaimed. "You're my magnificent king, my god, my Eros. No, listen: tonight, I want to be your she-wolf, your Messalina. The ardors of lust are devouring me, the desire to make love to you!"

A little pomposity, perhaps, a little exaggeration in the note, but what fire, what ingenuousness! I was completely carried away.

And her palms slapped her firm and opulent breasts, which she extended, their nipples erect, toward the man.

He was annoying me, that one! Doubtless propped up on the pillow, smoking a last cigarette, he uttered

---

[30] The Palazzo Farnese in Rome contains Annibale Carracci's cycle of frescos *The Loves of the Gods*.

vaguely approving grunts between puff. Did he understand the rare beauty of the spectacle? Did he appreciate the inestimable luck of possessing a *true* courtesan, one in ten thousand?

"I'm your Messalina, you bacchante, your maenad, your lustful slave. Oh, take me, embrace me, ravish me in the heavens of ecstasy!"

The last rustle of lingerie. A door grates, is wedged by a chair; the mirror-fronted wardrobe doubles the spectacle of their nudity for them, and the bed groans under the precious burden of indecency.

"See what a beautiful couple we make! See the wild harmony of your virile flesh combined with my pale complexion! Oh, you're my beautiful male. What joy you'll give me with your admirable member! And me! You see these beautiful breasts, you see this beautiful bottom, this superb bottom? They're yours, entirely yours; they're instruments devoted to your pleasure. Take everything!"

Sacred woman! Her brio and her enthusiasm were provoking my imagination t the point that being able to see the scene would, I believed, have told me nothing.

The frescoes of the Pompeiian brothel, those in the Secret Museum of Naples, were revived in my memory, and reconstituted the tableau of that sister of Lais and Phryné...

What triumphs could she not claim in the world of gallantry! Which of the fashionable professional beauties possessed such an enthralling mastery?

Bedclothes bitten, fingernails digging into flesh, hair thrown backward with an abrupt thrust of the head—and there was the click of colliding teeth, the impetuous gallop, the supreme gasp...and immobility.

I witnessed all that without missing a single detail, lying on the bed next to my stupid sleeper.

A cool draught flowed in through the wide window, from the blue and nuptial night, in which the solitary cricket accompanied the whistling of the tireless swallows.

While the wild maenad and her "beautiful male" rested, amid the moistness of love, I ruminated the desire to know the marvelous artiste who had put on that unforgettable performance for me. And I lay there for a long time following the progress of the constellations in the sliver of sky between the houses and the station, where a rocky peak was silhouetted, Hellenically.

The glimmer of the street-lights melted into the first light of dawn; the stars disappeared; the mountain was clouded in pink. The first cicadas began clicking, and my fever was numbed momentarily by the multiple titillations of their solar rhythm.

A coming-and-going in the next room reassembled my consciousness. The station came to life; footsteps and voices in the square dominated the confused awakening of the city, beneath the already-warm light. Just then the waiter knocked, following my instructions.

"Half past five!"

Should I board the train at seven for the Îles d'Or?

No! Only one thing as important, at present: to see the beautiful "Messalina," perhaps to speak to her—who could tell?—to conquer her; to make her deploy her talents for me, alone...recompensed, to be sure; I wouldn't stint. And, dressing hurriedly, I kept track of every gesture of the others, behind the wall, as they got ready to leave.

Singular. The amorous blandishments had ceased. The lush and spicily sonorous voice that had celebrated the furious obscenity a little while ago, was no longer uttering anything but everyday banalities. In a bad mood this morning, she was making bittersweet comments to the "beautiful male." As for him, he was a different man—loquacious, urgent, more submissive than was reasonable...stupid. His "Yes, my love" and "Here you are, my beauty" were more those of a placid bourgeois than a fatal individual, the careless foreigner that I had reconstituted.

But I was not about to knock my goddess off her pedestal for the sake of quibbles. They were taking the seven-ten to Bandol, where they would be staying. Enough of the Îles d'Or! A free traveler, I would follow them. I would go to Bandol; I would go to the devil, for Her!

Suddenly, my ex-bed-companion moved. Honestly, I had forgotten all about her! Tangled in the sheet, she was still asleep. Her white stockings, which she had kept on, had a lump between the ankle and the knee, designating the purse. Adieu, little brute!

They were ready. Suitcase in hand, standing by the partly-open door, as excited as a student on the lookout for his first mistress, I waited.

One more bag to pack, apparently. Finally, the "beautiful male" declared: "I'll go down first to order the chocolates."

An unexpected stroke of luck! The blot clicked in its socket; the handle turned. Heavy footsteps went along the landing, and down the stairs...

I saw a round back, a yellow valise and the black straw boater disappearing.

She was alone! And her door was still open!

I went forward, throwing all my chips into the pot, trusting to my inspiration, in approaching the woman, equally prepared for lyricism or conquering brutality.

Frightful luck!

She was at least fifty, smoke-preserved, with a severe expression. Coarse acned features; a double chin dotted with long grey hairs, her neck awkwardly gathered into a whalebone chemisette. She was sitting on the edge of the bed stuffing a moleskin bag; her pudgy hands, one of whose fingers was encrusted with a wedding-ring, emerged from black silk sleeves, and her similar dress compressed a gelatinous mass of ugly fat. Shapeless behind, breasts overflowing the receptacles of the corset. Jewelry in imitation jet, including a portrait-brooch, completed that paragon of womanhood, of odious housewifery, of shrewish and intransigent Virtue.

I stood there open-mouthed, as before a conjuror, hypnotized by the convexity of her tinted glasses, which she had fixed on me. An instantaneous sadistic desire ran through me, to rush at her, knock her down, pull up her skirts to expose that "beautiful bottom" and apply a magisterial kick thereto, avenging my deceived illusions, my concupiscent fever...

Suddenly standing up in the trappings of her threatened virtue, however, she overwhelmed me with a majestic: "Lecher!" and shut the door in my face.

I ran down the stairs with spasms of crazed laughter and tears of rage, to find the black boater that I had seen up above sitting in the restaurant in front of two empty cups, buttering his croissants with and unsteady knife.

He was reminiscent of a pet white rat, a poor tailless rat: minuscule eyes with puffy eyelids, one shoulder lower than the other, his meager skeleton parceled up in a schoolmaster's overcoat.

My heart failed me on hearing the footsteps of "Messalina" coming downstairs. I settled my bill, grabbed my suitcase, and ran to the harbor tram, which moved off, grating on a curve in the rails, amid the implacable hosannas of cicadas celebrating the sun of Love.

SF & FANTASY

Henri Allorge. *The Great Cataclysm*
Guy d'Armen. *Doc Ardan: The City of Gold and Lepers*
G.-J. Arnaud. *The Ice Company*
Charles Asselineau. *The Double Life*
Cyprien Bérard. *The Vampire Lord Ruthwen*
Aloysius Bertrand. *Gaspard de la Nuit*
Richard Bessière. *The Gardens of the Apocalypse*
Albert Bleunard. *Ever Smaller*
Félix Bodin. *The Novel of the Future*
Alphonse Brown. *City of Glass*
André Caroff. *The Terror of Madame Atomos; Miss Atomos; The Return of Madame Atomos; The Mistake of Madame Atomos; The Monsters of Madame Atomos; The Revenge of Madame Atomos*
Félicien Champsaur. *The Human Arrow; Ouha*
Didier de Chousy. *Ignis*
Captain Danrit. *Undersea Odyssey*
C. I. Defontenay. *Star (Psi Cassiopeia)*
Charles Derennes. *The People of the Pole*
Georges Dodds (anthologist). *The Missing Link*
Harry Dickson. *The Heir of Dracula*
Jules Dornay. *Lord Ruthven Begins*
Alfred Driou. *The Adventures of a Parisian Aeronaut*
Sâr Dubnotal *vs. Jack the Ripper*
Alexandre Dumas. *The Return of Lord Ruthven*
Renée Dunan. *Baal*
J.-C. Dunyach. *The Night Orchid; The Thieves of Silence*
Henri Duvernois. *The Man Who Found Himself*
Achille Eyraud. *Voyage to Venus*
Henri Falk. *The Age of Lead*
Paul Féval. *Anne of the Isles; Knightshade; Revenants; Vampire City; The Vampire Countess; The Wandering Jew's Daughter*
Paul Féval, *fils. Felifax, the Tiger-Man*
Charles de Fieux. *Lamékis*
Arnould Galopin. *Doctor Omega; Doctor Omega & The Shadowmen*
Léon Gozlan. *The Vampire of the Val-de-Grâce*
G.L. Gick. *Harry Dickson and the Werewolf of Rutherford Grange*
Edmond Haraucourt. *Illusions of Immortality*

Nathalie Henneberg. *The Green Gods*
V. Hugo, P. Foucher & P. Meurice. *The Hunchback of Notre-Dame*
Michel Jeury. *Chronolysis*
Gustave Kahn. *The Tale of Gold and Silence*
Gérard Klein. *The Mote in Time's Eye*
Louis-Guillaume de La Follie. *The Unpretentious Philosopher*
Jean de La Hire. *Enter the Nyctalope; The Nyctalope on Mars; The
Nyctalope vs. Lucifer; The Nyctalope Steps In; Night of the Nyctalope*
Etienne-Léon de Lamothe-Langon. *The Virgin Vampire*
André Laurie. *Spiridon*
Gabriel de Lautrec. *The Vengeance of the Oval Portrait*
Alain le Drimeur. *The Future City*
Georges Le Faure & Henri de Graffigny. *The Extraordinary Adven-
tures of a Russian Scientist Across the Solar System* (2 vols.)
Gustave Le Rouge. *The Vampires of Mars The Dominion of the
World* (w/Gustave Guitton) (4 vols.)
Jules Lermina. *Mysteryville; Panic in Paris; To-Ho and the Gold
Destroyers; The Secret of Zippelius*
Jean-Marc & Randy Lofficier. *Edgar Allan Poe on Mars; The Katri-
na Protocol; Pacifica; Robonocchio; Tales of the Shadowmen 1-9*
Xavier Mauméjean. *The League of Heroes*
Joseph Méry. *The Tower of Destiny*
Hippolyte Mettais. *The Year 5865*
Louise Michel. *The Human Microbes; The New World*
José Moselli. *Illa's End*
John-Antoine Nau. *Enemy Force*
Marie Nizet. *Captain Vampire*
C. Nodier, A. Beraud & Toussaint-Merle. *Frankenstein*
Henri de Parville. *An Inhabitant of the Planet Mars*
Gaston de Pawlowski. *Journey to the Land of the 4th Dimension*
Georges Pellerin. *The World in 2000 Years*
Ernest Pérochon. *The Frenetic People*
Pierre Pelot. *The Child Who Walked on the Sky*
J. Polidori, C. Nodier, E. Scribe. *Lord Ruthven the Vampire*
P.-A. Ponson du Terrail. *The Vampire and the Devil's Son*
Henri de Régnier. *A Surfeit of Mirrors*
Maurice Renard. *The Blue Peril; Doctor Lerne; The Doctored Man;
A Man Among the Microbes; The Master of Light*
Jean Richepin. *The Wing*
Albert Robida. *The Adventures of Saturnin Farandoul; The Clock of
the Centuries; Chalet in the Sky*

J.-H. Rosny Aîné. *Helgvor of the Blue River; The Givreuse Enigma; The Mysterious Force; The Navigators of Space; Vamireh; The World of the Variants; The Young Vampire*
Marcel Rouff. *Journey to the Inverted World*
Han Ryner. *The Superhumans*
Brian Stableford. *The New Faust at the Tragicomique; The Empire of the Necromancers (The Shadow of Frankenstein; Frankenstein and the Vampire Countess; Frankenstein in London); Sherlock Holmes & The Vampires of Eternity; The Stones of Camelot; The Wayward Muse.* (anthologist) *The Germans on Venus; News from the Moon; The Supreme Progress; The World Above the World; Nemoville; Investigations of the Future*
Jacques Spitz. *The Eye of Purgatory*
Kurt Steiner. *Ortog*
Eugène Thébault. *Radio-Terror*
C.-F. Tiphaigne de La Roche. *Amilec*
Théo Varlet. *The Golden Rock. The Xenobiotic Invasion; Timeslip Troopers* (w/André Blandin); *The Martian Epic* (w/Octave Joncquel)
Paul Vibert. *The Mysterious Fluid*
Villiers de l'Isle-Adam. *The Scaffold; The Vampire Soul*
Philippe Ward. *Artahe*
Philippe Ward & Sylvie Miller. *The Song of Montségur*

MYSTERIES & THRILLERS

M. Allain & P. Souvestre. *The Daughter of Fantômas*
A. Anicet-Bourgeois, Lucien Dabril. *Rocambole*
A. Bernède. *Belphegor; Judex* (w/Louis Feuillade)
A. Bisson & G. Livet. *Nick Carter vs. Fantômas*
V. Darlay & H. de Gorsse. *Lupin vs. Holmes: The Stage Play*
Paul Féval. *Gentlemen of the Night; John Devil; The Black Coats ('Salem Street; The Invisible Weapon; The Parisian Jungle; The Companions of the Treasure; Heart of Steel; The Cadet Gang; The Sword-Swallower)*
Emile Gaboriau. *Monsieur Lecoq*
Steve Leadley. *Sherlock Holmes: The Circle of Blood*
Maurice Leblanc. *Arsène Lupin vs. Countess Cagliostro; Lupin vs. Holmes (The Blonde Phantom; The Hollow Needle); The Many Faces of Arsène Lupin*
Gaston Leroux. *Chéri-Bibi; The Phantom of the Opera; Rouletabille & the Mystery of the Yellow Room*

Richard Marsh. *The Complete Adventures of Judith Lee*
William Patrick Maynard. *The Terror of Fu Manchu; The Destiny of Fu Manchu*
Frank J. Morlock. *Sherlock Holmes: The Grand Horizontals; Sherlock Holmes vs Jack the Ripper*
Antonin Reschal. *The Adventures of Miss Boston*
P. de Wattyne & Y. Walter. *Sherlock Holmes vs. Fantômas*
David White. *Fantômas in America*

SCREENPLAYS

Mike Baron. *The Iron Triangle*
Emma Bull & Will Shetterly. *Nightspeeder; War for the Oaks*
Gerry Conway & Roy Thomas. *Doc Dynamo*
Steve Englehart. *Majorca*
James Hudnall. *The Devastator*
Jean-Marc & Randy Lofficier. *Royal Flush*
J.-M. & R. Lofficier & Marc Agapit. *Despair*
J.-M. & R. Lofficier & Joël Houssin. *City*
Andrew Paquette. *Peripheral Vision*
Robert L. Robinson, Jr. *Judex*
R. Thomas, J. Hendler & L. Sprague de Camp. *Rivers of Time*

NON-FICTION

Stephen R. Bissette. *Blur 1-5. Green Mountain Cinema 1; Teen Angels*
Win Scott Eckert. *Crossovers* (2 vols.)
Jean-Marc & Randy Lofficier. *Shadowmen* (2 vols.)
Randy Lofficier. *Over Here*

HEXAGON COMICS

Franco Frescura & Luciano Bernasconi. *Wampus*
Franco Frescura & Giorgio Trevisan. *CLASH*
L. Bernasconi, J.-M. Lofficier & Juan Roncagliolo Berger. *Phenix*
Claude Legrand, J.-M. Lofficier & L. Bernasconi. *Kabur*
Franco Oneta. *Zembla*
L. Buffolente, Lofficier & J.-J. Dzialowski. *Strangers: Homicron*
Danilo Grossi. *Strangers: Jaydee*
Claude Legrand & Luciano Bernasconi. *Strangers: Starlock*

ART BOOKS

Jean-Pierre Normand. *Science Fiction Illustrations*
Raven Okeefe. *Raven's L'il Critters; Rave's Faves*
Randy Lofficier & Raven Okeefe. *If Your Possum Go Daylight...*
Daniele Serra. *Illusions*